BIRDLANE ISLAND

V.C. ANDREWS®

BIRDLANE ISLAND

G

GALLERY BOOKS

NEW YORK AMSTERDAM/ANTWERP LONDON
TORONTO SYDNEY/MELBOURNE NEW DELHI

G

Gallery Books
An Imprint of Simon & Schuster, LLC
1230 Avenue of the Americas
New York, NY 10020

Following the death of Virginia Andrews, the Andrews family worked with a carefully selected writer to organize and complete Virginia Andrews's stories and to create additional novels, of which this is one, inspired by her storytelling genius.

First Gallery Books trade paperback edition October 2025

Interior design by Erika R. Genova

Manufactured in the United States of America

10 9 8 7 6 5 4 3 2 1

Library of Congress Cataloging-in-Publication Data has been applied for.

ISBN 978-1-6680-1587-2
ISBN 978-1-6680-1586-5 (pbk)
ISBN 978-1-6680-1589-6 (ebook)

BIRDLANE ISLAND

PROLOGUE

I never thought much about the geese that flew over Birdlane Island. The sound of them seemed to rise from the earth and climb to the sky. Usually I would look up and turn to watch them flying until they disappeared, but I never made more of it than what Daddy had told me in his quick, matter-of-fact manner: winter was coming to Maine, and the geese were heading south. They usually did their fall migration in September and October.

This year was a little warmer than usual, and they flew over Birdlane Island closer to November. I always wondered what it would be like feeling as free as a bird, unafraid of leaving the island—or any land, for that matter. Watching them turn and glide filled me with such longing. I had reasons to feel restricted, entrapped.

But besides all that, I thought having a bird's-eye view of us was an exciting image. How could I come close to having that? I wondered. And then one morning I remembered that there was a place that could give anyone an idea of what it was like for the birds.

Even though I was forbidden from going there by myself, I was determined to venture to the high cliff on Birdlane to watch the geese disappear off to my right this year. The south loomed as a mysterious place that just had to be filled with birds. I imagined that if they all flew at the same time during the day, it would look like night. I didn't just want to look up at them today; I wanted to look *at* them, look to see if I could see the world through their eyes and, for a moment at least, feel the wonder they did. The only possible place from which to do that was the high cliff.

The cliff was known to the islanders as the Birdlane Crow's Nest, the highest point, because from there you could see all around the island. You could see the ocean all the way to the horizon. Big ships like the one Mommy had worked on slid along as if the sky was a wall of ice. I often imagined myself to be right beside her, the wind blowing through our hair, the sea embracing us.

I don't know why it suddenly became so important for me to go see the geese this particular morning, but it was one of the first things I thought about when I woke up. I had celebrated my tenth birthday on the last day of May, and although it was months ago, I was still enjoying the fuss, especially the fuss Grandfather had made over me.

Every birthday for me was a milestone. I tried to ignore the reason and do my best not to answer any questions about it. No one outside of my family talked very much about it, except maybe Aunt

Frances, Daddy's younger sister, who was a private-duty nurse. She always seemed to dwell on sad or troubling news. I didn't believe that was natural for a nurse who saw so many people suffering from one thing or another. I had met many nurses who were completely the opposite of Aunt Frances. Fortunately for me, she worked mainly in Bar Harbor and lived there.

Actually, she no longer had close friends here. Whenever she was here and brought up my health issue, Daddy would rage at her. Supposedly, they were twins, but I didn't see a close resemblance, maybe because she had always been so much thinner, with big, beady black eyes. Arguing was almost ninety percent of their conversation. Once, he asked her to leave our house. That happened shortly before my birthday, and when my birthday came, maybe fortunately, she was on an assignment, nursing a wealthy elderly lady who lived just outside Bar Harbor, so she couldn't attend. She would surely have said something to infuriate or annoy my mother and ruin my party.

We had a barbecue, and many of our neighbors had been invited. With several of Grandfather's and Daddy's important employees and their wives in attendance, I had never heard "Happy Birthday" sung so loudly. It was truly as if we were shouting down fate because of what I had learned about myself. Mommy's face was a full moon of happiness. Daddy, who disliked showing his emotions, at least looked very satisfied. I thought the laughter and the music still hung over our house.

I particularly recalled how Grandfather Charlie laughed and pinched my cheek. He wanted me to sit on his lap even at the age of ten. He had bought me the most expensive present, a beautiful new bedroom set he and Mommy had secretly chosen. Maybe Daddy was told, but he acted like he thought it was too expensive. And then he said, "She had a perfectly adequate bedroom set."

Grandfather scowled and said, "Which was why I bought it. She deserves more than simply adequate."

Daddy quickly retreated. Sometimes I thought our family was like a cobweb of nasty comments. You could ignore them or stay stuck to them all day.

That one comment about my bedroom was the only unpleasant moment at my party, but Mommy and I were used to Grandfather and Daddy bickering. Mommy said Daddy resented Grandfather for making him work his way from the bottom up in the business. We couldn't blame any of that on Grandmother Harriet's having died six years before I was born. She'd had an unexpected heart attack. But according to Mommy, Daddy and his father had always argued. With Daddy's sister, Aunt Frances, also having nasty chats with her father and Daddy, it did sound like an unpleasant family world.

This morning I didn't want to think about any of that, and anyway, the geese suddenly pushed aside my birthday memories. I had heard them calling to me in my dreams. Dreams were as hard as geese to capture and hold. Sometimes I was sorry I had awoken; I wanted to stay in my dream. Perhaps that was what I was doing that particular morning, trying to stay in my dream.

"Where are you going, Lisa?" Jamie Fuller asked when I burst out of our house as if the wind was behind me and lifting me down the few short concrete steps at our entryway, which was the only one in our neighborhood that had a distinctive dark-oak oval door. It closed so softly that Mommy often thought it was still open.

Right now, Daddy was at work and Mommy was busy with our

company's business paperwork. Grandfather had hired her to assist with the business accounting. She had agreed as long as she could work from home. Daddy told her, "He hired you to keep an eye on me." She didn't disagree.

As always, I shouted to her that I was going out, and, as always, she replied with "Don't go far."

Everyone my age was annoyed with all the warnings and restrictions the adults threw at us. I often felt as if there was an invisible leash and collar on my neck. I know it made me angry and defiant, but always a little afraid, too. Today I was not going to be.

Jamie stood absolutely still, waiting for my answer.

"I want to go to the Birdlane Crow's Nest to wait for the geese," I told him. "They're going to fly over soon. You can see them so much better there."

He looked toward our house. He was surprised because going to the top of the Birdlane Crow's Nest was somewhat of a dangerous thing to do, especially alone, even if you were older, very strong, and one hundred percent healthy.

"Your parents know?"

"Not exactly. Daddy is at work, and my mother is busy. I just said I was going out. She said okay."

I didn't like lying to Jamie and told myself that, technically, I wasn't. But I hadn't added that she had said not to go far. *All mothers say that*, I thought. It was what he'd think, too. In fact, what drew me to Jamie was the way he could voice what I was thinking or feeling. Sometimes it was like he could crawl inside me and see the world as I saw it.

"Oh. Okay," he said.

The foot of the cliff was nearly a mile west. I had wanted to go there many times, but Daddy, especially, told me, "You can't do those sorts of things. I don't need any extra problems right now."

He never did. When Mommy advised me against doing strenuous things, I could feel her love and concern; when Daddy did, I always felt he was worrying more about himself and how I could put an extra burden on him. Mommy was soft and gentle with her restrictions. With Daddy, it felt more like doors being slammed shut in my face. Mommy never let me feel like any sort of extra weight on our family.

"That's a steep climb, you know," Jamie said. He suddenly sounded more like my father.

"So? Don't make me afraid, Jamie Fuller."

I squinted at him with as much fire in my eyes as I could manage. He knew that when I was determined to do something, I would do it.

"Okay," he said. "But just wait a minute. I'm not letting you go by yourself."

I smiled to myself. I knew he would say that, but even so, I loved hearing it, hearing how much he cared for me and about me.

He was tightening the chain on his bicycle. He was always good at fixing things. His mother had told my mother that Jamie was born with a wrench in his hand. When I was five, I believed it. Jamie was nearly a year older than me and lived with his parents only three houses away from ours on Slope Street. I can't remember the exact day we began to do things together, but I do recall that Mommy was much happier about it than Daddy, who kept threatening to build a larger house closer to the sea "so that people recognize we've risen above being an ordinary fisherman's family."

"Why? To compete with your father and live in a mansion, too?

You can be such a snob sometimes, Melville." Mommy called him a snob so often, I began to think of it as his first name.

Jamie's father owned three lobster-fishing boats but was still entirely dependent on the profits from the catch to support his family. Their home was far more modest than ours, with barely any yard. Jamie was still sharing a bedroom with his older sister, Edna, even though she was practically engaged to Philip Booth, who commanded one of his father's three boats. They, and practically everyone I knew, had grown up and gone to school on Birdlane Island. People who had done so or had lived here most of their lives were affectionately called "Birdies."

Daddy didn't like to be called that even though he had grown up here. He was proud of our family business, despite his complaining that his father didn't give him the authority he deserved. He often complained about not getting enough recognition from Baxter employees. Maybe he really did think we should be treated like royalty. I know he wanted to look very wealthy and tried to have only very wealthy friends.

"We should be sendin' Lisa to the Montessori School in Bar Harbor," I had just heard him say yesterday. "We have more in common with those parents, and she will certainly have more in common with those children than the children of people on the fringes of poverty."

"You were once one of those children," Mommy reminded him. "The son of a lobster fisherman."

"But I'm not now."

"Thanks to your father," Mommy muttered loud enough to be heard.

"Even so, nothin' wrong with bein' proud and livin' like it."

"We're not sending her to the mainland school," Mommy had insisted. We often called Bar Harbor "the mainland" because you had to cross Frenchman Bay to get there. After a moment, she had firmly added, "You know why we can't do that."

They were both silent, so I imagined Daddy had walked away; however, Mommy had realized that I had overheard them arguing about my being sent to a "proper" school. She saw me outside the living room door, practically crouching in a corner.

"Don't pay any attention to your father's bluster," she had told me. She hugged me without saying another word. Later that day, when I told Jamie what Daddy had wanted, he looked upset.

"You're no mainland kid," he had said. He said that from time to time as if he was afraid I would want to be.

As the years went by, Jamie spent more time with me than he did with other kids in his class, especially the boys. I knew that they often mocked him about it. Rarely did he react. He would simply shrug and walk off, come over to join me, just as he did that day I had decided to go to the high cliff to watch for the geese like some barrelman in a crow's nest.

Our parents wouldn't be happy we had climbed our way up there. There was practically a natural stairway of grooves that had formed since the Ice Age. That was what Jamie said. He knew lots more about Birdlane than I did. He told me that archaeologists had found the remains of stone and bone tools in Frenchman Bay, some of which went back thousands of years and lots of which were exhibited in the Abbe Museum in downtown Bar Harbor. Most of it was from the Native people in Maine, the Wabanaki. I hadn't been there yet, but Jamie had. Even though it took only ten minutes to cross the bay, Mommy had always wanted me close to home when I was very young.

If Daddy tried to take me along on one of his business trips, she would say no. "You won't keep your eyes on her, Melville Howard Baxter." His close friends, most of them business associates, called him Mel, but Mommy never did.

Of course, now I knew what she meant and why she was so firm about her decisions concerning me, as firm as the legs of an old pier planted hundreds of years ago in the bay. But back then I thought she was being a little unfair to Daddy. And to me!

Jamie periodically looked back as we walked toward the cliff. I was sure he was worried that we'd be seen and maybe he would be blamed. His parents would be just as mad about it as mine would be. I felt a little guilty about having him go with me. I wouldn't want to hurt Jamie even accidentally. We walked on, him checking every once in a while to see if I really wanted to do it. But I didn't hesitate, not even for a moment.

The grooved steps were narrow, and there was nothing to hold on to if you got dizzy or stumbled. Even older boys had fallen, the most famous one being Gibson Carper, who fell halfway down and broke his neck. He was nearly fifteen. But that was nearly twenty years ago and more like an old wives' tale to me.

Once we reached the top of the cliff, Jamie and I sat on a small flat area not far from the edge and waited. All those high bluffs we saw would lovingly shield the house on the island that was, curiously enough, shaped like a bird in flight. Winter's breath was already in the air. The surf roared more loudly with the waves splashing higher on the rocks, some of them so washed they glistened like jewels. Many were jagged and looked dangerous. Sometimes the sea looked angry, but most of the time it looked inviting, beckoning. Walking on the beach and being dazzled by the leaping spray was always exciting.

Jamie and I sat closer, enjoying the aura of warmth around our young bodies. My hair danced around my head, and as he gazed at the sky spotted with long, thin clouds that looked like they had been spread over the darkening azure with a butter knife, he squinted; his eyes were an amber color with a copper tint to them. Of course I didn't know everyone's eye color, but Mommy once said that Jamie's eyes were the only eyes that shade on the island. Maybe there were only a few more like his in the whole state of Maine.

I didn't pay as much attention to other boys' faces as I did to Jamie's. His smile always began in his eyes and rippled down to his lips the way the seawater at high tide ventured over the rocks at the shore and, like tiny fingers, tried to touch shiny stones farther and farther inland.

Sure enough, this morning, as my dream had told me, the geese appeared. At first they were nothing more than a smudge against the sky, a shifting shape that looked like a fast-moving cloud approaching; they were that close together. At this height we could see their eyes, steadily focused on where they were going. With the distinct black markings on their necks giving them an air of quiet authority, they flew in a sharp V, each bird following the last without hesitation. Their feathers gleamed, and their pale underbellies caught the light as they passed overhead. They were Canada geese, travelers of great distances. As they soared, I watched their wings, broad and sturdy, lift them higher, and their eyes seemed to hold quiet determination. Mommy had told me that they could sleep with one eye open and one eye shut, watching for predators. Their eyelids shut from bottom to top, so it was easy to think they didn't have eyelids at all.

I used to try to sleep with one eye open but couldn't do it for more than a minute, if that.

"How do they know winter's coming?" I asked Jamie, who wore a small smile of wonder at how accurately I had predicted their coming, his lips just barely softening.

He brushed his hair back and turned a little to get a better view. He was already fighting with his father, who thought his dark brown hair was too long. There were only a handful of boys in our school who defied their Birdlane parents to wear their hair anywhere near as long as he did, even seniors. They wanted to be more like boys on the mainland who modeled themselves after rock stars.

Jamie said his father had told him the geese had a built-in thermometer. Of course I knew that wasn't exactly true.

What really interested me was wondering what would happen if any one goose didn't go with the flock.

"He'd hafta go," Jamie said as they disappeared off to our right.

"Why? 'Cause he'd freeze?"

"No," he said, "because he'd be lonely."

"Lonely," I repeated, and looked at them all disappearing, fixed on the horizon toward the south. Their flight was accompanied by a melodic chorus of honks among them. How sad that made me feel. I knew there were tears in my eyes from the imagined vision of one goose losing the flock and drifting in the wind.

Loneliness.

In the end, that made the most sense. It was really why you did most things: to avoid being alone and having your own echoing voice be the only voice you heard.

After which there would be the silence or the emptiness of your own thoughts searching fruitlessly for someone to hear them.

And that was when you were most afraid.

So I knew that I always would smile at the geese honking together, refusing to remain in the wrong season at the wrong time.

Eventually, I would refuse, too.

CHAPTER ONE

It wasn't until I was about to enter kindergarten that my mother sat me in the captain's chair to talk to me about something, with my father standing in the doorway of the living room, listening. She had a familiar light yellow folder clutched in her hand. Daddy was about to be on his way to his office building to work when she announced that she was going to explain things to me about myself. He stopped with surprise and stepped back to the doorway.

"Things?" he asked.

"About her health," Mommy said sharply. "Your sister said a girl her age would understand and should know."

"Advice from my sister?"

"She is a nurse, Melville."

"The only advice she's capable of giving is how to be miserable," he said.

Mommy smirked and turned back to me. I had seen her looking into the yellow folder she had in her hand often, but I did not know where she kept it or why it was so important to her, to me. She never left it laying around anywhere in the house where I or anyone else could peek at what was inside. I used to think it was just some secret business information about our lobster and fish company.

Mommy was sleeping more often in the smaller bedroom right past mine toward the rear of our house, so it could have been kept in there. When I first asked her why she had suddenly decided to sleep in that bedroom, she said it was closer to me and until I was older and more in charge of myself, it was just a good idea. That puzzled me at the time, the time before the captain's chair, but I didn't ask any more questions about it.

Daddy didn't seem to be terribly upset with her sleeping and moving her things there. He often kept his feelings under wraps. The only thing I heard him say was that he had more room in their bathroom with all her "beauty gimmicks" gone. Mommy gave him a look that could spear a bluefin tuna.

Her violet-blue eyes got brighter and bluer when she was angry or going to say something very important, and that was the way they were when she told me to sit in the captain's chair. I could never turn away from those eyes. I heard people, especially my father, say that she had a kind of "violent beauty." Looking at her was like looking into a flame.

Before she started, she brushed her honey-brown hair away

from her face. My hair was her color and always kept about the same length, which made me feel pretty because everyone thought she was. I couldn't imagine being more beautiful than my mother, even though older people were always promising me that I would be someday.

"Your mother is the most attractive woman on Birdlane when she is unaware anyone's lookin' at her," Daddy once said. I thought that was nice until he added, "Just like most women who put on airs when they know someone's lookin' at them."

I quickly sat in the captain's chair. My father was the one who mostly used this brown leather chair with nailhead trim. It was the most important place in the room, because everything else, the two facing sofas and the oak wood coffee table, was arranged so that whoever sat in the captain's chair commanded everyone's attention.

I knew it was going to be an "adult" conversation. Nothing would be disguised; there would be no "baby" talk, no putting the truth into magical characters or animals that talked like people, and I wouldn't be permitted to look elsewhere or be distracted. I had to sit up straight and put my hands in my lap, but that was never easy for anyone sitting or talking here, because there was a lot to distract him or her in our living room.

Framed in a high-gloss black finish was the front-page article in *Fishermen's Voice* announcing my grandfather Charlie Baxter's creating the Baxter Fish Enterprises Company on Birdlane Island to buy and sell Maine seafood. Every Birdlane fisherman in one way or another now worked for the Baxter company. We had our own office building on Main Street. Grandfather's office had big picture windows that looked out at Frenchman Bay. Daddy complained about his own office not having that view. He wanted more acknowledgment. Grandfather had finally made him officially the vice president.

At first we sold only on the East Coast, but today we were selling all over the country. What made our company front-page news back then was that Grandfather Charlie was only twenty-two years old when he stepped off a lobster-fishing boat and became what my father called an "entrepreneur."

I had to pronounce that carefully because Daddy thought it was such an important word, especially since Grandfather had created the most successful business on Birdlane Island and the one that employed the most people besides fishermen. Almost everyone in one way or another—the store owners and all the professional people, like lawyers, doctors, and dentists—was dependent on it, because if the fishermen didn't make money, they didn't, either.

On another wall hung one of Grandfather Charlie's original lobster traps. He'd had the others bronzed and given them to us. The opposite wall had ten pictures of Grandfather on his boat; three of them included Daddy as a young boy. He said he wasn't much older than I was at the time. He added that sons of fishermen were expected to grow up faster than other children. I wondered about daughters, but it was rare to see any girls working on fishing and lobster boats. Mommy had told me that girls usually didn't want to get "fisherman claw hands," hands that had calluses and got really sore.

In most of the pictures of Grandfather's boat, you could see some of the lobster catch. I always felt sorry for the lobsters, which Daddy and others often called "bugs." I would avoid saying how much I felt sorry for them when I was growing up. The one time I did, when Daddy had two of his and Mommy's friends to dinner, his face turned lobster red and his head nearly exploded with anger.

"That's our bread and butter!" he cried. "You should have respect and gratitude, not pity!"

"Melville," my mother said, sharply enough to sting his ears. He simmered down like boiling milk when the burner on the range was lowered.

Unlike the parents of other children my age, mine were very concerned about shocking me with reprimands, my father less so than my mother. Even when she was upset with something I had done or was doing, she spoke in a soft but firm voice. When I was very young, I didn't think that was so unusual, but after my mother had sat me in the captain's chair, I painfully understood the reason. I would have rather been yelled at.

I had been to see Dr. Bush, who ran the small clinic on Birdlane Island, and I had vague memories of being taken to see a doctor at Mount Desert Island Hospital in Bar Harbor. I could recall the scary-looking equipment he used when examining me. But it was some time since I had seen the specialist and had gone to see Dr. Bush. No one really had told me anything I understood. Aunt Frances had tried to say something once. I remembered that just as she began her sentence, both Mommy and Daddy practically pounced on her.

Mommy opened her special file and took out a paper with official-looking doctor's office information at the top. She turned it so I could see the picture. It was a visual of the heart. Mommy held it with her left hand and pointed to it with her right forefinger.

"You know what this is," she said. I nodded. "You know that it pumps our blood around our body." I nodded again, even though I never fully understood that. No one had really ever explained to me where our blood came from and where it went.

She took out another paper that showed a picture of the heart cut so you could see into it.

"There are four valves in the heart that keep our blood flowing in the right directions. You don't have to know their names right now or what each one specifically does. You just have to know that one of yours wasn't working correctly when you were born."

That frightened me, and I looked at Daddy, who smirked and shook his head.

"If you think it's time to get that technical, why don't you let a doctor tell her?" he said.

Mommy didn't turn completely around. "Because he wouldn't care as much as her mother, and he'd hide behind science so he wouldn't have to show any emotion. She'd be scared to death."

"Well, whaddya think you're doin' to her now? Especially if you're followin' Frances's advice."

Mommy looked at me closely. "She's all right. She's a big girl."

Daddy grunted. "I'd feel gawmy doin' that," he said, "gawmy" being a word we used in Maine to mean clumsy, awkward.

"You're not doing it. I am. You don't have to stay, Melville," Mommy said. "Go to work. I'll take care of it."

Daddy started to turn to leave but then turned back.

"Go on," he said. "I'd like to hear how you tell her about it, too."

Mommy pressed her full lips together for a moment and took a breath, which I knew was her way of swallowing back anger. She fixed her eyes on me again with an intensely serious gaze.

"When you were born, the doctor who delivered you heard a whooshing sound in your chest, and that was when we really had you examined and were told you were fine but we should always keep an eye on you. Now that you're going to start attending school, I want you to help by keeping an eye on yourself, too."

I looked at Daddy, who tilted his head a little and this time looked more surprised, like he did when he said, "I wonder why I didn't think of that." It was truly like he was blaming his own brain, as if it was one of the Baxter employees.

"How do I do that, Mommy?"

"I'm going to tell you. If you feel you have to gasp or are gasping, you know, like when you run too fast, and if during the day you feel very, very tired or you get dizzy, and if you feel a pain here," she said, pressing her right hand over her heart, "we want to know right away. Stop whatever you are doing and tell us or get someone to tell us, understand?"

"Who?"

"Well, when you start school, we want you to tell your teacher and have him or her call us. Don't ever be too shy or embarrassed to do that, Lisa. Will you promise to do that?"

"Yes," I said. My voice sounded so tiny and thin.

"If you close your eyes and think about it, you can feel your heart beat, can't you?" Mommy asked.

I could, and nodded.

"Good. If you ever feel it isn't beating the way it always does when you're not running or playing, especially if it sounds like it's skipping, you tell either me or your father or, again, your teacher. Tell someone to call us, wherever you are."

"What happens then, Mommy?"

"We'll take you back to the hospital in Bar Harbor, and the doctor will fix your valve."

"Why can't he do that now?" I asked.

"Well, right now it's okay."

"And you don't fix it if it ain't broke," Daddy said.

"Your father finally said something good," Mommy said.

"You're a wicked woman, Theresa," Daddy said, and walked away to go to work.

Mommy shook her head and put the pages back in her folder.

"Why did Daddy say you were wicked, Mommy?" I asked.

"Because he has a limited, Maine vocabulary," she said. I didn't understand, but before I could ask another question, she said, "You can go out now, Lisa. And play like always. Just remember all that I told you. When you get older, you'll understand it even more."

She stood up, and I slipped off the captain's chair, but I didn't have to get older to know that I would never think about myself the same way again, and I wouldn't play like always. After the captain's chair morning, there were so many things I would hesitate to do that other children my age would do without a second thought. Sometimes I felt I should jump into the cold sea to shock myself into thinking less about my heart.

And sometimes I would do things in defiance, angry that I had to be more careful than any other girl my age—or boy, for that matter. Maybe that, more than anything, was what drove me to go up to the Birdlane Crow's Nest that autumn morning.

Mommy never said I shouldn't tell anyone about my heart, so I told Jamie. I didn't tell anyone else until I was much older. I had never seen Jamie look so serious and even a little frightened as he did after I blurted what was in my mother's special folder.

"Don't you worry, Lisa," he had said, pulling his shoulders back and standing straighter and firmer. Jamie could look very grown-up sometimes. Despite his age, his father made him do a man's load. He often went out with his father's lobster-fishing boat even though he was younger than my father was when he went out with Grandfather Charlie. "I'll look after you, too, and make sure your parents know anything they have to know."

He looked so serious. It was then that I thought Jamie was going to be more than a friend. Sometimes I was sorry I had told him, because he would stop whatever we were doing, even stop walking, and ask me how I was. When I wanted to avoid thinking of my captain's chair time, Jamie would remind me. It got so I snapped back at him.

"I'm fine, Jamie. Stop asking!"

I knew that hurt him, but it never stopped him. Even after he graduated from high school and went to work full-time on his father's lobster boat, he would always ask me how I was almost the moment he saw me. It was never a simple "How are you?" like people asked each other when they met. Jamie's question was most often "How do you feel? Have you had any of the symptoms your mother described to you and your doctors told you to watch for?" Or "Did you get very, very tired today?"

I never had, and that seemed to please him more than it did me. One good thing was he never asked me in front of my friends—or anyone else, for that matter. For most of my young life, few people, least of all my classmates, ever knew my heart had made that whooshing sound when I was born. Jamie could keep the secret in his closed lips as tightly as an oyster could keep a pearl in its shell. Eventually, though, they would all know and look at me differently.

But even if Jamie hadn't asked his questions, I couldn't have kept the secret of the yellow folder from hovering in my mind like a storm cloud. I was annoyed at the way Jamie studied me sometimes, but also grateful that he was watching over me, especially because we spent so much time together.

Often at night I would listen to my heartbeat after I had gone to bed. I never asked Mommy what would happen if one of those symptoms occurred while I was asleep. Would I wake, or would I die before I had a chance to wake? Actually, I was afraid to ask the question, because the answer might force me to fight sleep and I might get sick or hurt my heart.

Sometimes, when I was growing up, I thought I caught my mother watching me more closely. Had I done something that frightened her? I sat thinking about every little move I had made, wondering if I had missed a symptom. I supposed it was only natural that there would come a time when I would panic. To this day, I blamed myself for what happened. Maybe I had gotten overconfident because I really hadn't had any of the symptoms Mommy had warned me to report. More than once Daddy had said, always when Mommy wasn't nearby, "Don't think about it. You've outgrown the problem. You've mended yourself."

Mommy never really answered me if I asked her if that was possible. "We'll see" was her standard response. When would I see? How long would it be before I would see? Doctor visits now were far more frightening events.

My latest physical exam earlier in the following summer was good, but I had gone only to Dr. Bush and not the Mount Desert Island Hospital clinic. I had heard Mommy tell Daddy that maybe it was time to return to the specialist and get a more intensive exam.

"What for?" Daddy had said. "She's doin' fine. Chout, Theresa. You'll make her so nervous that she'll just sit and worry all the time. She'll miss out on doin' things kids her age do."

Mommy didn't answer, but her silence was not reassuring. Besides, there were many more silences between them by the time I was fifteen. I wondered, of course, who was right: Mommy, who always wanted me to think about it and be careful? Or Daddy, who wanted me to forget about it and be more like any normal child? He did blame Mommy for my not wanting to do more sports at school. Instead, I chose to be in art club, where I could sit in the classroom for hours if I wanted and work on the details of a picture I was drawing and preparing to paint.

Mr. Angelo was my art teacher. He had returned from college and years working in Europe to teach art in our small school. His parents, descendants of a Birdlane Island family, had left him their home so he could live in a beautiful place at little or no cost like a fortunate starving artist and keep trying to become a famous artist. As soon as I first began with him, he told me he had given up on that idea.

"When I was about your age," he said, "and I was obsessed with my artwork, other kids would make fun of me."

"Why? How?"

"My parents thought it was amusing maybe to name me Michael."

For a moment, I didn't understand.

"Michael Angelo," he said, and my eyes widened. He laughed. "My friends would tease me and say, 'You're not Michelangelo. Change your name.' Instead, I decided I would teach art and become famous for discovering another real Michelangelo. Maybe it's you," he said. "You have an extraordinary ability to capture perspective, and I think there is a kind of maturity in what you choose to draw and paint. Don't give up on it as quickly as I did. Sometimes success takes most of your life."

"But isn't everything harder for a woman to do?" I asked. Daddy had certainly said or implied that many times, which was why he was always suggesting I work toward being a secretary or, like Mommy, a bookkeeper.

Mr. Angelo smiled. "Well, there's a ways to go to make things easier for women, at least as easy as anything is for men. But look at what happened last July: a woman was nominated for vice president . . . Geraldine Ferraro. It's not 1684. It's 1984. If you have the will, I think there's a way," he said, "whether you're a woman or a man."

His words excited me. I wished I could get Daddy to understand that I wasn't doing art to avoid being too physical and bringing about one of the warning symptoms. I really enjoyed it. "The more you act nervous about yourself, the weaker you'll become," Daddy had told me a little angrily one day because I had spent so much after-school time in art class. "If you were a boy, I'd have you on one of my lobster-fishing boats by now."

"Just because I'm a girl doesn't mean I can't work on a boat," I had told him. Lately I was thinking I might go out with Jamie one day just to prove it to him. I certainly would feel safe with Jamie. "I've seen fishermen's wives on boats."

"Some of those wives have mustaches," he said.

"What?"

"Forget about bein' a fisherman or fisherwoman. Just join the girls' volleyball club or somethin' to work those muscles, and don't spend all that time indoors doodlin'. Act more like a Baxter." Long ago I had lost count of how many times he had told me that.

"I love my artwork, Daddy," I said. "It's not doodling. You don't know that much about art. I won't give that up. If you took away all my artist's equipment, I'd draw pictures on the walls. You'll have to accept that's who I am."

"How many people make a good livin' bein' artists?" he snapped back.

"There is more to life than just making money. Even Grandfather says that."

"He'll say whatever it takes to please you," he replied.

For a moment I paused. His words sounded more full of jealousy than anger. I thought he realized it and immediately relaxed his shoulders and softened his tightened lips.

"Maybe that's true for women. But if you end up marryin' a fisherman's son, you'll have to do somethin' more than diddle in art to survive."

I always knew what he believed. Girls couldn't make important decisions, especially for themselves. All of those who had important jobs, the bosses, even the managers of stores selling women's clothing, were men on Birdlane Island. It was different on the mainland, in Bar Harbor. I had seen many women in charge of businesses there. Crossing the bay was like crossing to another world where there was more fashion and excitement. The busy streets and larger stores made me feel like Columbus discovering a new world. And it was there that I could see other people's art, some famous art that included female artists, too.

"That doesn't frighten me, Daddy."

"Well, it should," he said. He always thought it was important for him to have the last word in an argument. Before I could respond, he walked away.

Early in my life I learned not to go running to Mommy to complain about Daddy. First, I clearly understood how he would react. He wouldn't stop to reconsider what he had done or said. He'd have his back up and double down on whatever he had said or done. I didn't want to feel that helpless, either. Despite my health issue, I always wanted to be strong enough to take care of my own problems. Much of what went on between Daddy and me went unheard. The only one who managed to get some of it out of me was my grandfather.

It had become almost a ritual of ours for me to spend Saturday lunch at his mansion. He had asked me to come one day when I was twelve, and I had been doing it often since then. I certainly didn't want to go running to him to complain about something Daddy had said or done, but Grandfather had always assumed something would happen, not only between Daddy and me but between Aunt Frances and me or Mommy. She could be quite bitter and sharp with her remarks. Mommy never let her get away with her sarcasm or disdain, and although I knew it was impolite to snap back at an adult, I made sure she knew I wasn't going to just stand silently and take any of her bitterness, either. Daddy was right: Grandfather would defend me.

On this particular Saturday, Grandfather had a surprise for me at the Crest, his mansion. It would make Mommy nervous and for some reason infuriate Daddy. Perhaps he could sense what was going to follow.

CHAPTER TWO

As soon as he could afford it, Grandfather had redone, with great expansions and modern upgrades in the kitchen and bathrooms, what had been in his family for generations. It was one of the oldest and, at the time, one of the biggest homes on Birdlane Island. The family hadn't been able to afford to keep it up—just heating it cost a fortune—but Grandfather now could. He had the driveways redone and all the windows, as well as the floors and the stairway. When it was ready for him and my grandmother, he called it the Crest. It had a magnificent view of Frenchman Bay. He named it after the highest point of a wave. Since it was the highest building on Birdlane, that made sense.

You had to drive up a winding road that ran along the rocky shore and then turned sharply to climb the rest of the way to the house, which loomed atop the windswept hill. Its grand facade was a magnificent blend of Gothic Revival and Victorian elegance steeped in both opulence and secrecy. The mansion was encased in gray stone with rich decorative elements, pointed arches at the windows, and intricate tracery, and the gabled roof whispered stories of bygone days. The house, surrounded by lush gardens and winding pathways, offered a picturesque and serene escape from the world.

As you drove closer to the mansion, the road revealed a grand circular centerpiece lush with meticulously kept greenery and beds of blooming flowers reaching out from the darker foliage as if they longed to escape. Redwood steps led you to the formal entrance towering ahead, with its two grand front doors guarding the history within the mansion.

Upon entering, a grand foyer with a sweeping spiral staircase made of polished mahogany led the way to three of the six bedrooms. Each room in the mansion seemed to breathe its own unique atmosphere, capturing stories from the past.

Grandfather always dreamed of redoing it and began the restoration shortly after he had started his business and its growth had practically exploded. From the way he had described it to me, he had no idea his company would become such a major Maine enterprise. He called it "a shocking delight."

"I have had only three in my life," he said to me. "Meeting and marrying your grandmother, the business, and you."

Grandfather's housekeeper, Anna, was at the door as usual to greet me. She had been at the Crest from practically day one after Grandfather's restoration had been finished. Anna was in her mid-fifties, had curly graying black hair, and was short and puffy. Grandfather often kidded her, saying, "Don't poke yerself, Anna, or you'll shrink to the size of one of Lisa's dolls."

"Go on with you," Anna would reply. She knew all about me, about my health issue, but was considerate enough not to mention anything or stare. However, I knew Mommy had told her to keep an eye on me and report anything suspicious.

Anna was from away, some small village in England called Butingford. Sometimes she talked about it, sounding homesick, but always adding how grateful she was for the opportunity to work for such an important family in so posh a house. She said that meant the house, Grandfather's mansion, was rich, beautiful, and impressive like "some lord and lady's home in England."

I knew that Anna liked Mommy very much in particular. I'd say she even loved her, because Mommy didn't treat her like someone might treat a servant; she was more like a dear old friend, even a relative, since early on. Mommy once said that some people in Maine acted like we were still in the Revolutionary War and hated the British.

Anna was especially good at handling Grandfather, who could be quite grouchy sometimes, seemingly only when Daddy or Aunt Frances was around.

Anna would click her lips and shake her head. Most of the time, Grandfather would "pull up on the reins" and calm down.

"He's got his ways," Anna would tell me, "but who doesn't? Most men just need you to scratch their back a bit and get that itch gone."

Maybe most men, but not Daddy, I thought.

"Oh, don't you look lovely," she said when I arrived.

"Thank you, Anna."

"He's in his usual chair on the northwest patio."

I nodded and entered. Grandfather liked this side of the Crest because it didn't face the ocean. "I see it all day, all my life," he had told me. "Sometimes it's good to look elsewhere."

At first I couldn't quite understand how someone could tire of something as vast and beautiful as the sea. But standing there with Grandfather, trying to look at the side that turned its back to the sea, I began to grasp the comfort he found in facing this way. The rolling hills and the full cluster of trees brought a sense of peace.

His face exploded in that wide joyous look that always made me feel better and more energetic.

As long as I had known him, I thought Grandfather Charlie was a better-looking man than Daddy, even now, in his late seventies. He still had a full head of graying dark brown hair and that perfectly trimmed mostly gray mustache that to me suggested a movie-star British general. He certainly talked and moved like one. His posture didn't falter an iota. I was sure Daddy either had inherited or consciously imitated the way Grandfather stood with that military perfection, especially when confronting other people. You almost wished you could say, "At ease."

"Hi, Grandfather," I said.

"Every time I look at you, I see more of your mother," he said. "C'mon, sit down." He patted the chair beside him. "How are things at school?"

"Good. I'm practically getting personal art lessons from my art teacher."

"Mr. Angelo," he said. It always astonished me how much detail

Grandfather knew about me and what I did. I didn't think my father had told him, but if he did, there was a good chance it was in the form of a complaint.

"Yes."

"My grandmother thought she could be an artist. There might be some of her paintings in the basement. Brought it all with me when we first moved into this place."

"Really? I'd love to see them."

"I'll have them found and brought up. When you finish something you're proud of, bring it for me to see. I have plenty of wall space that needs beautiful things."

"Oh, I don't know if they are that good, Grandfather."

He lost his smile. "There is one thing I want put for good in some closet," he said, "and that's lack of self-confidence. Those people who suffer that never succeed at much."

"You sound like Daddy."

"Occasionally, he listens to me."

Anna appeared in the doorway.

"What'cha making for us?" Grandfather asked instantly.

"That Cobb salad you've been wanting."

"How come it took so long to get it?" he asked, half kidding. I could see the twinkle in his eyes.

"Shortage of Cobb," she tossed back at him.

He laughed. "And some of your special lemonade, if you please."

As soon as she left to prepare our lunch, Grandfather turned to me and said, "Never let that woman go."

"Why would I? How could I?"

He turned and looked long and hard out the window at the

trees and well-trimmed bushes. There was a rise to a small hill. Another view of the ocean was on the other side of it.

"Your seventeenth birthday is next weekend, correct?"

"Yes. And you agreed to have my party here."

"Agreed? I was the one who suggested it."

"Oh, Mommy didn't say."

"Today I'll be giving you some pre-birthday presents. Your grandmother Harriet wouldn't like it, but she'll forgive me."

He turned with his smile.

"She did that many times: disapprove of something I did or said. She wouldn't yell; she would just click her lips and widen her eyes."

"I wish I had been born earlier so I would have known her."

"Me too. Wish you had."

Anna arrived with our lunch and set it out.

"Let's eat this rare lunch first," Grandfather said.

Anna shook her head and smiled at me. "He's had it many times, including just last Sunday."

"You ever see such an insolent servant?" Grandfather joked.

She tapped him playfully on the shoulder and left us.

"It is delicious," I said. I ate and watched him, trying to keep from blurting out, "Tell me. What pre-birthday present?"

Grandfather, on the other hand, ate calmly, gazed out at the scenery, and, when he was ready, turned to me. I knew no one else, in the family or out of it, who had his patience. How many times had he told me that there were no accidents with patience? Probably a hundred times.

He paused, laid down his fork, and reached into his sports jacket pocket to produce an envelope.

"I want you to read this and then give it back to me. It will be in my safe-deposit box at the Birdlane National Bank. This," he said, holding up a key, "is the key to the box. I'll keep it taped to the back of my desk drawer. After you read the papers, I'll answer any questions you have. I trust you and know you will keep it to yourself unless it is necessary to reveal at some future date."

I reached for the envelope slowly. He didn't release it. He held it and stared at me with his piercing gray-blue eyes.

"Understand? This is trust in its most pure form, Lisa."

"I understand, Grandfather."

"Good," he said, and released it.

I think my fingers trembled as I opened the envelope and took out the papers. Grandfather watched me start to read and then turned away to look out again at the scenery. As I read, I could feel my throat tighten. It was as if I was trying to swallow tea that was not yet cool enough.

After I read both documents, I sat speechless.

Grandfather turned back slowly. "Even now," he said, "your grandmother would have forbidden my showing that to you."

I glanced at the papers again to be sure I had read them and this wasn't some dream.

"Do my father and Aunt Frances know this?"

"The deal I made with your grandmother was we would never tell them. Everything was arranged outside of Birdlane, and as I said, only my personal attorney was involved."

"But . . . why . . ."

"Your grandmother was unable to have children of her own. She had what they called ovulation disorders. We tried many times and finally went to top specialists in Augusta who confirmed her situation, even confirming with some top New York City doctors.

"Both of us were disappointed, but I didn't want her to think it had any effect on our relationship. My attorney suggested adoption to me, and for weeks I kept the concept under lock and key, and then one night I brought it up as gently as I could. She didn't hesitate; in fact, she was going to try the idea out on me but was equally afraid.

"And then, as if designed by fate, something happened, and we were able to take advantage of it. Your grandmother put out the word that she was pregnant just before we were to take a prolonged winter holiday. People accepted and believed. Word came to me from sources I had alerted that there was a terrible accident, and a woman pregnant with twins was in a coma. The babies were removed, healthy and alive. We were there. Your grandmother went away to 'give birth.' We always took a long winter vacation from which I'd return myself to do business. For her to return with a child, in this case two, seemed normal to everyone. No one has ever questioned it. Or, maybe, dared to. They were twins, and your grandmother thought they made us the perfect family, a boy and a girl."

He slowly took the papers back, reinserted them in the envelope, and put it back into his inside pocket.

"These are the real birth certificates."

"So you are saying that my father and Aunt Frances still don't know."

"There were many times when I was tempted to tell them, but your grandmother would have been devastated, and I doubted that in the end it would change them much."

"But now Daddy and Aunt Frances are certainly old enough to know this," I said.

"As I said, it wouldn't change anything, only make them both more defensive, even angry. They'd certainly have more reason to go after each other, which practically became a necessity as they grew up and challenged each other for your grandmother's and my attention and affection. I was never properly good at the affection aspect as it was."

"But they look so different. Aunt Frances is so tall and thin, with a narrow face and that slightly darker complexion."

He smiled and leaned toward me. "Maybe she has more Wabanaki blood than Melville." He laughed, but I didn't.

"Seriously, there is a way of explaining it. Twins who don't look alike are called fraternal twins because they develop from two separate eggs fertilized by two different sperm, meaning they share only about fifty percent of their DNA, similar to any other siblings, and can have distinct appearances, unlike identical twins, who share the same genetic makeup and usually look very similar."

I let it all digest for a moment. He sat quietly, watching me think.

"So, technically, I'm not really your granddaughter," I said.

His face stiffened, grayed, any hint of a smile and glee gone.

"You are more my granddaughter than ever. I know you're closer to me than you are to your father, and I'm closer to you than to him. Don't ever think otherwise. I love few people, with your mother and you being the top two. Grandmother Harriet wouldn't tolerate any other thought. Look what I've shared with you."

"Not even my mother knows this?"

"No. I told you who were the only two. Now there are three who do."

"What about their birth certificates showing that you and Grandmother were their parents?"

He smiled. "You're a smart one all right. We had friends in high places who got your grandmother and me what we needed."

He thought a moment.

"And as I told you," he said, patting his pocket, "I have their real birth certificates with these papers. Their authenticity is easily checked if necessary. You know it all now, and I am sure you'll keep it locked away unless it's ever necessary to release."

I wasn't sure how I felt about his confidence. The shock of knowing was one thing, but having it locked in my heart, carrying the burden of the secrecy, was another. Would I ever look at Daddy and Aunt Frances the same way, and would they ever look at me and realize what I knew? And what if they did find out and discovered I had been given their secret before them?

"I don't know, Grandfather. I think I wish you never told me."

"I wouldn't have if I didn't believe in my heart that you'll need to know this. I am as confident of that as of anything, and you'll thank me for this."

"Daddy is so proud of being a Baxter."

"And right he should be. He's always had my family name. Earning it is a different thing, but that's another discussion."

"But why did you say I would need to know later?"

"Knowledge is power, Lisa. Leave it at that for now."

Anna reappeared before I could press him further.

"You two could have eaten more," she complained.

Grandfather didn't respond. I looked away, and I know she

sensed a sensitive moment was at hand. She cleared away the dishes and left.

"Is this why you don't invite us to live here, Grandfather?"

"No. Partly. I see enough of Melville at work."

"But it has to be so lonely for you, in so big a house."

"Your room is always there for you."

"But I wouldn't like leaving Mommy, even for a weekend, and she wouldn't leave Daddy, despite how they argue at times. He'd resent it and make things harder for her, maybe for us both."

"Well, it's agreed you'll have your seventeenth birthday party here. Your mother's done all the planning, and besides . . ." He leaned toward me. "You can invite your poor fisherman boy."

He had a wry, teasing smile on his face. I knew how he liked to poke Daddy sometimes. "You can make it some sort of sleepover for some girlfriends if you like. I know you kids do those things now."

"Everyone invited is excited about seeing the Crest."

"Don't show them the skeletons in the closet," he kidded. "Let's take a walk around the property," he said, rising. "When you look at it from every angle, every detail, you make it part of yourself." I rose to join him.

Lately Grandfather had been telling me more and more about the Crest, his voice carrying a weight I hadn't noticed before. Sometimes he sounded more like a real estate agent trying to sell it than the owner. It was as if he was trying to convince himself it was still worth something, that it was still strong despite the years. Today he showed me small cracks in the foundation and some gutters that needed replacement. He said the issues were nothing serious. He had a very good house manager who oversaw any repairs and the landscaping, Brad Lester, who always gave me a big hello and a smile. He was a man in his fifties who had been born and raised on Birdlane. People like that did seem to take more pride in their property.

I knew Daddy had always been jealous of Grandfather's house. He neglected so much about our own, which usually meant Mommy had to see to things. Because of what Grandfather had shown me, it was difficult to think of Daddy the same way. Could I keep that from him? Would it feel like he was more of a stranger? I didn't want to ask any more questions. Truthfully, I didn't want to know any more. I always feared my face was a windowpane: one look from either Daddy or Aunt Frances, and all the secrets could be seen. I didn't know what made Grandfather so confident about me, but he did say lack of self-confidence would lead to failure. I wasn't going to disappoint him.

Afterward, Arthur, the family driver, took me home. When we arrived on Slope Street, I saw Jamie waiting for me in front of my house. He looked like he had been pacing.

As soon as Arthur stopped in the driveway, I got out and Jamie came over. We watched Arthur back out and drive off.

"What's happening?" I asked. He looked so serious.

"I think I got your father enraged at me."

"How?"

"I just rang your doorbell. I guess your mother isn't home. He might have been deep in some business work, and when he opened the door, he practically ripped it off its hinges. I thought he was just going to slam it shut when he saw it was me. I apologized and said I was just looking for you to give you a birthday present."

"But it's not until next weekend."

"I know, but I want to be the first to give you a present this time. I know your sixteenth birthday was special, but you're going to be seventeen, and soon you'll . . ."

"What?"

"You'll make big decisions in your life for yourself. I mean, you could do most anything without your parents' permission."

I stared at him a moment and then took a deep breath. How much dramatic and earth-shattering news could I stand without just screaming? The world I knew was changing by the minute. This wasn't the time for anything more serious, but how could I say that to Jamie without his asking what was wrong? Who could read me better than he could?

"Is everything all right?" he asked at my silence.

"Yes, yes. My grandfather is showing his age, but it's all right. You could really wait on the gift."

"I'd rather not. Okay?"

"Okay," I said, gazing at the front door. By now Daddy was surely peeking through a window. Where was Mommy? "Let's go inside," I said.

"Your house? But . . ."

I just started for the front door, and he hurried to catch up. The moment we stepped in, Daddy appeared.

"What's this?" he asked.

I could count on the fingers of one hand how many times Jamie had been here. He never was without Mommy present.

"We're going to discuss my upcoming birthday party at the Crest. You can join us," I said, heading toward the living room.

"I have more important things to do. Your mother went shopping in Bar Harbor," he said.

"Thank you, Daddy," I said, almost in a dismissive tone.

His face actually reddened. I turned and motioned for Jamie to follow me to the living room. He looked at the captain's chair as if Daddy were sitting in it and then perused the wall of awards and mementos.

"I've always been impressed with all this."

"You can try the chair," I said.

"Oh, no, this is fine," he said, sitting on the sofa.

He immediately took out a white box wrapped with a red ribbon tied in a fisherman's knot. I sat beside him and glanced at the door to be sure Daddy wasn't standing just outside it, listening in.

"Happy birthday," Jamie said, handing me the box.

I laughed and took the gift. "Thank you."

Jamie nodded at the present he had given me. "I saved up all year for that. I hope you like it."

"Oh," I said. "You didn't have to buy me something so expensive."

I opened it and took out the small, flat box, carefully lifting the lid to find a blue and white sapphire bracelet.

"Oh, Jamie, it's beautiful."

"They call it a tennis bracelet, but you don't wear it to play tennis. Mr. Lowe, the jeweler, told me the story."

"Story?"

"Why it's called a tennis bracelet. I thought something with a famous history would have more meaning for you on this special birthday."

"Tell me the story."

"First, let's put it on," he said, and he helped me do so. "Just like he promised . . . a perfect fit."

I held my hand up to admire the bracelet. "It is so beautiful. What is the story?"

"It comes from a tennis match . . . the 1978 US Open. During the match, Chris Evert dropped her diamond eternity bracelet and lost it somewhere. She made them pause the match so she could look for her bracelet."

"Eternity bracelet?"

Jamie blushed. It wasn't like him to do so.

I smiled and reached for his hand. "Why was it called that?"

"It was meant to show the eternal love between two people."

I looked toward the door again to be sure Daddy wasn't listening to us. And then I got up and closed the door. Jamie looked frightened.

"We're entitled to privacy," I said. "Your gift is really special, Jamie."

Suddenly, I felt more drawn to him than ever, my heart tingling with warm excitement. It was as if I was seeing him for the first time, everything inside me wanting to touch him in ways I had never thought to do but now longed to. I pulled him a little closer and kissed him. His amber eyes widened with surprise and delight. Then he leaned completely into me and kissed me back, but longer and with more feeling than any thank-you kiss. This was my first real love kiss. All his pecks on my cheek were void of this passion. With this kiss came his hands moving down my shoulders to get a firmer embrace. I leaned back, and he braced himself over me, gazing down at me.

It seemed odd to think of yourself as recuperating from a kiss, but I was trying to get my heart to stop pounding and the feelings running through my body to slow down. Jamie had a look of surprise on his face, too. Both of us were playing with runaway horses. Our gazes locked. Neither of us could speak for a few moments.

"I never kissed a girl like that," he said.

"Why don't I believe you?"

He laughed. "I'm not saying I never wanted to; I just never did."

"Then you'd better do it again," I said, "so you never forget."

"How could I forget? But you're right, I'd better do it again."

He lowered himself to kiss me and slide his body against mine.

"I've wanted to do this for so long," he said. "I mean, kiss you like that. All-out"

"All-out?"

He laughed. "Put myself and what I feel deeply into it."

"Why didn't you try before, then?"

He shrugged. "Scared, I guess. Don't tell anyone," he quickly added. "I'll get ribbed to death. Most of my friends think I already have, but I deliberately never confirmed or denied it. They can let their imaginations run away with them. I thought you might get upset and never want to see me again."

"I wouldn't get upset with you. You're supposed to be a good fisherman. You should know when you've made a good catch," I said.

He laughed so hard that I thought it brought tears to his eyes. He kissed me again and again and then brought his leg gently over mine as his hands moved down my sides and then slowly moved toward my breasts. He paused. I was holding my breath, anticipating the feeling.

"I really love you," he whispered, and ran his palms over me, creating an explosion of excitement that flowed over me, through me, settling in my thighs, which I pressed against his. *Defiance*, I thought. *Is it that or love?*

"Lisa," he said, "we will get married one day unless you become a mainland girl. Birdies are never good enough for them."

I did think I loved Jamie; I did, but there were so many things I wanted to see and do, and if I said them, I would sound more like a mainland girl. First, I did want to become an artist, and Mr. Angelo had taught me that a writer, an artist, anyone who wanted to create, had to want to have more experiences, see new things, hear new music, and widen his or her vision. It was why he didn't regret having traveled before settling back on Birdlane.

How could I do both, love Jamie and widen my vision? Be the woman I wanted to be?

CHAPTER THREE

Before I could find an answer, we heard a knock on the door. Jamie practically leaped to his feet in one motion, and I sat up.

"Come in," I said, and Mommy appeared, bright-faced, her hair having been blown about by the boat ride back from Bar Harbor.

"Hi," she said. "I found the perfect dress for your birthday party."

"Oh, I can't wait to see it."

"How is everyone in your family, Jamie?"

"Everyone's fine, thanks, Mrs. Baxter."

"And your lunch with Grandfather Charlie?" she asked me.

My first test, I thought, and who better to be the participant but my mother?

"It was beautiful up there, and he was delightful as always."

Mommy looked behind her shoulder. "And your father?"

"Working on something," I said.

"Okay. I'm sure Grandfather is excited about your party next weekend. He's approved everything. He doesn't have that many opportunities to show off the Crest."

"He could," we heard Daddy say. "Lots of great new business deals to celebrate." He paused, looked at Jamie and me, and walked on.

Mommy smiled. "We're going to the Earl for dinner tonight," she told me. "Don't forget."

"Okay," I said.

"See you soon, Jamie," she said, and left for her room.

Jamie rose. "I'd best be getting on home, but there is so much more I want to tell you," he said.

"I have the time. Sit and tell me it all before you leave. I'm not into doing any homework."

He laughed and sat. "Okay, so I made this deal with my father. The deal is I work like I'm working for a year, and then I get half the business. I'm in charge of three of the six boats, and I get the profits they make. It won't make me a millionaire like your father, but it's a good living. And I didn't have to make any initial investment. It's all there for me. 'Course, I worked for it. But I didn't demand it. He offered it."

"That does sound like a good deal for you."

"I hope it's not just for me. There's another part to it, the agreement. My father was a little surprised I asked for it, but he agreed. Not easy to keep secrets from my father. He—and your father, too, I imagine—has that Birdlane bird's-eye view. They're a step ahead of you all the way. Both are and will never stop being fishermen. You have to anticipate every change in the wind and turn of the current."

"Well, what is it? What else did you ask for?"

He turned to me, beaming.

"I get the cabin on Crystal Lake, which you know is only five miles from here, the only lake on Birdlane. It will be mine, deed and all," he said proudly.

"You mean to use as a home?"

"Exactly. It has a full kitchen, a small living room, and a good-sized bedroom. All the furniture is there and still quite good. Can't get a better view of the Birdlane Island seashore. You know that. You've been there often. Remember, you wanted to make it your dollhouse when you were little."

"Yes," I said, smiling. "I left one of my dolls there looking out the window."

"It's still there."

"My mother thought that was funny, too."

"Well, now what I'm saying is, I'd have a business and a home by the time you graduated from high school. Your doll would never leave that window until we could afford a real house."

I was silent, although the words were waiting at the tip of my tongue. This was a Birdlane man's marriage proposal. The woman was supposed to jump to yes or fill in the gaps. Their shyness made the men that way. But I couldn't help pretending I didn't understand. Maybe I didn't want to. We were just talking about my rushing my life, and now this!

"What are you saying exactly, Jamie?"

"After that year I worked, you'd be eighteen," Jamie said. "You wouldn't need your father's permission to get married. I know in the beginning moving out of a palace and into my cabin will be quite a step down, but we could have our own life, children, everything. Maybe after a while your father would approve of it, but I want to be sure you understand, although he might not, probably wouldn't, that I'm not asking you to marry me so I would get money. I'm not some fortune hunter. I really love you, Lisa, and always have."

Jamie was everything any young woman should want in a man, I thought. He'd always been hardworking, responsible, and caring. Maybe we would make each other happy. We would have children and make an effort to be good parents, and maybe the pleasant years would pass uneventfully as we grew older together, loving and needing each other.

If I looked back at all the things he didn't do because of his devotion to me, I wouldn't hesitate to say yes, but would that yes be a yes of appreciation or one of deep-down, eternal love, the love his birthday present signified? Now that I was confronted with such a choice, my mind was electrified with the reasons to say yes and the reasons to say no.

Why was Jamie so confident at seventeen? True, he was months away from being eighteen, but he seemed and sounded so much older than other boys in the senior class, even some of the graduates I knew. Was that what came with being a fisherman, especially on Birdlane Island? You weren't judged by what age you were but by what you accomplished when you competed with much older men.

When Jamie's agreement with his father was done, he'd be so young compared to other boat business owners. But he had grown up working in the business, just like Daddy had. Jamie's confidence came from his experience. He knew what he could and couldn't do. He was really asking me to trust him with my life, my future. Perhaps what he had said about me was just as true for him. We were both older than our ages.

But did I want to be? Very few of my classmates ever talked about what they wanted to do when they were older or what they wanted to be. At seventeen, you certainly weren't too young to think about it. The big decision should have been made at the start of the senior year. Were you going to go to work after you graduated, or were you going to go to college? Mr. Martin, the school guidance counselor and assistant principal, said if you went to college, you probably wouldn't have to decide on a major until you started your third year.

I thought most people liked to put off the decision as long as they could. Some were quite immature about it. Listening to them talk, most of them wanted to be rock stars or movie stars. Daddy wasn't so wrong about the young people in school. They dreamed aloud of leaving Birdlane and living in some big, exciting city with bright lights and parties every day. It seemed almost nobody in my class or the ones just above and below was happy being a Birdie or thought of themselves that way. Some were very dramatic about it, like Joan Hatfield, who had burst out crying at lunch, saying, "I'm suffocating on this island. I feel like jumping into the sea and swimming way out."

"You'd drown," Juliana Albee had said. She took everything literally.

"I'm drowning here!" Joan had cried.

Maybe I was more like her than I thought.

Jamie's proposal, his plan, made me think deeply about so much so quickly, but I didn't want to wake up twenty years from now and look longingly at the horizon, forever wondering if I would have been happier going beyond it, searching like Ahab in the book we had read in English class, *Moby-Dick*, for my own white whale.

"You're not afraid to be a fisherman's wife, are you?" Jamie asked during my deep, thoughtful silence.

"What? Why would I?"

"It's not terrible to have that fear. My mother has admitted her fear many times. Storms, the dangers out there . . . there have been some tragic accidents over the years, like the Kendricks, father and two sons. I'm a good sailor, and I maintain my father's boats, the engines."

"I know you do, Jamie. I'm from here, too, born and bred to the sea. We know what it's like to go out and challenge the sea almost daily. Our first breaths are of sea air. I know women from far away don't know or feel that. Your mother was from Montpelier, Vermont, right?"

"Right," he said. "My father always calls her 'the city girl.' She gets dizzy just looking at the waves. She's never been on any of his boats and hates waving goodbye from the dock. You've heard my father laugh at her."

"Right," I said, smiling.

He looked down, the sadness enveloping him like a shadow. Thinking so deeply, philosophizing, worrying, remembering the worst things, all at once, could turn a day without clouds into a gloomy one. I hated to see Jamie feeling sorry for himself or thinking even for a second that he wasn't good enough for me.

"So it's safer to marry a librarian," I said, "who might get hit by a car one day carrying too many books?"

Jamie laughed. It felt good to pull him out of any darkness. At least I could do that for him.

"So what about my plan, my idea?" he asked, with so much eagerness and hope in his eyes.

"I'm not saying no, but we have time to think about all that, and as you said, you have a whole year after graduation to become your own boss."

He nodded, but he wasn't happy with my answer.

"Ayuh, ayuh, ayuh," he said, suddenly becoming more of a Maine Birdlane person. It was our way of saying a strong yes. Maybe Maine and Birdlane ran too deeply in my blood for me to even think I could leave.

"I do love you, Jamie. I depend on you more than anyone I know."

He leaned over to kiss me again, softly on the lips, while he stroked my hair. Then he laid his head on my lap and looked up at me.

"I'm warning you," he said, "I'll be ruthless if anything or anyone tries to take you from me."

I touched his lips, and then he took my hand and kissed it.

"You really do love me, don't you?" I asked.

"Ayuh, ayuh, ayuh."

I laughed and looked at all of Grandfather's mementos on the wall. Maybe I shouldn't want any other future than the one he dreamed of us having. But I couldn't help the feeling of reluctance.

Not long ago, when Mommy and I were looking out at the sea, she became very quiet. I felt she had gone somewhere else for a few moments.

"What are you thinking so hard about, Mommy?" I had asked.

"How important the dreams for yourself can be, and how sad it is when you've deserted them."

"Have you?"

She had smiled and stroked my hair. "Everyone does at one time or another, Lisa. What you have to do," she had said, looking back at the sea, "is learn how to survive it."

Now, at dinner, because I was so quiet, I was afraid Mommy would start asking me pointed questions about my visit with

Grandfather. Daddy went on and on about business issues, usually finding fault with some decision Grandfather had made. Mommy kept softly saying, "We're supposed to be enjoying ourselves, Melville. Put business aside for now."

He just glared at her and turned to talk to someone else at another table. Fortunately, she was fixated on what I would wear to my party and some of the new things she had seen for me in Bar Harbor.

"It's amazing how although it's almost June, they're advertising fall clothes," she said. "You'll come in with me after your party and we'll do some shopping."

"Yes, there are a few things I've seen in magazines that I'd like."

In between things I said at dinner, I kept thinking about what Grandfather had shown me and what Mommy's reaction might be if she knew what I knew. Would anything be different between my parents? Mommy never bragged about the wealth and success of the Baxter family. She'd just smile when compliments were given to her or simply say "Thank you" and move on to a different topic.

People on Birdlane, especially at restaurants, would always give us big hellos. Mommy's smile was wide, deep, and sincere enough to make up for Daddy's merely nodding. I wondered, did he have any real friends or just associates who had to pander to him, hoping he would pass their names or information on to Grandfather?

He's not going to be able to handle the truth, I thought. It would be like his legs had been swept out from under him if he found out. I hoped there would never be a reason to expose it, even though Grandfather seemed so sure there would be.

Because Grandfather was so excited about hosting my birthday party, it seemed bigger and better than the sweet sixteen held at our house. How could anything compete with the Crest, anyway? Daddy stood off to the side with some of the fathers who had brought their daughters, and Mommy spoke to the mothers. Jamie and I were called out to start the dancing after the food had been served. There were enough balloons, I thought, to lift me up if they were all tied to me. Because Grandfather put no limit on the guests, I was able to invite my whole class, and all of Jamie's friends were invited.

After the cake and singing of "Happy Birthday," I looked at Daddy. Mommy was whispering something to him. He looked at Grandfather and then crossed the floor to ask me to dance. I glanced at Grandfather, who gave me his tight smile and nodded his head. Daddy saw him, too.

"The old man needs to approve everything, even when you brush your teeth," he mumbled.

"Why are you so critical of Grandfather when you want so much to be just like him?" I asked.

He held me away from him a little farther. "You have that wrong," he said. "If anything, he should be more like me. He's grown too soft for business. He should retire. Maybe you can convince him."

"I hardly think that," I said. "He's as witty and bright as ever."

Daddy smirked and stopped dancing. "I have to speak to someone. Enjoy your party."

He walked away, leaving me looking a little silly in the middle of the dance floor. Instantly, Jamie was holding me and dancing.

"Are you all right?" he asked.

I took a deep breath. Mommy was talking to a group of other women. No one was looking my way. All my friends were having fun. Daddy was already gesturing heavily in some kind of an argument with a couple of the fathers.

"I'm going to leave the ballroom. Don't follow right away. I'll wait for you in the hallway and we'll get some fresh air. I'll show you the side door in a pantry that opens to the cliff."

Jamie nodded and released his grip on my hand. I turned and slowly walked to the entrance of the ballroom. Fortunately, there were people standing in front of Grandfather Charlie, so he didn't see me leave. I walked down the hallway to the left and waited for Jamie. He saw me and hurried to join me. Without speaking a word, I led him to the pantry and out the side door. I headed for the large old oak at the rear of the mansion. There wasn't a sea view here, but it was very private, tucked away at the southeast corner of the property. I plopped down under the tree and embraced my legs. He sat beside me quickly.

"What's wrong?" he asked immediately. "Did your father say something unpleasant to you?"

I continued to look down. There was no one besides Mommy to whom I had entrusted any secrets. Over the years, Jamie and I told each other very private things about our own families. I didn't have even a girlfriend who was closer to me when it came to those sorts of secrets. But telling Jamie what Grandfather had shown me would truly be betraying a trust. Despite how much I wanted to do it, I couldn't.

Before I could ponder it any longer, Mommy appeared outside the side door.

"Lisa," she called. "What are you doing out here?"

"Just getting a breath of air," I said, standing quickly.

"Your grandfather wants to say good night. He's going to bed. The party's not going to last much longer."

"Okay, we're coming. Sorry."

"It's all right," she said as we drew closer and she looked at Jamie. "I know what it means to share a moment when everything seems so overwhelming."

Could she have said anything better?

I took Jamie's hand, and we hurried back to the ballroom. Grandfather studied my face as I approached him. He could see that I had not betrayed the secret. He smiled and I hugged him and thanked him for the party.

"I've been thinking," he said. "I'm going to invite your parents and you to move into the Crest. I'm getting along in years now. It's important to me that we spend more time together, feel more like a family."

"That would be wonderful, Grandfather."

"For the future, a little challenging but a lot of joy. Anna will be very happy," he said. "I'm going to sleep. Enjoy the rest of your party."

"Wow," Jamie said, overhearing. "It'll be great visiting you here."

I looked at Mommy. Grandfather had already told her, but I knew I had to brace myself for one of her and Daddy's stormy arguments. She recognized my fears and leaned over to whisper, "Don't worry. I'll promise him I'll share one of the bigger bedrooms upstairs, but I'll still have one of my own."

Mommy didn't bring it up on the way home. She said she wanted to wait for Grandfather to offer the invitation in person. As we both anticipated, Daddy's reaction was to be unenthusiastic. He mumbled something about being a guest, but Mommy stayed on it, and he eventually agreed to a move in the fall. There would be a nice profit to be had on our house, too. As Daddy had said, a Baxter house was an extra value for a buyer.

Mommy was the happiest I had seen her in a long time because of our moving to the Crest. Grandfather gave her complete authority to make any changes she wanted in the bedrooms and the formal living room. "Good to have a woman's touch again," he said.

Daddy was glum and disinterested. "Still feel like a guest," he muttered.

After we moved and were living in Grandfather's home, Jamie felt more comfortable visiting. That didn't change Daddy's attitude toward him. He was still "a fisherman's son." Daddy made that sound almost like a curse word.

"How you can belittle the people whose work production you so depend on is beyond me," Mommy told him.

"It's a matter of where you are in society," Daddy replied.

I thought about him and how much more the truth would hurt him because of what he thought of himself and the meaning of our family name. On the other hand, Grandfather didn't have these kinds of "I'm superior to everyone else" thoughts, and he liked to mingle with the fishermen. He would often spend hours with them at the Wharf Bar and Grill.

Daddy said it was an embarrassment. "We have to negotiate prices with these people," he'd complain.

Grandfather would just smile and say, "You don't understand, Melville. If someone is your friend, he feels worse about undercutting you."

"Chout," Daddy would say, and then walk away.

The last time that happened, Grandfather turned to me and said, "This is not brain surgery, our business, no matter what your father is saying. We negotiate a fair price with the fishermen, remembering they have to make a good living or they disappear, and then where would we be? We work on the packaging and negotiate with delivery companies and our customers. Your father has done a good job of finding markets, but he makes it all sound too difficult, and being a successful businessperson doesn't make you better than anyone else. Your grandmother would not permit either of our children to look down on other people."

I wondered why Grandfather was telling me all this—and so vehemently, too.

It wouldn't be all that long before I knew.

CHAPTER FOUR

A month after we had moved into the Crest, I was working very hard in school on a painting of Frenchman Bay with lobster-fishing boats coming home. The shades of red and blue were very important with the sun moving toward the horizon to hide until morning. I didn't want the boats to look like they were all the same distance from the pier. In my mind, one of them was Jamie's father's, and he was on it. I knew Mr. Angelo was keeping an eye on my work even though he was fiddling about, organizing his materials.

Maybe it was the intensity of my work or maybe it was just the fear that I would do a poor job of it and disappoint Mr. Angelo, but I was in such deep concentration that the floor began to feel like the deck of a lobster boat navigating the wavy sea, the few times I had been on one with Grandfather Charlie. I think I groaned and brought my hand, paintbrush and all, to my forehead before I tilted too far to my right and brushed the easel, causing it to topple as I slipped to my knees.

Mr. Angelo came rushing over and helped me to a chair.

"Are you all right?" he asked. I nodded, but I was very frightened and he surely could see that.

"My painting," I said.

"It's fine. No damage." He put it back on the easel. "Just hold on," he said, and rushed out to get our school principal, Mrs. Curtis. The two of them came hurrying back.

"How are you, Lisa?" Mrs. Curtis asked, remaining just a step or two back from me as if I might be suffering from some infectious disease. She was a tall, thin woman with light reddish-brown hair and firm cheeks that looked stretched tightly enough to tear before they reached her jaw. Some of the older students called her a "killer whale" because she looked so stern standing outside her office when class ended and the bell rang. She'd study everyone as if she was searching for a broken rule and would pounce as quickly as a whale. Often, she'd pluck out someone, usually one of the boys, and take him to her office for a stinging lecture or a punishment like detention.

I had caught my breath, but I was still frightened. This was one of the symptoms Mommy repeatedly had warned me to report.

"Just a little dizzy," I said.

Mr. Angelo brought me a glass of water. He smiled and patted my hand.

"Just try to relax," he said.

What I think surprised me the most was how although every teacher, even the secretary in the high school, probably knew of my heart valve issue, they rarely caused me to feel self-conscious about it.

Mrs. Curtis's secretary appeared, looking a bit frazzled. She held her hands to her chest. She took deep breaths like she had run from the office to here.

"I couldn't reach Mrs. Baxter. Her maid didn't know where she was."

"Did you call her father?"

"I called his office, and his secretary told me he was in Augusta on business. Her grandfather got the message and said to have her brought home. He is almost there himself and said it would be quicker than him coming here to get her, and he'd see to it that Dr. Bush came to their house."

"I can take her," Mr. Angelo said.

Mrs. Curtis looked at him strangely but then nodded. "If there is any worrying change, you have my permission to go right to the Bush clinic on the way, but call me instantly on arrival there. She's still under my care until her parents are present."

"Yes, ma'am," Mr. Angelo said. He smiled at me and took the glass of water.

I was feeling better, but I didn't want to say anything that would reveal how frightened I really was.

Mr. Angelo brought his car to the front of the school and got out to help me in. I didn't look back for fear that others inside were watching us, watching me. I got in, and we drove off.

I suppose Mr. Angelo was more nervous than I was. He talked the whole way to the Baxter mansion, raving about the work I had already done on my picture of the bay and describing the first time he had tried to capture it in a painting of his own.

"Funny," he said, "but sometimes when you're far away, your hometown images are more vivid than they were when you were there. You look like you're feeling better," he added, after glancing at me as we started up the hill.

"I am," I said. "Thank you."

"Oh, my pleasure. Anyway, I get to see the view from the Crest," he said, smiling.

Grandfather was waiting at the front door. Anna appeared beside him as we drove up.

"Thanks," he told Mr. Angelo. He took me by the arm and handed me off to Anna. "Take her to her room. Dr. Bush will be here shortly. We'll see if we have to make arrangements to go to Mount Desert Island Hospital."

"I feel okay, Grandfather. Where's Mommy?"

"Some shopping spree in Bar Harbor with the Ladies Auxiliary of Birdlane. The sea is rough today."

"I can hear how the wind has grown stronger."

"Yes, but these island women think they're all seasoned sailors. I've made efforts to contact her, but I just heard the ferries are grounded until there is more calming."

"How will she get back?"

"Let's not worry about that right now. I'll find a way. Let's concentrate on you."

"What about Daddy?"

"He has yet to call back. Just go to your room," he said. I looked back to see Mr. Angelo drive off. I really hadn't gotten a chance to thank him properly.

Anna held my arm all the way to my room, which was on the first floor. We had six bedrooms, but Mommy felt that having me go up and down the spiral stairway all the time wasn't necessary. It was her soft way of saying I had to be extra, extra careful. Would I ever be like other girls my age?

Anna helped me undress, get into more comfortable clothes, and then into bed.

"I'm really feeling a lot better," I told her.

She smiled. "I'm sure you'll be fine."

"I'm so embarrassed. Everyone in the school is probably talking about me."

"Hardly a reason to worry about that. My mother was just like you. She'd wake up with a flu or something, have a temperature, and start cleaning the house, not a complaint uttered until she practically collapsed. 'Face your demons down, don't ignore them,' my father would preach."

"He was a preacher, right?"

"A minister, yes."

We heard Dr. Bush arriving and Grandfather rushing him to my room.

Dr. Bush was a stout six-foot-tall man with a brushed rust-colored mustache and bushy matching eyebrows. Since he had begun taking care of me, his hair had thinned and grayed. He had kind, compassionate light blue eyes and was always very soft-spoken and gentle with me. I could barely feel his fingers on my wrist. That bothered me because he made me feel so fragile. Sometimes I felt like shouting "Feel my muscles" or something.

I lay back while he carried out his exam. Grandfather stood in the doorway, watching.

"She's doing fine," Dr. Bush said. "Nothing wrong that I can see."

"Maybe I'll still arrange to have the cardiologist at Mount Desert

Island reexamine her as soon as possible. I'm sure her mother is going to want that."

"Sure. Never hurts," Dr. Bush said, not taking any offense.

Grandfather walked the doctor out. Anna brought me some tea with honey and a biscuit.

"Any news about Mommy?" I asked.

"Your grandfather sent a boat to Bar Harbor and called the police chief. You know your grandfather. No moss grows on that rock."

I nodded and smiled. My eyelids suddenly felt so heavy.

"Did Dr. Bush give me anything?"

"No, you're just naturally exhausted from it all. Who wouldn't be? Rest. I'll keep you up on everything," Anna said. I nodded and closed my eyes.

I had no idea how long I had slept, but I woke to the sound of crying. I rose slowly, whispering "Mommy." Anna was there before I reached the bedroom door. She seized my arm.

"Back to bed," she ordered softly. Even so, her voice cracked with emotion.

"What is it? Why are you crying?"

The terror in her face frightened me more than anything. She was afraid to speak.

"There has been an accident," she said as soon as I had sat on the bed.

"Wait," I heard Grandfather say. He appeared in the doorway with Dr. Bush at his side again. Grandfather looked pale, his eyes red.

"Best you lie down," Dr. Bush said. They both stepped in, but I didn't move.

"Where's my mother?" I asked. My voice was dry, hollow, as if someone else was speaking through me.

"There has been a dreadful accident," Grandfather began. He stepped closer.

Dr. Bush took my hand. I glanced at him fearfully and turned back to Grandfather. Anna had stepped back and was sniffling.

"Preliminary reports tell me that the boat lost its engine power, was caught in a wave, and capsized. The skipper was able to get to your mother, but . . ."

"But what?"

"Either the edge of the boat or something on it struck her in the head when the boat overturned."

"She died instantly," Dr. Bush said. I think he thrust that into the description to make me feel better that she didn't struggle or drown. But it didn't diminish the effect it had on me.

For a few moments, I was too overwhelmed to cry.

"It's best I give you something, Lisa. The impact on our bodies when we have tragedies is bigger than people know."

I said nothing. I stared ahead while he gave me a shot.

Grandfather was letting his tears streak down his cheeks. "She was the daughter I wanted," he said, almost too low for me to hear.

Anna stepped out of the room.

"Have you reached Daddy?" I asked.

"I left a message for him to call me when he gets to his next meeting. Your aunt said she'll stop by tomorrow. Made it sound like an ordinary visit," he said, mostly to himself. "There's lots for us to do now, but you rest, because you'll need your strength. I'll be leaning on you," he added.

What Grandfather was saying was finally taking hold of me.

Mommy would never walk into my room again? She wouldn't ever be here watching over me? She wouldn't be kissing me good night and waking me in the morning? She wouldn't be here to watch me grow into the woman she had promised I would become, beautiful, healthy, and strong, a woman just like her? She loved my artwork and had recently begun to take me for walks on the Baxter estate to look at the sea and the scenery, imagining the pictures I would draw and the paintings I would create. Would that never again happen? Would anything look the same without her?

Dr. Bush guided me backward to rest my head on my pillow. I felt my eyes closing again and tried to keep them open. *I won't be treated like a child*, I thought, and then I heard him say, "Don't fight it, Lisa. Let's delay all the troubles for a while longer. We want you strong."

I let my eyes close.

When I opened them, I saw Jamie sitting beside my bed, his arms on it and his head resting against them. I reached out slowly and touched his hair.

"Lisa," he said through his tears. "My family is devastated. Even my father is crying. The whole village knows, and it's like the end of the world down there. Many fishermen have docked in a show of sympathy, and even some stores have closed their doors."

"I still don't believe it."

"I know. It was a true sea accident, with the engines dying and the boat and the skipper at the mercy of the roused sea, especially with those wind gusts."

I started to sit up, and he leaped to help.

"Is my father back?"

"Not yet. Your grandfather is in his office."

"Well, where's my father?"

"He was on his way to some second meeting and didn't hear about it until he got there. He's coming from there, I think Phippsburg."

"He probably finished his meeting first," I said dryly.

Jamie didn't respond. Then he took my hand and said, "I'm sorry, Lisa."

My mother's accident was one thing; my father's reaction was only going to point up how cold and empty their relationship had become. Had it ever been anything more?

Not too long ago, when my mother and I were sitting near the cliff and looking out at the sea, I simply asked her why she had married Daddy. I didn't think she was going to answer, but after a long moment she turned to me and said, "If you don't have solid home roots, you lose any sense of belonging and just drift. When I joined the cruise staff, I rarely went home. My father's business took us first to Bergen, Norway, but we didn't settle down there. His business took us to many other locations, including the Middle East. I never really established long friendships. By the time I came to Birdlane on a cruise, I was exhausted with loneliness.

"Melville was much younger then, of course, already quite well-to-do as his father's vice president. I admired his self-confidence, which has unfortunately metamorphosed into pure arrogance. He was a handsome man and had a lot more personality, some sense of humor; I'd go so far as to say he was charming. The first time he saw me with a group from the cruise ship, he was attending to some fisherman's boat at the dock, and I was just standing there looking out at the sea and admiring the view from the island. He came over and stood beside me. I didn't even know he was there for a few moments, and suddenly I heard him say, 'How can I help you? I really want to.'

"I don't know if I would go as far as to say it was a flaming romance, but he did have everything I wanted, the stability and, yes, even the power and position. I know it all sounds like an excuse, but that's how it was."

"I'd better see to Grandfather," I said now, starting to get up. "It's all falling on his shoulders right now."

Jamie helped me walk down the hallway to Grandfather's office. We were both surprised to see that Daddy was there. He looked at Grandfather before he rose to greet me with a quick hug.

"We're just finishing up the arrangements," he said, as if we were talking about a business meeting.

"Mommy is gone," I said. I didn't even see tears in his eyes.

"For now, it's best to concentrate on what has to be done," he said. He looked at Grandfather.

"The funeral is in two days. She is with the funeral director in Bar Harbor," Grandfather said.

"I want to see her."

"According to what I heard, Dr. Bush thinks it would be wiser for you to gather your strength, Lisa," Daddy said. "We can only go through this once."

I shook my head.

"I can take her," Jamie said.

"You can take her?" Daddy nearly shouted.

"Well . . ."

"Yes, he can. And he will, in the morning," I said. "Grandfather?"

"Okay, Jamie. You can use our company boat. For now, though, please rest, Lisa. I'll have Anna bring your dinner to your room."

"Jamie will be eating with me," I said.

"I've got to make some calls," Daddy said angrily. "And, frankly, I'd rather be alone before we get inundated with mourners."

He walked out of Grandfather's office.

"He was never good at dealing with sadness and disappointment. Practically shrunk inside himself at his mother's funeral. Your aunt can meet you at the funeral parlor."

"I don't . . ."

"Let her do something. I still practically pay for her existence. Her nursing salary is inconsistent."

"Okay, Grandfather."

He nodded and lowered his head.

Back in my room, I fought to stay awake again. Whatever Dr. Bush had given me lingered. I fell asleep before dinner and then almost right afterward. When I woke again, Jamie was leaning back in the chair, his eyes closed. I woke him and told him to go home.

"Okay. I'll come get you at eight tomorrow morning if you want."

"Yes."

He kissed me and held me for a long moment before he turned and left quickly so I wouldn't see him cry.

Grandfather was up early but looking years older. I asked about Daddy. "He went to the company building. Work is his solution to grief. It's his solution to everything," he muttered. "I'll be going with you," he said. "It's too much to lay on that young man, and anyway, I want to go. We can't just leave her alone."

I started to cry, finally. Grandfather put his arms around me, but I felt how fragile he was, and most of the day I was looking after him as much as I was mourning Mommy. I had never really liked Aunt Frances, but her nursing skills were important when it came to Grandfather. He seemed to grow more fragile every moment at the funeral parlor. She knew how to keep him steady and occasionally took his pulse, making it look like she was only holding his hand. While we were there, I barely shed a tear. I told myself that when I cried, I was admitting that Mommy was gone.

The funeral was different. Even someone made of stone would cry, I thought.

I had been to the Mount Desert Street Cemetery in Bar Harbor a few times when I was younger, but the one time that stood out in my memory was going there to visit Grandmother Harriet's grave on the tenth anniversary of her death.

The Baxter section of the cemetery was clearly set apart from other gravesites by the monument that was erected in commemoration of the local men who had served in the Civil War on the right and a beautiful line of pine trees on the left. One of the things I had learned in school, but especially at the cemetery, was that at the time of the Civil War, Bar Harbor was called Eden.

Grandfather Charlie liked to call it Eden all the time and joked that Adam and Eve had lived there. "A proper place for your grandmother Harriet to lie and wait for me," he had said.

It was the first time I had heard the idea that the dead waited for a loved one before they went on to heaven. "Makes the journey easier," Grandfather Charlie had said. Mommy thought it was a quaint, lovely, and romantic idea, but Daddy thought it was another example of religious nonsense. Grandfather had made sure that on Grandmother Harriet's tombstone there were two hands clasping. Daddy had nothing like that done for Mommy's tombstone. In my heart of hearts, I vowed that I would do something special in the near future.

It truly seemed as if the entire population of Birdlane Island came to Mommy's funeral and later paid their respects at the Crest. All my classmates, Mommy and Daddy's friends, local shopkeepers, everyone who came, seemed afraid to talk too much to me before the funeral. Maybe they were scared of seeing me cry and then feeling responsible for bringing on more grief for me. Only Jamie was clearly unafraid and clearly as sad as I was. He remained at my side as much and as long as he could. Every few minutes, it seemed, Daddy would see us and come over to tell me to talk to other people.

"Show respect and dignity," he ordered, and then added his mantra, "You're a Baxter." He looked angrily at Jamie as if Jamie was keeping me from doing that.

"I'm my mother's daughter. Respect and dignity for her is what matters most," I replied.

He turned red in the face and walked away.

In the days that followed the funeral, whenever Jamie was able to be at my side, he was, being a quiet support wrapping around the hollow ache that had settled inside me. Jamie filled the empty space with things for us to do, small distractions meant to pull me away from my thoughts, memories of my mother that pressed heavily on me when I was alone.

"As long as you feel all right, I will continue to find things for us to do," he said. "Everything has happened so fast; we never talked about your dizzy spell in the art room."

"Dr. Bush examined me that day. All was fine," I said.

I left out what he really meant: fine for now, but now was not forever. It was what everyone who lived off the sea and traveled it knew: you couldn't see beyond the horizon, but you had to imagine what possibly could lie ahead and be sure your lifeboats were in good shape.

CHAPTER FIVE

I didn't want to return to school, but even Anna said I'd feel worse and my mother would be upset if I didn't. Jamie sensed all that. When Arthur, one of Grandfather's drivers, brought me home every day, Jamie would come by to greet me. He often held my hand when no one was looking, his touch a silent promise that I wasn't alone. He even kissed me on the cheek now whenever he said so long, something he had previously been hesitant to do, especially in public. He was so shy. Daddy saw that as a weakness and never hesitated to tell me so. My reaction had evolved from accepting it to telling him he could use some shyness himself.

I didn't stay after school to work on my art yet. I couldn't help feeling guilty doing enjoyable things after Mommy's passing. Mr. Angelo, with his kind eyes and patient smile, said everything would be ready when I felt inclined and strong enough to continue. What made it even more difficult was that I had always looked forward to Mommy's comments about my artwork. I had looked to her more than I did to my art teacher. She was always very honest and serious about it. I sensed that maybe it was because she saw so much of me in my work. Watching the strokes of my brush, she could tell instantly when I was happy or when I was sad. Now I was like an actor who had lost his audience and was alone on the stage. How could he utter another line?

Meanwhile, Jamie continued to suggest things for us to do after I got out of school that would keep me from thinking about Mommy's tragedy, especially walks on the beach, during which we discovered things like stones so polished they could easily pass for expensive jewels. Sometimes I thought he was going to wear out his vocal cords describing sea life and making sure I didn't have a silent moment with my sad thoughts. The moment my eyes watered, he would do something silly like somersaults or racing toward waves as they approached the shore and retreating just in time. Of course, I remembered my sea walks with Mommy.

What I didn't remember, however, because Mommy was the one who kept track of my important medical exams, was that I had an upcoming appointment with the specialist in Bar Harbor. Grandfather was the one who received the reminder call because Daddy was on another job mission.

"But I don't feel sick, Grandfather," I said. "If I wasn't sicker after Mommy's funeral, I must be all right."

"I'm sure you are, but we owe it to your mother to do what she planned," he said. "I can't lose you, too," he added, but with a new intensity that took me by surprise.

"You won't, Grandfather," I said.

His smile was softer and more loving than any I could remember. This week, he was looking at me differently as well. I rarely caught him staring at me or watching the simple things I did, but he was doing that now. When I looked back at him, he turned away. He really appeared to be worrying about me.

I mentioned it to Anna.

"Oh, dearie," she said. "When terrible things happen, it takes time for them to settle in fully. Your grandfather knows how sad you are, and that makes him sadder still. He puts on a big show, bigger than your father does sometimes, but he's a softy."

She hugged me, and then she told me that people often shed their mourning like birds shed feathers, just a little at a time. She also said that whether mourners liked it or not, they learned to live in a world without their loved ones.

"Do mourners change?" I asked her. "Change who we were, who we are?" I wondered how I would.

"Oh, yes. We all change in subtle, little ways sometimes, and sometimes people who have a more difficult time change a lot. It's natural to grow a little bitter."

"Am I?"

"You've grown older," she said. "Quickly. And maybe a little wiser."

The day of my appointment, Daddy told me Grandfather would take me.

"If I miss this day at work, I'll have to put in five additional days," he said. "Besides, it's only a checkup. Your grandfather can handle it, and all the information will be sent to me as well."

Jamie wanted to come, too, but it was a school day, and I was beginning to feel guilty about how much of his time I was taking, especially time he should have been spending at work.

Grandfather and I set out for Bar Harbor. We were lucky. It was a clear, calm autumn day. When I turned to my right in the boat, I could imagine my mother with her eyes closed, smiling, with the breeze making her hair dance. Memories like that froze in your mind, I thought. Life was filled with beautiful paintings, but the ones that featured people you loved were very special. It was as if the whole world faded away around them.

As if he could see what I saw, Grandfather took my hand and sat with a gentle smile.

"One day I'm going to paint your portrait, Grandfather."

He laughed. "Do it from memory," he said. "I can't sit still long enough even for a photograph."

He was up helping dock the boat when we reached Bar Harbor. Daddy always made the driver do everything. He and Grandfather were so unalike that I didn't need any proof they weren't blood-related.

I thought my exam went well, but when I looked at Grandfather after the doctor had spoken to him, I wasn't so sure. I felt my heartbeat quicken.

"You're doing okay," the doctor said, "but we're going to keep a close eye on you, and if you have any more dizzy spells, I want to know it as soon as possible. Now, here's something I want you to use occasionally, and especially if you feel unsteady."

He handed me something to put on my finger and showed me how to use it and read it. It showed the level of oxygen in my blood.

"It's called an oximeter," he said, looking more at Grandfather than at me. "It was created for patients about four years ago or so."

Right now it showed my blood oxygen as being at 98 percent. I took it off my finger. It was one thing to think about my symptoms, even feel them, but I was afraid I would be using this so much, and more people would wonder about me, especially classmates. Jamie would probably think it was wonderful.

The doctor could read my thoughts. "It's not necessary for you to use it constantly," he said. "You'll make yourself worry too much, okay?"

I nodded.

"Maybe I'll use it, too, once in a while," Grandfather said.

The doctor agreed, a little more sincerely than I had anticipated.

"Is there something about your health I should know?" I asked Grandfather.

"No, I'm as fit as a fiddle."

He smiled, and we left to return home.

The biggest surprise of all after my hospital visit was how much time Grandfather would spend with me, rushing home from work at the company and never missing a dinner, whereas Daddy missed at least two a week.

I had yet to see Daddy show his grief over the loss of my mother, his wife. If anything, Mommy's death seemed to make him an angrier man, which was what Anna had said was true for many people. Daddy could start an argument with Grandfather on almost anything at the company, even something as small as the size of a secretary's desk or the style of chairs in the lobby. If they argued in front of me and Daddy walked out, Grandfather would explain everything in detail to me if it had to do with a customer or shipping.

One time in the late fall, they argued before dinner in the hallway, and Daddy just went off in a huff and left the house, slamming the front door so hard that I thought the walls shook. I came running to see what had happened now.

"Nothing special," Grandfather said. "His problem is he has to win every argument and negotiation, no matter what. In the end, he'll probably drive away more customers than he gets. He just misunderstood my work ethic. Negotiation means compromise. Remember that, Lisa." He turned to walk away and then paused. "There's something else to remember," he said, "something my father taught me."

He hesitated as if he was still deciding whether or not to tell me.

"Grandfather?"

"Sometimes you have to compromise with yourself for peace of mind. Don't be ashamed of doing it."

He walked on.

I saw Anna standing in the doorway to the dining room.

She smiled. "When men reach your grandfather's age," she said, "they want to get out as much of what they have learned in their lives as soon as they can."

She started to walk away, then stopped, turning back just like Grandfather had done.

"Look at me doing the same thing. If there ever was a pot calling a kettle black . . ."

Her laughter trailed after her. How lucky I was to have them both in my life, I thought, especially with Mommy gone.

When you're younger, you're not as conscious of time. You dream of being older so you can do more things, have more control of your life, but you don't realize the day or the year as much as you do when you're older. Grandfather said he was aware of every minute now. Maybe this was one of the results of a family tragedy Anna had described: you couldn't help but feel and be older and more aware of what would be coming tomorrow.

The fall seemed to slip by. You could almost smell winter in the ocean breeze. The water looked colder, the clouds heavier. Birds looked more frantic to me. It was as if they and the geese were afraid they wouldn't get away.

I returned to my art that I had been working on at the time of my dizzy spell. Mr. Angelo had safely stored the painting I was doing at the time.

"This is your first masterpiece," he said. "You have to complete it."

Jamie often half-jokingly complained that I loved art more than I could possibly love him. It was true that when I was working, I didn't even realize he was there. After I said "What?" five or so times, he usually slipped away.

When many of his friends went on to colleges, trade schools, and the military, Jamie had begun that serious work with his father, who had acquired the three additional fishing boats. Jamie was totally in charge of the three and very proud of it as well. He never stopped reminding me this was all part of his deal with his father and his plan for us.

One night when Daddy went on one of his frequent business tips, Jamie came to have dinner with Grandfather and me. Lately Grandfather brought work home, too, but it seemed to me he did that to show me what he and the company were doing. He liked having Jamie as an audience, too. I didn't know how many times Grandfather had said, "This isn't brain surgery. Your mother helped with this; you can get into it, too."

I did some of the accounting Mommy had done. Jamie thought that was something I should be proud of doing: "Just like me, you're becoming an important part of your family business."

"My father hasn't said anything about it. He looks just as annoyed as he did when my mother was doing it."

"I couldn't tell," Jamie said, smiling. "To me, he always looks annoyed."

Maybe laughter was the best response.

Our conversation inevitably led to talking about our future, our Birdlane home, and our family. Although Jamie grew more and more excited about it, I had this strange feeling, almost a frightening feeling, building in my heart. Jamie's vision of me seemed far too simple. I respected the Birdie women like Jamie's mother, women who were dedicated to their husbands and families, women who kept their homes running and managed a good part of their daily lives, freeing the men to concentrate almost solely on their fishing businesses and enjoying the companionship.

I kept looking longingly at that horizon, unable to stop the feeling that there was something more for me out there, something bigger, something that would complete me. Could I have both? Surely I loved Jamie.

Daddy was contradictory when it came to Jamie's family and those like them. Although he still often ridiculed and belittled the fishermen of Birdlane, he was just as obnoxious when it came to my decision to pursue a career in art by attending the College of the Atlantic in Bar Harbor. He also thought Grandfather's explaining everything to me about the family business was a waste of time.

"Your mother was good at accounting; that's about it when it comes to the Baxter company," he uttered once after Grandfather explained how he dealt with restaurant corporations with lobster specialties. "The only thing she could cook was the books." He usually laughed at his own jokes, no matter at whose expense.

"What can *you* cook? You'd burn tea," I told him. I saw him wince, but he didn't snap back as usual.

I don't think he and I were ever as close as most fathers and their daughters and sons. He was less inclined to offer compliments and soft, loving remarks than he was to offer criticism and give me an order, always claiming he was trying to make me a better Baxter. Now that I knew the truth about his identity, those sorts of comments from him had less and less impact. Truthfully, however, he was Melville Baxter more than he was my father.

Without revealing the secret Grandfather and I shared, I explained my feelings about Daddy to Jamie one night after dinner in late April. We took a walk to our favorite spot at the Crest, the oak tree toward the rear of the mansion. I brought a blanket. There wasn't a sea view here, but it was very private, tucked away at the southeast corner of the property.

"You look tired tonight," I said when we were sprawled on the blanket.

"I'm working practically two shifts to complete the deal with my father," he said. I studied him a moment. He looked so much more mature. Since he had graduated and begun this work program with his father, all his teenage characteristics and thoughts had drifted off, not that he wasn't always one of the most serious and responsible young men I knew at school.

I guess I can marry Jamie and raise a family here, I thought, but when I turned and looked into the darkness, I couldn't help feeling that a commitment like that would surely take the fire out of my dreams. Maybe Mommy hadn't realized hers, but I know she wanted me to realize mine. It was hard and would be hard to explain to Jamie. His goals were so real, so attainable. Mine were so "out there," so elusive, and so dependent on a lucky moment. Mr. Angelo had made that clear to me.

"It's not that you get lucky and that's that," he said. "It's that you're ready for luck when it shows itself. I wasn't; you will be."

Was it wrong for someone like Mr. Angelo to fill me with so much hope and expectation?

"If you don't dream, you'll never be disappointed in yourself. You'll always feel satisfied," Mommy had told me when she was really talking about herself. "But it's not worth the trade-off."

"You're in deep thought," Jamie said now, waking me out of it.

I smiled. "You're always there, trying to protect me, even from my own thoughts. I'll always be safe with you."

"And loved," he said, and brought his lips to mine.

A kiss was so much, I thought. First, it was a promise that could be mutual. It was also a moment filled with romantic anticipation. Something thrilling and exciting would surely light up your body and make it tingle in places you never expected. Jamie wasn't a schooled lover, but it was clear to me that he put everything he felt into his kiss. If I waited too long to press my lips back to his, I sensed he would feel a great letdown, a fear. Was I kissing him because I didn't want to hurt him or because I loved him?

He was whispering it and holding me tightly. What could my mother's kiss to my father have been if they had grown so far apart? Had she simply been a good actress? Was I as good?

"We'll have a wonderful life," he whispered. "I promise."

I kissed his neck, which surprised him, and he brought his hand to my breast. He rolled into me, and I let his hand travel everywhere. We were both moaning. The sexual pleasure kept me from thinking too hard. I put his hand under my skirt. He felt about and then stopped.

"I'd hate to think that I was taking advantage of you," he said.

"You're not."

He looked around. "This isn't the place I envisioned for it. I want it to be ours, everything . . . ours."

"You're a hopeless romantic," I said, and he laughed.

He turned over, and I laid my head against his shoulder. We were looking up at the stars.

"I want to be everything for you," he said. "Is that dumb?"

"No, but just be everything I need you to be."

"Oh, I'll be that for sure."

"Lisa!" We heard Anna calling my name. "Lisa!"

I stood up quickly.

"What's wrong, Anna?"

"You're grandfather has a big surprise for you," she shouted, not really seeing where I was.

I took Jamie's hand. He scooped up the blanket, and we hurried to the house. Grandfather came out of his office the moment we entered.

"Your art teacher couldn't wait until morning to tell you," he said.

"Tell me what?"

"Your painting of the bay and the fishermen's boats . . . was chosen to be displayed at the Doyle Art Gallery. We're very proud of you, Lisa, and we know your mother would be beaming. They're putting it up in the morning," he said.

I looked at Jamie. He should have looked happier, excited, but instead he looked worried.

I took his hand. "Tomorrow you'll take me there to see it. Okay?"

"Sure," he said. "Oh, I can't. Tomorrow we're going to fish at the cove inlet. My father has a plan utilizing all the boats."

"I'll take you," Grandfather said.

I looked at Jamie. Jamie couldn't have seemed more worried if I had found another possible boyfriend. I squeezed his hand.

"And then when you are free, we'll go again. Okay, Jamie? We'll go later in the day and then go to dinner. My treat."

"No, it'll be mine," Grandfather said. "I don't have all that much to celebrate these days. Okay, Jamie?"

I thought that was cute and thoughtful of Grandfather, making sure Jamie didn't think he was the recipient of a charitable act because he couldn't afford an expensive Bar Harbor restaurant.

"Sure," he said.

"Someday we'll hang it in our home," I whispered.

And he beamed.

"You could be a great politician," my mother once told me. "The way you manipulate your father."

I had laughed. But was I doing that again? Only this time manipulating Jamie? I hated to think I was being dishonest, but sometimes you did things more to help those you cared for than for yourself.

I had the feeling this wouldn't be the last time.

CHAPTER SIX

When we told my father, his first question was, "Is she gettin' paid for it?"

"In respect for her worth as an artist. Did you ever put a value on that, Melville?" Grandfather asked him. "Respect?"

"Yeah, I tried buyin' some groceries with it, but they wouldn't sell," Daddy said dryly.

Grandfather shook his head. "If you look down on everyone and everything but the almighty dollar, Melville, you'll eventually break your neck."

"Little late for those sorts of lessons, Father. You're takin' off work to visit the art gallery?"

"There's nothing urgent pending, Melville. You can come along and take pride in your daughter's work."

"I got the Pendletons comin' to meet in the mornin'. I want to get that delivery cost to North Carolina reduced. It doesn't fit the model I created."

"You created? That ratio has been there since you were twelve," Grandfather said.

"It's gotta be fixed," Daddy insisted. "Last I checked, we're not a charity."

"Whatever," Grandfather said. "We're leaving at eight thirty if you change your mind."

He didn't, but Grandfather didn't say another word about it. I was too excited to care as well. Once we got to the dock at Bar Harbor, it only took about five or six minutes to arrive at the Doyle Art Gallery, which occupied a whole building. It was a much less costly imitation of the famous Building of the Arts because of its four large columns and steps to the portico and main entrance. I used to dream about this, and now the dream had come true. Mommy would surely have been even prouder of me than Grandfather. I couldn't help feeling guilty being so happy.

"You're thinking about your mother, aren't you?" Grandfather asked. I nodded. He put his arm around my shoulder to give me a hug. "She's with us. Just like your grandmother," he said.

We started for the building. Eddie Doyle himself was awaiting me at the main entrance. He was an elderly man with a full gray beard and bushy eyebrows, but his kelly green eyes resembled the eyes of a man half his age because of their bright, eager look. He was stout and smiled a Santa Claus smile the moment he saw me.

"Talented *and* beautiful," he said. "Mr. Baxter. How are you?"

"I'm good," Grandfather said. "Shall we take a look?"

"Absolutely. Let me take you in," he said.

We entered the first room of the gallery. All the paintings were of famous people in Maine's history. I had read up on the gallery and knew it had separate rooms for types of paintings, two for impressionistic and abstract and four devoted to realism, as well as a large room for sculptures.

My painting hung between the two front rooms. It was very prominent. Mr. Doyle had put it in a bigger, more impressive gilded frame. Below it were two other landscapes of the Maine coastline. Both were breathtaking because of the way the colors enriched the almost photographic scenery. The ocean gave the illusion of moving. It was impossible to look at them and not feel as if you were there. Although I had the honor of being featured, looking at the other two paintings, I could see how much I had to learn.

"Whose works are these?" I asked Mr. Doyle.

"That's Kyle Wyman's work. He's going to be our artist in residence this year. By the way, he chose your painting."

"He did?"

"Yes. Since he was chosen to be our artist in residence, we thought he should be the one to choose the best amateur painting. Every successful artist was an amateur at one time," he said, smiling. "Kyle has a painting of a Maine seashore hanging in the Maine State House in Augusta."

He leaned toward me to whisper.

"I want your help working to keep him here longer. You know how these creative people have no patience when it comes to settling down anywhere."

"Matisse did in France and . . ."

"I'm talking about the new generation of young, restless men especially," he said. "I'm sure you're not like that."

Maybe I am, I thought, but just smiled.

"Be happy to meet him and try when he comes," I said.

He handed me Kyle's brochure.

"He studied in France at the École des Beaux-Arts, and many other places, too," I told Grandfather.

I knew he didn't know what that meant, but he raised his eyebrows. "Talent recognizes talent," he said.

A surge of excitement passed through me. The world grew just a little bit bigger. I would get to know an internationally famous artist. And, more important, he would know me!

After we toured the gallery, Grandfather took me to lunch at the Bee Hive, a very elegant sandwich shop. So many people worked in Bar Harbor now. All the good restaurants looked crowded, not that I had spent as much time here as I wanted to spend.

Grandfather talked a lot more than usual about the family business. "I know your father tells you very little, except when he wants to brag about something he has done."

"Mommy told me things, but Daddy always believed I'd go off, get married, and have nothing to do with it."

"Yeah, well, he doesn't know you as well as I do," he said.

I was a little puzzled about what he meant, but before I could ask, Aunt Frances arrived.

"I thought you said you couldn't make it," Grandfather said.

"I switched shifts with someone. Saw your painting," she told me as she sat. "Very nice. I ran in and out to see it before I got here. Are you going to pursue a career in art?" she asked with Daddy's exact disapproving tone.

"Yes, Aunt Frances. I'm going to attend the College of the Atlantic."

"Oh. So your father will be supporting you for some time," Aunt Frances quipped, and looked at the menu.

"First, he's not the one supporting her, and where did you get that sarcastic, nasty tone? Not from me or your mother," Grandfather said.

I wanted to say it was inherited, but I bit my tongue.

"I just speak the truth, Father. It's part of my profession. We don't tell patients what they want to hear, only what they must hear."

"Lisa isn't a patient," he said.

Aunt Frances shrugged. "What are you having? I think the honey burger is outstanding," she said.

I laughed to myself, remembering how Mommy used to call her Olive Oyl, Popeye's cartoon wife, because of her figure and how fickle and nasty she could be. I think she once mentioned that to Grandfather, who had thought it was funny and perfect.

After our food was brought to the table, Aunt Frances said she was surprised at Grandfather taking a whole workday off.

"Not like you, Father. Thinking about retiring?"

"Hardly," Grandfather said. "Our business, with the good people we employ, can practically run itself."

"My brother doesn't think so."

"Most people work to live; your brother lives to work."

Aunt Frances laughed.

Grandfather looked at me and then leaned toward her. "Maybe some of that should rub off on you. My guess is you just didn't take your assignment today."

"That's not true," she said, in a tone that convinced me it was.

I had just begun eating when Grandfather's boat skipper appeared in the restaurant doorway and searched the room.

"Grandfather," I said, nodding toward the door.

The skipper saw us and rushed to our table. Grandfather greeted him. "What's up, Murphy?"

"Just had a message over the radio. The Fuller boats were involved in a bad accident."

"And?"

"Bret Fuller's son was untangling a net and got crushed."

Grandfather stood. "And?"

"He's being rushed to the hospital."

"Oh, maybe I'll get some work," Aunt Frances said.

I know I was screaming at her. My mouth was wide open, but I couldn't hear any sound.

"Take us to the hospital," Grandfather told Murphy. He looked down at Aunt Frances. "You take care of the bill," he ordered.

She looked like he had asked her to commit suicide. He put his arm around me and we walked out of the restaurant.

I was still shivering when we got into the car. Grandfather held my hand.

"Let's not think the worst," he said. "He was brought to the hospital. He'll be all right."

I tried to smile with hope and closed my eyes until we arrived at the hospital. Jamie's mother and father and his sister were in the lobby. Some of the other fishermen were there as well. Everyone turned when we walked in. Grandfather went right to Jamie's parents.

"We're waiting for the doctor," his mother said, and looked at me.

She suddenly reached out to pull me to her. We hugged. Everyone was quiet. Jamie's father started to describe the accident to Grandfather. The doctor appeared in the doorway and nodded at

Jamie's father and mother and his sister. They quickly went in and I stepped back, more terrified than I was when I had gotten dizzy and fell in my art class.

Everyone was quiet again. Grandfather stood beside me with his hand on my shoulder. One of the fishermen turned to him and asked, "Didn't you lose someone in a storm, Mr. Baxter?"

"Hurricane Edna. My mother's first cousin. We named Melville after him," he replied.

I looked up at him. Mommy's tragedy loomed in my mind again. I was surprised no one had mentioned this after that had happened.

"No one ever told me that, Grandfather."

"Some things we avoid talking about," Grandfather said. "It keeps the tragedy alive when you do."

I hope we won't be talking about Jamie years from now, I thought.

Minutes seemed like hours, but finally Jamie's parents appeared. Everyone rose and gathered around them.

"He's suffered a severe leg fracture," his father began. "They need to operate and put some rods in to keep his bone intact. He had crushed ribs, but they're going to be okay. They're going to operate in a few hours. He had some internal bleeding, of course, so . . . so . . ."

Jamie's mother put her arm around his father. He took a deep breath. His sister was crying, but silently.

"So, he's still what they call critical. We're going back in, but we won't have news for a number of hours. Best you all go back to doing what you do," he said.

I looked at Grandfather. He had been through terrible experiences, including my mother's fatal accident, and his face wasn't going to betray any hope. He honestly wasn't sure, and he certainly was not going to candy-coat what was happening just to make me feel better.

"Can we stay?" I asked him. He looked at Jamie's parents. They were so close to me, so caring; it was sometimes like they were *my* parents.

"Just immediate family here," his father said.

Grandfather nodded. "We'll take a room at the Bar Harbor Inn. Murphy will stay in the hotel lobby and come to us immediately with updates."

Aunt Frances appeared and looked at everyone. Before she could speak, Grandfather offered Jamie's parents her services if needed.

"Do what you have to do to be on hand," he told her. "Let's go to the inn," he said to me after Jamie's parents and sister went back to the surgical area.

"Why is he critical, Grandfather? Can't I give him blood or . . ."

"He'll get transfusions," Aunt Frances said, growing serious and more professional now. "You don't give people just anyone's blood. Type has to match."

"Why does he need blood, anyway?"

"It's just that operating on someone who's lost lots of blood endangers blood pressure and . . ."

"That's enough," Grandfather told her. She seemed disappointed, as if she enjoyed telling people hard things. "Okay, let's go. We'll rest, keep updated, and return," he told me.

I felt more like I was floating, like I had lost all contact with everything and everyone around me. Mommy would call this kind of day a "yin-yang." The day had started out bright and beautiful, full of excitement, and then suddenly turned dark and ugly and full of fear.

Grandfather called Daddy from the inn and told him what had

happened and where we were. When he hung up, I could see he was unhappy with the call.

"What did Daddy say, Grandfather?"

"He said the Fullers had a contract to produce and deliver a certain number of pounds, and if they didn't, we should cut their price."

I stared at him a moment and let the words sink in.

"He's not your son, Grandfather."

"I know. Think I can get my money back?"

I found a laugh, and he smiled.

"I'll get us an update in an hour. Just try to rest," he said, and left for a while.

All sorts of memories of Jamie rambled through my mind. I hated that I was thinking of them. It was like preparing myself for another tragedy. "If you have bad thoughts," Mommy had told me, "tell yourself to stop thinking of them. Act like there is someone else inside you that you want to shut up."

I closed my eyes. I didn't know how much time had passed, but suddenly Grandfather was shaking my arm.

"The operation is over," he said. "He'll be in intensive care for days, so we'll go home."

"How is he?"

"He's stable. They put the rod in his leg. It's too early to tell how that will be."

"When can I see him?"

"They'll call us. As soon as you can, you will," Grandfather promised.

I felt helpless leaving Bar Harbor without seeing Jamie. Once we were out at sea again, the reality set in. This was our gold mine; everything we owned we owed to the sea and the fishermen. But it could be so treacherous. Weather ruled our lives as much as or more than those of most people.

And yet, like anything as vast and unpredictable, the sea held its majestic beauty. Birdies grew up with it practically in their blood. I wanted to hate it for what it had done to Mommy and Jamie, but I couldn't deny the colors of the water, the gracefulness of calm waves, the birds and the fish that would rather be nowhere else. How many calm days had Mommy and I and Jamie spent sailing on calm waters, feeling the ocean breeze in our hair? Its singing put us to sleep, and the moonlight turning it into sparkling jewelry comforted us. I knew that, despite what had happened to him, Jamie could never hate the sea.

It was our home.

We didn't hear from the hospital until three days later, and that was because of Aunt Frances, who served as Jamie's private-duty nurse. Grandfather paid for it. I wanted to go see Jamie that day, but we had exams. He had no phone by his bed in the ICU. I was so frustrated that I almost forgot the last sheet of questions on the English test.

The hours were restrictive, but I could go the next morning. They permitted only two at his bedside, so I had to wait in the lobby for his parents to come out.

"Oh, we're so happy you came, Lisa. Jamie's very depressed." His mother hugged me. I could feel how shaky she was.

"You'll cheer him up," his father said. That suddenly loomed as a big challenge. "You've come through a bigger tragedy."

I'm not through it, I thought, but I nodded and walked in toward the ICU. I saw Jamie lying back and staring up at the ceiling. I knew what all this meant to him. He would lose his dream just as I was marching ahead with mine.

He sensed I was coming and looked at me with a face full of guilt. Aunt Frances stepped in front of me before I reached his bed.

"He's on a sedative," she said. "It won't work if you rile him up."

"Why would I rile him up?"

"I'm just telling you," she replied, and walked away.

"Olive Oyl," I wanted to shout at her, but I just continued to Jamie.

"Why do only rich people have good luck?" he asked as soon as I was at his bedside.

"They buy it," I said.

To my joyful surprise, he smiled.

"What kind of fisherman has only one good leg?" he asked.

"Captain Ahab. *Moby-Dick.*"

"Serves me right for not paying attention in English literature class," he said. He turned away for a long moment.

"Jamie?"

"You know this changes everything. Captain Ahab or no Captain Ahab."

"Let's wait and see."

"Your aunt is pretty realistic. She said I'll need close to a year of therapy, and then who knows?"

"My aunt is an expert in depressing people, probably because she is always depressed herself. The only reason she became a nurse was to lord it over people. She just happens to be good at nursing."

Jamie thought a moment and then suddenly brightened. "I forgot all about your painting. Did you see it in the museum?"

"Yes. It's a great honor."

"Maybe you'll make a lot of money selling paintings and support us both," he said. "I don't mean it," he quickly added. "A man should be able to support his family."

"Why can't a woman?"

He closed his eyes. I watched him for a moment and realized he was drifting off. My aunt came up to my side.

"You should let him rest. It's when he's healing."

"Okay," I said, rising.

I waited a moment, but he didn't open his eyes.

"How long are you here?"

"As long as I have to be and your grandfather pays for it," she said.

"Did you ever do anything for anyone without being paid for it?"

She stared at me a moment and then gave me that wry smile of hers. "I sold Girl Scout cookies once," she said, "but ate a box myself."

I walked away. Grandfather's driver, Arthur, and car were waiting to take me to the dock.

"Please take me to the Doyle Art Gallery," I asked him.

I didn't want to ride home with this air of sadness. Good news was like sunshine after a storm. I wondered if I was being selfish thinking of bringing joy to myself while Jamie was lying back there in the hospital.

You're no good to him with this dour look on your face, I told myself.

The moment I walked into the gallery, Mr. Doyle popped out of his office.

"What a coincidence," he said. "Kyle Wyman doesn't start for months, but he was on someone's yacht and they pulled into the harbor, so he thought he'd stop by and look at your painting on the wall."

"Really?"

"That's what he said, but maybe he's looking at his own," he whispered, and winked. "To be an artist, you have to be very confident and proud of yourself. Maybe a little arrogant," he added.

I wasn't sure I liked hearing that. It sounded a little too much like my father.

I reined in my excitement and followed Mr. Doyle to meet his artist. Since he had chosen my painting, perhaps he would look at me differently from the way he looked at other young admirers.

CHAPTER SEVEN

Kyle Wyman was standing with his back to us in the portrait room, staring at a painting of William King, Maine's first governor. I remembered him from history class.

I could see that Kyle was at least six foot two or three and had surprisingly broad, athletic shoulders. He wasn't what I would imagine an artist to be. He more closely resembled a cosmetically perfect construction worker, with his black silk collared shirt and crisp-looking jeans. He even wore shoe boots. The shirt was tight enough to show his muscular arms. How heavy are a canvas and a brush? I wondered. He didn't turn when Mr. Doyle announced my arrival. Instead, he began talking as if I had walked in on his lecture.

"In the eighteenth and early nineteenth centuries, paint was made from three basic ingredients: linseed oil as the vehicle, pigments as the colorants, and turpentine as a dryer. These elements combined created what we call oil paint."

"I knew that," I said, and he turned. "My high school art teacher explained that a while ago. He favors the baroque period and romanticism."

"Man of eclectic tastes," Kyle said. "There is always the danger of spreading yourself too thin. I would say that's true for most of life. True art captures what's real, no matter what style or period it's created in."

"And your imagination?" I asked.

"It's real to you; now you have to make it real to someone else."

"Maybe it isn't that important. Maybe pleasing yourself is enough," I said.

I felt like we were challenging each other. Perhaps he was surprised that I wasn't intimidated. He seemed frozen for a moment, and I took a better look at him.

His dark brown hair, cut neatly at his ears and the nape of his neck, had thin streaks of gray in it that seemed to enhance the silvery blue in his eyes. I had a suspicion that the gray wasn't natural. He didn't look much more than thirty. He had high cheekbones and a lightly tanned face, with strong, full, manly lips. He resembled a male model or a movie star more than a successful working artist who spent most of his day inside, carefully moving a brush over a canvas. I thought he had a two- or three-day beard, but so neatly trimmed that I suspected he treated his face as if it was, in and of itself, a work of art.

I tried desperately not to gape and look like I was overwhelmed, like a teenager meeting a rock star. Maybe my effort was obvious. My quickened heartbeat betrayed my feelings. I even felt a small flush in my cheeks. But I couldn't look away.

He relaxed his lips toward a smile but held it frozen as he looked at me. I thought it was more like he was studying me, making me more insecure about my own face as every imperfection I imagined streamed through my mind. Maybe he had imagined me through my painting that he had chosen. Was I a disappointment? It was impossible to really know from his look.

"Impressive young lady," he told Mr. Doyle.

"You knew it. You chose her work," Eddie Doyle said. He turned to me. "And it wasn't because of who you are and what your family is to the economy of this area. All you did was sign 'Lisa B.' on your picture."

"Of course, I know who you are now," Kyle said.

"I'm just me," I said succinctly.

He widened his eyes. "You're as convincing in real life as you are in your work."

"I don't make that distinction," I said. "To me, art *is* real life."

"Wow. I might need a bodyguard working here, Eddie."

He laughed, and I relaxed.

"To be honest, I knew about your family, and when we started for Bar Harbor, we paused so I could look at your grandfather's mansion. I'm sure you can get quite inspired looking out from there. You painted your picture from there?"

"Yes."

"Pardon my skepticism. I can't tell you how many daughters of rich people I've met who in the end wanted to know the best makeup for them just because I worked with colors. Maybe they thought they'd be in one of my paintings."

"That would be just wasting your time," I said.

"You're kind of young to worry about wasting time," he replied.

"If I have any talent, wasting it is a sin," I said.

He smiled and looked at Mr. Doyle.

"You have talent. That's why your painting is here," Kyle said firmly.

I shrugged. "Mr. Angelo, my art teacher, told me that Picasso said, 'Every child is an artist. The problem is how to remain an artist when he grows up.'"

"Very clever. Must be a good teacher." He looked at his watch. "I'd better get going. I'll leave you with this."

He turned slightly so as to address the portrait again.

"What fascinates me about these old portraits is how detailed they were, to bring out the best qualities of the visage. You know, the first thing you think about when you do someone's portrait is, how can I do it and still flatter them?"

Eddie Doyle laughed. Kyle's smile widened.

"If you saw what half of these people in these portraits really looked like, Eddie, you'd empty the room."

"Ah, what is an art gallery, Kyle, if not a world of illusion?"

"You agree?" he asked me.

"Maybe all life is," I said. "I remember my mother sitting with me at our big oak tree and reciting a famous Japanese haiku poem about that."

"Haiku?"

"Three lines, seventeen syllables in Japanese. English translation isn't exact, but her favorite was 'A man sat under a tree dreaming he was a butterfly, or was it a butterfly . . . '"

"'Dreaming he was a man.' I know it." He looked at Mr. Doyle. "I'm looking forward to working. Perhaps we'll see each other when I return."

"Looking forward to it, too."

His smile widened. "Better get going. Have to pick some people up. See you in a few months."

As I watched him walk out, I thought this was another yin-yang moment. I had just left Jamie in the darkness of his injury, holding my tears as far back as I could. Now I was feeling this surge of excitement, not only because of who Kyle was but also because of how he had looked at me and talked to me. I tried to smother the feeling, but Mr. Doyle didn't help when he said, "He was very impressed with you, Lisa. To tell you the truth, so am I."

"Thank you, Mr. Doyle."

"I'll see you soon. I'll set up a celebration event in the near future or maybe wait for Kyle's return."

"Whatever works best for the gallery," I said, when I really wanted to say, *Yes, wait for Kyle Wyman.*

I returned to the dock for my ride back to Birdlane. As we were pulling out, I saw the yacht Kyle was on and all the young men and women with him. I felt like sticking pins in myself for wishing I was on that yacht instead of thinking about poor Jamie and the next time I could visit him.

"That's a Palmer Johnson classic," Grandfather's driver, Arthur, told me as he looked at the yacht. "Friends of yours?"

"No. I just met someone who is on it."

"Well-to-do, for sure," he said.

I watched the yacht leaving the area for a few more moments and then looked to Birdlane as I always did to get that sense of coming home.

I was able to visit Jamie twice more that month. He was transferred to the Coastal Breeze Therapeutic Center just outside Bar

Harbor. Grandfather paid for it and paid for him to have a room as well, because he had to have physical therapy sessions four times a week, and traveling between there and Birdlane was an ordeal. After a couple of months, Grandfather told me what they were concluding about Jamie's injury and operation.

They weren't happy with how much he was able to bend his knee, and the injured nerves were taking longer to heal. They talked about another operation. Fortunately, part of the treatment at the center involved psychotherapy, so there was some attempt to counter Jamie's deep depression. He didn't know what I knew about his evaluation. The doctors included Grandfather in everything they told Jamie's parents.

When Daddy found out how much Grandfather was doing for Jamie and his family, they had another argument.

"Who do you think you are, Father?" Daddy began one evening after dinner. "Santa Claus? There are many fishermen's families who would like some of your charity. Who they goin' to come to when you're gone?"

"Not you," Grandfather said.

"You got somethin' right." He glared at me as if this was all my fault and, as usual, marched angrily away.

"Let's hope the dead can't hear the living," Grandfather said. "His mother would be turning in her grave."

"Mommy would have arguments about things like that with him, but usually she'd be the one to walk away."

"Yeah, well, your father likes to lick his wounds."

"Thank you, Grandfather, for helping Jamie."

"Half the time, I think I'm doing it to annoy your father." He laughed.

I wished I could get to see Jamie more at the therapy center, but between schoolwork and my effort to do a new painting, I was limited. I wasn't sure I was helping him that much anyway. I seemed to remind him of all the hopes he'd had for our future.

"I can't be in the boat with one good leg," he kept saying after every hopeful thing I thought to tell him.

"There will be other things for you to do."

"What? This is what I've done all my life," he said.

"You're young enough to start something new, Jamie."

He didn't say anything, but I could see he didn't believe it. I wanted to scream at the ocean on the way home that day. All that we had came from it, but all our sadness and tragedy came from it as well. I stopped thinking about it the moment the Crest came into view. I thought about my new painting and the way the house loomed above the cliff, embraced by soft, puffy clouds. Was I doing it because I was really inspired or because Kyle Wyman had suggested it?

Even though I was cramming all I could into my days and weeks, the year seemed to move slowly. I was excited about attending the College of the Atlantic in Bar Harbor, but my doctors continued to remind me that I had to restrict my physical activity and keep my log, checking my vitals and reporting anything unusual to them. At times I felt as restricted as Jamie was feeling.

His good news was that the doctors decided not to operate again but to have him continue his therapy with a therapist visiting him twice a week on Birdlane; again, this was something Grandfather financed. Jamie was reluctant to leave his house and be seen with his crutches, but I got him out to restaurants and up to the Crest from time to time. His mood improved, but he still felt quite lost.

I found I wasn't thinking about Kyle Wyman only when I was

working on my painting or someone mentioned something about art. His smile seemed to have imprinted itself on my mind. For no reason at all, I'd look out at the sea from the high cliff at the Crest and think of him either on that yacht or smiling at me with that look of delighted surprise.

At first, I blamed it on my restricted life. How many good-looking young men had I met? My life had been school and whatever trip Mommy had taken me on, but with her gone and my father totally absorbed in his business, I was seldom taken anywhere. I did visit shops in Bar Harbor, often accompanied by Anna, but her time was restricted with all the domestic duties she had. Most of my high school girlfriends were a little, maybe very, afraid to do vigorous things with me. I couldn't blame them after my incident in art class. I easily imagined their parents warning them not to have me do anything that could lead to a health issue they'd be blamed for causing.

I was convinced, however, that the reason for my looking for excuses for my infatuation with Kyle Wyman was the sense of guilt it brought along with it. It was foolish, I told myself. All I'd done was discuss art with him and appreciate how he appreciated my work. Who wouldn't think about someone like that? And look how much older than me he was . . . at least fifteen years.

I had never had a schoolgirl crush on anyone. Jamie had just been there all the time. And pasting pictures of rock stars on my bedroom walls wasn't anything I wanted to do. I was usually silent when my girlfriends raved about this singer or that. Maybe I should have been more like them. Maybe I was growing up too fast. I could certainly blame that on my heart issue and how careful and sensible I was. Was it possible to be too sensible? Was I wearing raincoats in the sunshine?

In a little less than four weeks, I would be celebrating my eighteenth birthday. Most of my classmates who were looking forward to that lost some of their excitement when the national drinking age was raised to twenty-one, but with voting rights and other considerations, it was easy to think of yourself as more adult, more in charge of your life.

I couldn't help but be jealous of them, even though they all thought that because of the family wealth, I should be the person to envy. Truth was, since my diagnosis, I always felt people were scrutinizing me more, anticipating something. To me, everyone was a few notches extra nice, almost as if they believed they had to tiptoe around me—everyone, that was, but my father, who treated illness and physical injuries as just minor annoyances, things that interrupted the flow of commerce.

"You were told what to do to take care of yourself; take care of yourself," he said recently when I had moaned to myself about another blood test, another doctor's visit. No matter how blue the sky, I always had that black cloud over my head.

One sunny afternoon in early May, I had come home early from school, not because of my health but because my last-period teacher was out and the class was going to be a study hall. I could get in a few extra hours at the cliff to work on my painting.

Suddenly, Grandfather's car drove up, and he got out quickly. He was carrying an armful of bound papers and headed right for me, walking faster than usual, and not easily, either.

"Your father will be the death of me yet," he began. "He forged my signature on a demand letter that he sent to Jamie's parents, cutting their contract because they haven't delivered their allotted pounds of lobster and fish. I had to spend half the day with our attorney keeping him out of jail and righting things with the Fullers. Here," he said, handing me the bound papers. "This is a list of all our providers, distributors, et cetera, their contract information. In short, the essence of Baxter Fish Enterprises. I want you to have it, read it at your leisure. This is a family business; you're a big part of the family," he concluded, and then he turned and started back to the house before I could utter a sound.

He looked like he had just aged ten more years as he hobbled along. From the looks of the sky, I knew we were in for a storm soon, so I put the papers in my basket and began wrapping up my painting and supplies. I couldn't stop thinking of the pain Jamie's family had just endured. Their costs could easily send them into bankruptcy.

I think it was my rage building against Daddy that made me move as quickly as I did, cursing and muttering to myself as I entered the house. After closing the door behind me, I struggled to put down my things safely so I could organize them.

The moment I felt it, I feared that Grandfather was going to blame himself.

Out of the corner of my eye, I saw Anna coming down the stairway. She was looking at me and suddenly started descending with total disregard for her own safety.

I often wondered what that moment before your death was like, that realization that in a second or two you would cross into darkness. Would you be wondering if you were going to heaven or hell or just floating out into space? Would you think at all about your body, any pain or ache, or would you somehow have stepped out of it?

I didn't fall so much as I sank. It felt like I was melting down to my feet. Maybe Anna prevented me from hitting the floor hard. I don't know. The sense of the world bouncing beneath me caused me to open my eyes and see long enough to realize I was being carried to a helicopter, there was an oxygen mask on my face, and Dr. Bush was at my side. I didn't know until later that Grandfather had a helicopter on constant call to take me to Bar Harbor. It was especially important this afternoon, as the sea was already churning in anticipation of a storm.

I could feel myself being lifted toward the sky, heading to Bar Harbor, carried along like the Canada geese that flew in perfect formation, drawn by instinct to a place that was both familiar and distant. I had a presence there; I was part of the city, of the lights and the tourists jabbering on the streets, my painting on the wall in the gallery, all of it waiting to welcome me, the place where I would either live or die today.

I closed my eyes.

Or, rather, they closed themselves.

CHAPTER EIGHT

When I opened my eyes again, I recognized Dr. Knox. Grandfather was standing off to the right side. The constant beep of the heart monitor helped me focus more. Of course, I had a different oxygen mask on, but I thought we had just arrived.

"Relax, Lisa," Dr. Knox said when he saw me try to speak. "You've just had a very serious operation. It went well, but your recuperation is just as important, if not more. You're going to be in here a while and then in a private room. You'll have to restrict your activity even when you're able to go home. Cooperation and no resistance to it all is the best formula to return to health. Just nod if you understand me."

I did.

"Mr. Baxter," he said to Grandfather, who stepped up to the side of my bed.

"Where's Daddy?" I asked Grandfather.

"He's on a phone call in the doctor's office. One of our trucking companies had an accident and spilled our products all over the side of the road in New Jersey. But he did wait first to hear about your operation and condition."

"What is my condition?" I asked Dr. Knox. "What new restrictions are there?"

He smiled.

"What?"

"Once you've healed, you'll have no restrictions, Lisa."

I couldn't believe I was not in a dream. Those were the words I had dreamed of hearing my whole life. How many times had Mommy promised me I would? Probably a thousand.

"How did this happen? The last thing I remember is sinking toward the floor."

Dr. Knox said, "Well, it was a delicate procedure that we avoided as long as we could. It became unavoidable, and we performed it, and it went exceedingly well. Except for some follow-ups, I don't expect I'll need to see you—not that you're not a nice person," he added, laughing.

I could see how upbeat and excited everyone was. This was real; this was no dream.

"You're okay, Lisa. Relax," Dr. Knox said, patting my hand.

I was afraid to believe it, but the smiles were too real. I finally let it settle into me.

"Just think about all the things you wanted to do and now will."

I didn't wait to be alone. I started to make a list on a piece of paper of things I wanted to do but was always afraid to do. Just running up the hill to the Crest would be a wonder for me.

I couldn't wait to share this news with Jamie and then remembered he could never run up that hill again; he might not even be able to walk it.

Dr. Knox stepped back, and he and Grandfather talked. I felt myself drifting again. I saw the images of other men, most looking like they worked in the hospital, but one stood out because he was dressed in a cable-knit white sweater and had a full, shaped head of coal-black hair.

One of the nurses told me to expect hallucinations and dreams that didn't seem to make any sense to me. "Our chief of psychiatry told me that all the images and memories we don't even realize we have are always alive and moving in our minds. Coming out of anesthesia or something similar lets them emerge for a moment or two. They don't disappear forever. Could easily be something you remember from childhood," she said.

"This felt . . ."

"What?" she asked, smiling.

"Now," I said. "Not from childhood."

She widened her eyes. "Just don't spend any time worrying about it."

In the beginning of my recovery, I wasn't worrying about spending much time doing anything. I slept a lot. Daddy came and went, usually for a short visit before heading to a business meeting. Toward the end of my stay in the ICU, Grandfather brought Anna to see me. He left her with me while he met with someone on a business matter in Bar Harbor.

"You look so much better than your father described," she

began. "Not that he spent much time describing anything. He treats words like money."

I laughed.

She held my hand and looked around. "So many flowers."

Some of the flowers had been sent from the school, my teachers, and the class after there had obviously been a collection to buy them for me. There were roses from Jamie. Anticipating when the first dozen would fade, he had sent another with Anna.

"Thank you, Anna."

"Your grandfather put . . ."

Anna looked back at the door and then leaned closer to me.

"Your grandfather put Jamie on the list for visitors when you are moved to the private room. Your father might have some spies in here." She smiled and then stopped. "You don't look happy about Jamie coming."

"Jamie has his own burdens now, and returning to the hospital will only make them heavier."

"Sometimes when you have troubles, it's better for you to think about someone else's troubles. Diminishes your own," she said. "It's no good for him to wallow in self-pity."

"I'm sure you're right, Anna. I was just tired of people worrying about me."

"Well, soon that sounds like it'll be over."

"I know. I'll start helping you clean the Crest. That oughta convince them."

She laughed. "You'll find more creative ways to exert your new energy. You have a lot of catching up to do."

"I do, don't I? And I will."

"Good. Oh. Your teachers and Jamie will be getting your schoolwork together for you to do at your own pace."

"Is my picture all right?" I asked.

"Your grandfather decided to keep it in his office. Safe and sound."

"I'm not sure I want to continue it," I said. "I feel like I'm doing it for someone else."

"Really? Who?" Anna asked.

Grandfather returned before I could answer.

"Time to go?" Anna asked.

"Yes. Lisa, you're going to be moved to your private room tomorrow," he told me. "And we'll put your aunt back to work."

"Jamie didn't like her," I said.

"Liking her may be asking too much. Let's see if she can do the job I paid her nursing tuition to do and earn back the investment," Grandfather said.

"You sound like Daddy," I told him.

He smiled. "Good business sense is all right; he just applies it to everything in his life. I think he was five when he asked your grandmother if something she was doing was worth it. Okay. See you soon," he said, nodding at Anna.

She kissed me, and they left.

Aunt Frances was there when they started to move me to my private room the following morning. Anyone who saw her and me would think we hadn't met previously. I never had seen her so arrogant in her role as a nurse. She spoke to other people as if they were miles below her. It was still hard to think of my father and her being brother and sister but from another set of parents. Of course, they had no idea about this, and it was strange for me to have that knowledge without them having it.

When I was comfortably set up in my room with all the monitoring equipment, Aunt Frances went over everything as if she was reading from a textbook. At the end, I said emphatically, "Thank you, Aunt Frances."

She paused and looked hard at me. "I don't discriminate with my patients. Everyone is treated the same."

"How reassuring," I said.

She could have burned through me with her glare as she left.

"Sometimes it's not good to get close to some of your own relatives," Mommy once said. She surely was thinking of Aunt Frances.

Two days later, I had finished dinner and lay back just wanting to think about the world that was going to open for me the moment I walked out of the hospital. I was so into imagining all the things I would do that I didn't see him enter and sit beside the bed. Maybe he was deliberately as quiet as a ghost.

Suddenly realizing someone was there, I gasped and pulled myself to the side. He was smiling widely.

"Good reflexes," he said.

"How did you get in? It's after visiting hours."

"Maybe I look like a doctor and not an artist," he replied.

"How long have you been here?"

"About forty-five seconds," he said. His eyes were dazzling with laughter.

"No, I mean Bar Harbor."

"Oh. I arrived this morning."

"And you came here to see me? How did you find out about me so fast?"

"You sure you want to be an artist? You sound more like a district attorney," he said, his smile holding.

"No, it's just that . . ."

"I worry about my protégés. Your grandfather stopped by the gallery about an hour after I had arrived today to show a friend your painting, and I heard him talking to Mr. Doyle about you. He stepped aside and filled me in. I'm so happy for your successful operation and apparently full recuperation from your health challenge," he said.

I stared at him a moment. He was wearing a fitted long-sleeved dark blue shirt and dark blue jeans. His silvery-blue eyes looked bluer. I thought the silvery-gray streaks in his dark brown hair had either darkened or been removed. Since he was the first older man who had shown interest in me other than my teachers, I was intrigued by everything about him.

I sensed he was amused at the way I was studying him.

"What sorts of things are you looking forward to doing when the doctor gives you the okay?" he asked.

I laughed. "That's what had me in such deep thought. Believe it or not, I've never driven our speedboat, swum in the ocean, water-skied, or even gone on long hikes. There are great hiking trails on Birdlane. When I was very young, I snuck off and climbed up a cliff known as the Birdlane Crow's Nest."

The moment I said it, I realized I had left Jamie's name out.

"All things I like to do," he said. "'Course, I've never been up to the Birdlane Crow's Nest. I've never been to Birdlane. Why don't you give a call at the gallery when your doctor gives you the green light?"

He leaned toward me as if he was sharing a secret.

"Until your next birthday, we'll call it art research," he said.

I was sure my cheeks had turned crimson. *Until I'm eighteen? What happens then?* I wondered.

He paused a moment, his face closer, and then sat back with his smile.

"Actually," he said, mostly, I imagined, to break the silence, "I'm bribing you. I hope you'll recommend my doing a painting of the Crest or support the idea if I bring it up with your grandfather."

"Really?" I think I sounded disappointed. That was his main purpose?

"For an artist, the subject of the work is half, if not more, of the effort. The Crest has so much to offer the imagination."

"Where are you from? Were you always artistic?"

"Born in Wyoming at my father's summer residence. I come from well-to-do people. My mother overruled my father and financed my work as an artist. When I succeeded, she practically rubbed it into his soul." He laughed. "How does your father feel about your work? I mean, I know your grandfather is very happy about it."

"Your father and mine must be related," I said, and he laughed again.

"All wrapped into one: beautiful, talented, and witty."

"I'm not sure all that is wrapped," I said.

His eyes widened. "Yeah, 'wrapped' isn't the right way to put it. I guess I'll have to come up with some original lines."

We heard voices approaching.

He rose. "I'll keep in touch and eagerly wait to hear from you. Continue your good recuperation."

Aunt Frances walked in and stopped as if she had walked into a wall.

"Who are you?" she demanded. "And how did you get in here?"

"I am Miss Baxter's personal art instructor," Kyle said, exaggerating how insulted he was by the question.

It brought a smile to my face, especially because of the stern look on Aunt Frances's. She could roll those eyes. It could make you dizzy watching them.

"Well, she's not going to do any artwork in here, and you're here after hours," Aunt Frances said firmly.

"Ah, there's where you're wrong," Kyle said, undaunted. "There are no after hours for great artwork."

Aunt Frances looked at me. I was stifling my laughter. Her face looked twisted, numbed.

"If you don't leave, I'll call security," she warned, and folded her arms.

"Oh, we're done," Kyle said. He started out and then turned back in the doorway. "A true sculptor frees the art from the stone; so an artist frees his subject from itself."

He glanced at Aunt Frances, who looked at him as if he had spoken a foreign language, and then continued out of the hospital.

"Does your father know you are seeing this man?" Aunt Frances immediately asked.

"My father, no. I doubt he cares. My grandfather knows."

"And he's paying him to be your art instructor?"

"Not that I know of, no."

She smiled and nodded. "A man like that isn't interested in dollars and cents, Lisa. You don't have a mother to guide you now, so I'll step in. Men like that have only one reward to satisfy, and it's between their legs. You are like a ripe piece of fruit. Your virginity screams out, and that man and men like him hear it well.

"I'm sure he's dumped compliment after compliment on you. He'll say anything and do anything to get into bed with you. I've been through all that, and my mother was a naive woman. Your grandfather was her only boyfriend. What kind of advice could she give me? To cover up her failure with me, she blamed things on me. Anything that happened to me was my fault."

"What happened to you?"

"I was raped at twelve years old," she said. "And on your precious Birdlane Island, too."

I couldn't speak for a moment. She slammed the cup of pills on the table.

"Take these and sleep. You're going home tomorrow and must have full rest for five days. The doctor will see you at the Crest. Your grandfather will send the boat for him."

On the way out, she paused in the doorway and turned back to me.

"It was a friend of your father's, too," she said. "He knew about it but refused to confirm it when I told your grandfather and grandmother. Of course, they didn't believe me," she added, and left.

I had to remember to close my mouth, it was so wide open with shock.

CHAPTER NINE

I was stunned for minutes after she left. How could it be that no one ever had mentioned it? Could it be that no one else knew? Or, as she had said, that no one believed her? Should I pity her, feel ashamed that I had never really liked her? I suddenly felt so lost and alone. Without Mommy, whom could I talk to about this? Certainly not Daddy. I didn't think I could talk about it even with Jamie, especially now because of his own problems. And I didn't want Grandfather to somehow blame himself for what had happened to her.

I gulped the pills and lay back. What Aunt Frances had said about my grandmother easily applied to me as well. Other boys had flirted with me, but none had gone as far as to ask me for a date. I doubted I would have gone even if they had. Jamie just seemed to be there, to be my boyfriend forever.

Was Aunt Frances right? Was I naive and too innocent, making me vulnerable? I had no doubt that Kyle had had many girlfriends and might even have one now. What did I really know about him? It depressed me to think that he was simply taking advantage of me. I pouted about it for a few moments and then thought, who was Aunt Frances to give me advice about relationships with men, even if that had happened to her? Maybe she was simply jealous. She always seemed jealous of my father, my mother, and, now that I thought of it, especially me.

It was almost as if she deliberately said something to steal away my new hope and excitement. If I told my grandfather what she had said about Kyle, he'd go into a rage. I swiped the air as if I could erase it from my memory and had turned to go to sleep when the phone beside the bed rang. It was Jamie.

"Your father's secretary told my mother you're coming home tomorrow," he said.

"Yes."

"My sister said she'd drive me to the Crest the day after tomorrow. I'll call first if that's okay."

"Of course it's okay, Jamie. How are you doing?"

"I sit with my leg on a stool. Dr. Bush said I should start putting more weight on it gently when I walk with crutches."

"Well, do what he says."

"It's easier to just sit here."

"Jamie, remember what my mother told me, something I told you years ago."

"What?"

"If you have so much self-pity, you won't have anything to offer people who need it."

He laughed.

A wave of fatigue washed over me. "I'm a little tired," I said.

"Sure. I understand."

"Get some rest, too. I want to see someone who is hopeful when I see you in two days," I said. I really was tired, but I wished I could have kept talking. I didn't want to risk my full recovery, however. *Got to be a little selfish sometimes*, I told my conscience.

When morning came, to say I was anxious was a tremendous understatement. I practically gobbled down my breakfast and couldn't take my eyes off the clock. About ten thirty, I was surprised to see Daddy arrive with Aunt Frances beside him. I didn't know why, but he had to explain his appearance, my own father. Why wasn't it just natural for him to want to see me?

"I had an early meeting with a distributor in Bar Harbor and told your grandfather I'd handle this. Frances will gather your things. I have the car waiting. She already came to the Crest last night and arranged your room according to what she says were Dr. Knox's orders and requirements. I'll inform the desk," he said, and stepped aside.

"Your father told me to bring you this to wear," Aunt Frances said, and handed me a nightgown, a robe, and my furry slippers.

"Why can't I wear regular clothes until I get home?"

"Oh, starting already," she said, tossing the garments onto the bed. "I told my father to double my salary. Stress." She closed the door behind her and stood there with her arms folded.

"I'm the one who isn't supposed to have stress," I said.

"Oh, don't worry. I'm on that," she replied threateningly.

"You don't have to do this," I snapped back at her. "There are private nurses on Birdlane Island, too."

She looked a little frightened for a moment.

"It makes my father happy, which makes my life easier, too," she said. "Let's just get you home and make you comfortable."

I shrugged. Why couldn't she talk to me in a kind way before? Why did she have to be threatening?

I put on the nightgown, robe, and slippers while she gathered any personal items.

"Just sit there," she said. "I have to get a wheelchair."

"Wheelchair?"

"It's protocol."

She left, and I plopped back on the bed.

Dr. Knox came in next, with my father beside him.

"Everything is looking good," he said. "The next week of recovery is important, so just follow your aunt's instructions, which came from me. I'll be there to see you tomorrow. Any questions?"

"Do I have to stay bedridden?"

"For the first few days. Then you'll take short walks in the house, accompanied. I don't want anything to happen to my perfect job," he said, smiling.

"Okay."

"Let's get moving," Daddy said. "As usual, we have a crisis of some sort at the business."

"With Bar Harbor Wilson Brothers?" I asked.

His eyes widened. "No. I took care of that." He looked at the doctor.

"You have a very alert daughter. Rare these days," Dr. Knox said.

Daddy grunted and stepped back for Aunt Frances and the wheelchair. Aunt Frances quickly came around to guide me into it, which I thought was a bit over-the-top. I was far from that helpless, but it seemed to please Dr. Knox. He followed us out the door and to the limousine. It was a cool, mostly cloudy day, but to me it was pure sunshine. About ten minutes later, Daddy's driver and, surprisingly, Aunt Frances lifted me, wheelchair and all, into the boat. Aunt Frances put a blanket on me and sat beside the chair, her hand on it, while we pulled away from the dock and toward Birdlane Island. I gazed at her out of the corner of my eye.

The veins in her forehead were prominent. She seemed to be gritting her teeth, her jaw taut. I had never really looked so closely at my aunt, but looking from her to Daddy, I could see why they thought they were twins. Although Daddy was handsome, he had a similar forehead and similar lips. It was just that he was filled out more and seemed more alert. She looked like she was constantly in an angry dream. There was a lot that was similar in their personalities, but they fought, being brother and sister. I rarely heard him give her a compliment, and she was always finding fault with what he did.

The boat rocked steadily as we sailed home, but everything about it felt different now. Without the warmth of my mother's hand to hold or the sound of her voice guiding me through the wind and waves, it all seemed hollow. My heart was strong now, but the emptiness inside felt heavier than ever. The sea stretched endlessly before me, carrying me home. For a fleeting moment, I could almost see her reflection in the water, bringing me a small sense of comfort.

When we arrived at the dock, Daddy drove off to his office, and we were taken to the Crest. Grandfather's limousine and his driver were outside at the front. Anna came running when we pulled up.

"Your room is all ready. Aunt Frances arranged it last night."

Aunt Frances began carrying my things into the house. She left Anna to assist me.

"Where's Grandfather?"

"He's getting some things together and will be in your room shortly," Anna said.

My room looked like the one I had just left at the hospital. All my posters, pictures, and awards were gone. The window had a sheer sheet over it. The hospital equipment was on two tables beside the bed. The bedding even looked like hospital bedding. I stepped back as if the room were on fire.

"I'm not going in there," I said. "I am coming home, not returning to the hospital."

Grandfather came walking quickly down the hall.

"What's happening?"

"She's changed my room!"

"I did what is necessary for a recovery room. It's doctor's orders. We have to keep her blood pressure controlled, and too much contact with the outside world right now is not advisable," Aunt Frances recited.

"Doing that to her room certainly won't keep her blood pressure from rising," Grandfather said. "I'm sure the doctor didn't mean anything this extreme. Restore her room."

"What?"

"Do it. I'll speak to Dr. Knox before I leave," Grandfather said.

She glared at me, huffed, and then walked off to get my things.

"Let's wait in the living room," Grandfather said. He embraced my shoulders, and we walked to the sofa and sat. "Unfortunately, Frances can be irritating sometimes."

"Where are you going, Grandfather?"

"New York. Our biggest distributor who handles . . ."

"Thirty percent," I said.

He smiled. "You've been reading the material. I'm so pleased, Lisa."

"Better than other things I was given. What happened?"

"Your father got into an argument with the corporate heads over nickel-and-dime issues. I'm attending their board meeting to see if I can calm things down. Not the first time."

"How long will you be away?"

"Two, two and half days' travel, but Anna will keep me informed, and I'll speak with Dr. Knox, who will see you tomorrow."

Aunt Frances appeared. "The throne is ready for Your Highness," she said.

"Ignore her. Just follow Dr. Knox's orders. I'll see if I can cut the need for her short."

We rose and headed back to my room. It looked like almost all was restored. She stepped back with a smug smile.

"Okay?"

"Just take care of her well. Your brother will be here for dinner. When was the last time you two ate together?" Grandfather asked.

"I think before we were born," she said sarcastically. "All he does is complain. Not good for my digestion."

Grandfather laughed, and I got into bed.

"See you soon," he said, and kissed my cheek.

Aunt Frances shook her head as she watched him walk off. "He never showed me half that affection."

"Maybe you didn't show any to him," I said.

She widened her eyes and handed me my pills and a glass of water.

"I'll be back to check your vitals. Now I have to settle into my room. Wish I could have brought all my things to make it seem like home."

"Don't you have a lot here?"

"Not the things I want since I left," she said, and walked out.

Anna came hurrying in.

"This just came for you. Special delivery from Bar Harbor," she said, handing me an envelope that obviously had a card in it. "Well?" she asked immediately.

"It's . . . from the new artist at the gallery," I said, showing Anna the inside of the card, where there was a thin pen drawing of me.

"My goodness. How long were you with this man?"

"Probably less than an hour in total."

"This picture of you is so amazingly good. How nice."

I stared at it. On the other side, he had written, "Welcome home. See you soon. Get well. Kyle Wyman."

"Great artists have special visual memories; their eyes are like cameras."

"I'll say. I'll put it on your dresser here," Anna said, and did so, so that I could look at the drawing.

Aunt Frances walked in. I didn't have to hear her say what her expression was saying. "Parasites," she muttered.

"Excuse me?" Anna said.

"Men when they spot an easy prey, which most women are. They do that sort of thing."

"Well, I shouldn't want to measure everyone with the same ruler," Anna said. "If you'll pardon the expression."

Aunt Frances glared. "You were only married once, correct?"

"Yes," Anna said.

"Not much experience with men, I guess."

"I didn't need much to understand that I had a wonderful husband. Unfortunately, he suffered an ailment that took him."

"So you don't have family," Aunt Frances said, which I thought was cruel.

"What? She has family. We're her family."

"If that's true, you got the short end of the stick," Aunt Frances replied, looking at Anna.

Nobody spoke for a moment, and then Aunt Frances shrugged and went to check my blood pressure.

"Too high," she said. "Best we leave her to rest."

Anna glanced at me and walked out. Aunt Frances looked at something else, shook her head, and then just left. Was I supposed to worry? Could she be doing this to me deliberately? I wondered.

She wasn't in my room most of the remaining part of the day, claiming again that she had to set up her room to make even a few days here comfortable. "So much of how I wanted mine to remain was changed," she complained, mocking me, I was sure.

Anna brought me my food, which Aunt Frances had to approve. It was ridiculous, as Anna never made anything that could cause an issue.

Daddy finally appeared while I was eating.

"Well, from what I've been told, you can finally stop being babied," he said.

Aunt Frances, standing by, looked so pleased with his comment.

"I don't think you've babied me, Daddy."

"By your mother and my father, mainly," he said.

"Like you weren't babied," Aunt Frances said.

He glared at her. "At least I wasn't a whiner."

"Oh, please, that's all you did; that's all you do."

"Oh, you two will have a great dinner together," I said.

"I'm here just to change clothes. I have to see our accountant for dinner. I have some questions and recommendations."

"Without Grandfather? Does it concern the Pantel distributors?"

"He babbles. Don't worry about it," he said. "Besides, what do you know about the Pantel distributors?"

I was silent. Of course, it had never occurred to him that Grandfather would give me detailed information about the business. I didn't want that to start some new argument.

His gaze went to the card and the drawing. "Did your fisher boy draw that?"

"No, he has other abilities."

"Not anymore. He'll be campin' outside our door, hopin' to marry into this family. Don't you start gettin' serious with some handicapped fisherman."

"That's a terrible thing to say, Daddy."

"You just do what I say. I'm still your father and, despite what your grandfather thinks, the head of this household. You do what I tell you."

Until I'm eighteen, I thought.

"You're raising her blood pressure, Melville," Aunt Frances sang.

"Ah, you two deserve each other," he said, and walked off.

She laughed and started out, then turned and said, "Remember, don't get out of bed and walk about until Dr. Knox sees you tomorrow. They'll blame me if something happens to you."

My phone rang. I expected it to be Jamie, but it was Grandfather.

"I'm at the airport," he said. "How are things?"

"All right, Grandfather." I wasn't going to let him worry while he was away.

"Well, I have some surprising news that might please you," he said.

"What?"

"I hired that artist at Eddie Doyle's gallery to do a landscape of the Crest. He'll work on his days off. He'll stay at the Crest those days."

"Really?" I looked at the card. "When did you hire him?"

"About ten minutes ago," he said, laughing. "He came to the airport to ask me. Mr. Doyle had told him I was leaving for New York when he mentioned his desire to him."

I was silent a moment too long.

"Is that okay?"

"Yes, as long as he didn't choose my painting to get the job."

He laughed. "That's my girl. You'll make a good businessman. I mean, businesswoman. Oops, I gotta go. I'll call you from New York."

"Bye, Grand . . . pa," I said. I called him that when I wanted him to know I loved him extra.

I closed my eyes and moments later fell asleep. I was sure it was only a dream, but I had this vision of the ghosts of the Crest gathering at the foot of my bed and watching me. When Aunt Frances came to check my vitals and enter numbers in her report in the morning, I told her what Grandfather had done.

"He's going to be here? That's like inviting the fox into the chicken coop," she said.

"Maybe you need more foxes going into yours," I replied.

Her head literally snapped back. She charged at my card from Kyle.

She ripped it in half.

"NOOOO!" I screamed.

Anna came charging down the hallway, yelling, "What's wrong? What's wrong?"

I was lying back on my pillow, looking up at the ceiling.

"What happened here?"

"She tore my card," I said.

Aunt Frances tossed the two pieces onto the bed.

"She needs guidance and discipline, and not from an old lady who has had very little experience with this sort of thing. She's a patient but still my niece. You work for the family. Go back to the kitchen. This is a family matter."

Anna moved to the torn card, picked it off the bed, and turned to Aunt Frances. "This isn't a family matter. It's a matter of meanness," she said, and left.

"When we take over the Crest, I'll give her two hours to pack all her things and get out," Aunt Frances said.

I didn't look at her and I didn't say a thing. I heard her click her lips.

Just as she walked out, the phone rang. I was hoping it was Grandfather, but it was Jamie.

"You don't sound too good. Were you crying?"

Jamie knew me. Why shouldn't he? We had spent practically all our lives together. I didn't tell him about the card, just how unpleasant my aunt was.

"She truly likes dominating people. She's the female version of my father, for sure."

My rage was ripping through my voice.

"We'll be there in an hour," he said.

They came in a half hour, probably because Jamie was so insistent. His sister, Edna, understandably was intrigued by the Crest. She hadn't been here much at all. She was so nervous she kept talking about her kids, her housework, everything. Jamie smiled and laughed at her. Then she said Jamie's father wanted to construct a special chair for him on one of the boats, and he stopped smiling.

"He doesn't want it," she said.

"Why not, Jamie?"

"I might as well wear a flag on my head," he said. "The only handicapped fisherman on Birdlane Island. I'll be like a kid handed a rod."

"Oh, Jamie, when I can, I'll get on the boat with you, too."

"See?" his sister said. "Don't be such a downer."

Jamie smirked and nodded.

Anna came and greeted everyone. I saw what she was holding. Instinctively I didn't want her to display it, but she was too proud of what she had done.

"This is repaired," she said, handing me Kyle's card.

It was amazing. You almost couldn't tell it had been torn.

"How did you do this?" I asked when she handed it to me.

"Tricks of the trade," she said.

"What is that?" Jamie's sister asked.

"A card the new artist in residency at the Doyle Gallery sent me."

I looked at Jamie, who was staring hard at the sketch of my face. Aunt Frances paused in the doorway, looked in, and kept walking. I looked at Jamie again.

"Did you pose for that?" he asked.

"No. Grandfather and I met with him after my painting was chosen. He's a nationally known artist."

"Must do great portraits," Jamie's sister said.

He was still staring.

"Not as much as landscapes. Grandfather has hired him to do the Crest on his days off."

"Wow," Jamie's sister said.

We heard the doorbell, and Anna hurried out. I recognized Dr. Knox's voice.

"That's my doctor," I said.

Jamie's sister stood instantly. Jamie rose. His silence was scaring me a little.

"As soon as I can, we'll go for a walk here. It will be good for both of us," I told him.

"Not when the artist is here," he said. "I don't want him drawing a picture of me hobbling along."

"No, he . . ." I started to speak, but Dr. Knox appeared in the doorway with a different nurse.

"We'll see you again," Jamie's sister said. "Okay?"

"Oh, yes, please do come again."

They both left.

"This is Judy Warner," Dr. Knox said. "She will be replacing your aunt as your private-duty nurse for a few more days."

A short, stocky woman with a jolly, pudgy face and short light brown hair smiled at me. She didn't look much older than me.

Dr. Knox gave me his exam and then said, "I should have known better than to have a family member be your nurse. Family brings additional baggage, if you know what I mean."

Of course, I did.

"I think we can move you along a little bit faster. Start taking some walks around the house and in two days start going outside, when the weather permits, of course. Let's not think about anything else. Okay, Lisa?"

"Yes, thank you, Doctor."

He left. I was going to call Jamie, but I didn't. It was as if I knew instinctively why not to.

I was almost back to my room the following morning when the doorbell rang and Anna answered it.

Kyle Wyman stood there looking in at me.

CHAPTER TEN

I looked at Judy. From the expression on her face, I wondered if she knew who Kyle was or was just impressed by his good looks. He did look even more handsome in a collared light blue short-sleeved shirt and tight jeans with loafers, his hair glistening. He stepped in as Anna stepped back.

"Hi," he said. "I thought you might be up. I decided to use my first day off here scouting a perspective for the landscape. I was hoping you could come out and do a survey with me. It's really nice out, an unusually warm spring day, they say."

"Oh, she can't . . ." Anna began, but Judy stepped forward.

"We can go outside if I walk right by you two," Judy said.

"Who is this?" Anna asked.

"This is Mr. Wyman, the new resident artist at the Doyle Gallery," I said.

"Oh. You chose Lisa's painting and did that drawing of her."

"Yes, ma'am, or rather, the painting chose me. Just like I imagine this house chose you."

Anna beamed, her smile so bright. I looked at Kyle. Was he born this charming, or did he develop it along with his art? Every time something about Kyle excited me, the feeling was accompanied by guilt over what Jamie would think, especially now that he had seen Kyle's drawing of me.

"I'll go put something on," I said.

"I'll show you some of the house," Anna told Kyle.

Judy stayed with them rather than following me to my room. I paused. Suddenly, what I was going to wear just to walk around the Crest was so important that I stood there pondering. I wanted to remain casual but chose a blouse my mother had bought shortly before her accident. When I looked at my hair, I gasped. It looked like an unraveling mop. I quickly ran a brush through it. *Maybe I should put on lipstick*, I thought, and then I thought I was acting too much like a lovesick teenager drooling over her idol posted on a wall.

I gave myself one more look and then walked out. Everyone was waiting at the door.

"Wow," Kyle said. "You'd never know this young lady had a serious operation recently."

Anna smiled, and Judy looked at me enviously. I know I was blushing. I felt a new sense of energy.

"Now, don't overdo it," Anna warned, as if she could read my mind.

I know her warning was born of real love, but I was determined not to have what I did decided by anyone else, least of all my father. This new energy gave me the feeling I was finally breathing—and breathing on my own.

"Oh, I think Lisa is someone we can trust at the helm," Kyle said. He reached for my hand. Judy opened the door, and we stepped out.

I don't think I ever walked out of the Crest without being impressed by the ocean. To the left below was part of the beach and a row of island houses. Today was beautiful; it truly felt like the first day of my life.

I paused to take a deep breath. Kyle laughed.

"How long have you been in Bar Harbor this time?"

"Not that long. Why?" he asked.

"Seaman's words . . . *helm*?"

He laughed again. "It's not pretentious. We had lots of expensive toys, one of them being a sixteen-foot sailboat."

"Had?"

We walked toward the cliff. Judy was close enough to breathe down my neck, but I suspected it wasn't to protect me as much as to hear the conversation.

Kyle shrugged. "I said my parents were wealthy enough to finance my development, as I told you, mostly thanks to my mother, but my father has since made a number of poor financial decisions. Truth is, he almost had to declare bankruptcy last year. I had to lend him money. For him, it was like taking castor oil."

"But not for you," I said, and he laughed.

He looked back at Judy. "Pretty smart girl, huh?"

"What? Oh, yes, she is," she said quickly.

"Point is, I had it to lend, but I'm not someone who will tell you

I don't care about money and I care only about my art. I like my art making money. I even sold a multimillionaire a painting four months ago just because the colors matched what he had in his entertainment room. I don't think he looked at my work twice. I know his wife hadn't seen it. He had an associate come to a showing of mine. But," he quickly added, "that doesn't mean I lack respect for my own work. I don't offer anything until I'm satisfied with it. Why they buy it isn't as important to me. Understand?"

"Yes," I said.

"I thought you would. I'm kind of surprised and quite happy that you are not some tasteless, spoiled rich girl."

I couldn't help but feel myself blush again, only this time I was happier about it. His smile warmed. For a moment I thought of a lobster going into a trap, but how could someone so handsome and exciting be a trap? Even if he was, it was flattering to know he wanted me to like him, really like him. I loved Jamie, but there was something about this that was quite different. I thought about it for a moment but only needed that moment to realize what it was.

With Jamie, I still felt like a high school girl.

With Kyle, I was feeling more like a young woman.

We paused at the cliff and turned back.

"I was thinking, almost from the moment I drove up here, that I should set up right by that oak tree," he said.

"The oak tree?"

"Yes. I remember you mentioning it when you were telling me about the haiku poem," he said, "and I took a quick look at it before I came to the door."

Did he memorize everything I had told him?

The tree had more meaning than that for me. It was Jamie's and my favorite place to meet and where we came the closest to making love.

"I'm not sure it should be in the picture, but there's a good view of the house from it. Let's take a look," he said, and started for it.

We paused at the tree. I watched him turn and study each angle until he nodded to himself and turned back to me.

"I think this works because I don't want too much of the ocean. You can't exclude it. We're on an island, and the house has to reflect that, but the focus of attention should be fully on the Crest. Right?"

I tried to look at it from his perspective, but with those silvery-blue eyes of his fixed so warmly on me, I couldn't think for a moment.

"Yes," I said quickly, embarrassed by my silence. "I see what you mean." I really did. What astounded me was how quickly he saw the view that the landscape should capture.

"I thought you would. Breeze is a little stronger now." He gestured for us to return to the house and looked at Judy. "We don't want to overdo it."

She giggled and followed us. He smiled at me and stopped when we got to the door.

"Eddie Doyle says your big appointment with Dr. Knox is late Tuesday morning. You'll get the final seal of approval."

"I'm that much of a topic of conversation?"

"You're a star in the gallery, so we talk about you."

His answer slightly disappointed me. Sometimes I wanted not logical replies but emotional ones. Maybe he saw the disappointment in my face.

"I was wondering, if your father and grandfather approve, could

I take you to lunch afterward, assuming all goes well? I'll deliver you to your grandfather's boat to go back to Birdlane."

"Lunch?"

"Also assuming you like being in Bar Harbor and that there are no other plans for your celebration. I mean, I understand if . . ."

"Of course I like Bar Harbor. It's always been an exciting place for me and my mother especially. In comparison to Birdlane Island, Bar Harbor, or what we call the mainland, is riveting with its bright lights, traffic, and variety of things to do."

I could see he was amused by my enthusiasm.

"I intend to go there a lot more often now."

"Breaking out of the—" he started to say.

I finished it. "The prison my body put me in."

"Watch out, world. Lisa's coming."

He leaned over to hug me quickly. A thrilling warm feeling traveled through me like a wave. He started for his car, a rental from the pier. At the car, he paused and turned back.

"We all live in our own prisons sometimes. Let your art free you."

"It has."

He nodded. I watched him drive away.

"What a nice young man," Judy said. "I must visit the gallery."

There's never an age when we all don't fantasize, I thought. My mother once told me, "Everyone carries around their own Snow White mirror."

Daddy came to my door shortly before dinner to tell me he was stopping by just to change clothes before going out to dinner. I began to wonder if he was seeing someone. I did suspect it once and asked Mommy. She said, "Some things are better left undisturbed." I didn't know what she meant, but I knew I shouldn't pursue it.

"The artist who is doing the Crest was here to get a perspective, Daddy."

"Probably more to get more money out of my father," he said.

"Not everybody is like you, Daddy."

He didn't reply. For a moment I thought he was going to say something nasty, but he just shook his head like last time and walked away. It felt good to leave him speechless.

Kyle was right. *Watch out, world. I'm coming.* I laughed to myself.

Jamie called me the next day. I didn't mention Kyle's visit and afterward felt guilty about it. It was truly as if I were hiding it from him, but I did promise to call him as soon as I had the doctor's exam results. He sounded the same, his voice low, without much energy. I asked him again about the special chair his father wanted built on the boat, and he got a little angry at me for even bringing it up. I apologized and again told him I'd call him as soon as I could.

Instead of lying there feeling guilty, however, I thought about Kyle's offer to take me to lunch. Was Daddy right in a way? Was Kyle giving me all this attention because Grandfather had hired him to do the Crest? For a moment I even wondered if he had chosen my painting with this in mind.

"No," I could hear my mother saying. "Don't discount yourself so fast."

So often, my mother told me how pretty I was, and other people did, too, but in the back of my mind was the idea that they were saying this so I wouldn't feel as bad about my heart issue. We used to joke about some of the boys in our class who primped their hair and had nervous breakdowns over a pimple here and there. But so many times I studied my face in mirrors and wondered, *Am I really so pretty? Do I really look so much like my mother?* Despite his moods and attitudes, Daddy was a very good-looking man.

My hope was that this feeling of being offered compensation, flattery to help me accept my physical condition, was soon to be gone. That would truly lift another weight from my shoulders. It was with all that in mind that I awoke the morning of my appointment in Bar Harbor with Dr. Knox. I thought about my tests and the final evaluation but was quite distracted by my hope to have lunch with Kyle. It was almost as if I wanted to learn as much about myself when it came to such a date as I did about him. I wasn't quite eighteen. How would I handle a man as accomplished and as worldly and experienced as Kyle Wyman? And would I recognize what he truly wanted from me?

Daddy showed up just as Judy had put together everything I needed for the short boat trip.

"Morning, Daddy," I said.

He grunted something that gave me the feeling Grandfather was making him come. To him, it was probably just another exam.

"Your grandfather tells me you might stay in Bar Harbor for lunch with this artist."

"Yes, maybe."

Why did he sound so displeased?

"You didn't ask me if you could," he said.

For a moment, I was surprised. Did he suddenly really care?

"I'm only going to lunch."

"Yeah, well, women are too emotional to make the right decisions when it comes to the important ones. Becomin' eighteen isn't goin' to change that."

"I think it will. You won't have to worry about approving. Think of the burden I'll be taking off your shoulders, with all you have to worry about as it is."

He stared at me a moment. Did he miss the irony, or did it make him too angry to speak?

"Whatever," he said.

"Let's go," I heard Grandfather call.

"The mastermind speaks," Daddy said, and started out. Judy and I followed.

Could there be a day more important to me? I wondered. Nothing else, not my upcoming eighteenth birthday, not my high school graduation, came even close. Leaving the house, I finally felt a little trembling of concern.

The sea was as calm as I had ever seen it, and the sky with its powdery clouds here and there made it what people in Maine called a "wicked good" day. But I wasn't thinking that much about the weather. As the breeze combed through my hair, I continued thinking about my exam. It was a key put in a lock. Would it open my life or just not turn? This exam was truly the seal of approval.

Daddy and Grandfather were up front arguing about something in the business, for sure. I couldn't hear them, but Daddy was stabbing the air while Grandfather just stared ahead. Suddenly, Grandfather turned to me, clenched his fists, and shook them. Daddy stared as though he had just realized I was on the boat.

I didn't really get very nervous until we got into the limo at the Bar Harbor pier. I was taking short breaths until Grandfather pressed my hand and smiled. Everyone was pleasant and optimistic-looking as they took me through the blood tests, X-rays, and other exams. I barely spoke. Grandfather and Daddy remained in the lobby, but from what I understood, Daddy spent most of his time on the doctor's phone, arguing with a fisherman's company. Finally, Dr. Knox arrived in my room.

"Our prognosis has been one hundred percent confirmed. I want you to finish the antibiotics you have, and after that do nothing more for an issue that is gone. The only restriction is never to be unhappy," he said, smiling.

Grandfather stepped up. "How do you feel?" he asked. Daddy appeared at his side.

"Funny, like if I take the weight of this blanket off me, I'll float up to the ceiling."

Grandfather laughed.

"Women," Daddy said. "Who else can make sense of that? Well, then, I'm off to see Branden."

"If you lose us that fisherman, you go back to fishing to make up for it," Grandfather threatened.

Daddy smirked and walked off.

"Branden?" I said. "That's one of our most reliable accounts, over ten years."

"Right. Your father thinks nickel-and-diming them helps our business. Forget that for now. Someone is waiting for you in the lobby."

"Oh, my gosh, Kyle," I said. I had been concentrating so hard on my exam that I had forgotten his invitation. "I'll get dressed."

"I suggested and then made a reservation for you two at Erik's Viking. It has that semicircular window view of the bay," he said.

"Then you approve of him, Grandfather, even though he's that much older?"

"It's not the age. I believe you are very mature and a very intelligent young lady. I'm not worried about you and your decisions.

Your mother brought you up. Now it's time for you to be in charge of your own social life."

"Thank you, Grandfather," I said with teary eyes. I hugged him.

As soon as I was dressed and had brushed my hair, I went to the lobby, almost as excited about this as I had been about the news the doctor had given me.

Kyle stood there smiling and holding a half dozen red roses. He looked even more handsome in his light blue leather jacket, tight jeans, and white loafers. He stepped forward quickly.

"Your father came out mumbling something about 'she's fine' and 'all yours.' We didn't even get properly introduced. How did it go? How do you feel?"

"It went well, Kyle. I have the final green light to live my life. It's a different feeling, something so new and yet something I expected, like . . ."

"Putting on your first bra."

"What?"

He laughed. "Something my younger sister always says. She even says it now when she feels something special."

"You never mentioned a younger sister. Now that I think of it, you've hardly told me anything about your life."

"We haven't been alone that long."

"True."

"I will now," he said. "Let's go have lunch and celebrate."

He handed me the flowers, kissed my cheek, and took my arm. He directed me toward a red sports car, top down, with the steering wheel on the English driving side.

"What is this?" I asked.

"My favorite car, a 1954 MG."

"English, but why have an English car here?"

"I got it in a trade with an English man who's a member of Parliament. And I love driving it, here or anywhere."

"Car? In a trade?"

"He really wanted one of my paintings of the English countryside where he lived. I was there for most of one year. We negotiated for a while, and I finally just asked for the car. To him, it wasn't that important. He would get another in a minute."

"You've lived in England, too?"

He laughed and started the car. "And in Japan, and in Australia."

"You've been to all those places?"

"I lift my paintbrush into the air, and wherever it falls, I go. My passport book is stamped full. I'd love to paint on the moon."

I laughed as he took off, whipping me back a bit as the wind combed through my hair. I screamed, and he laughed, waving his arm.

"More of this from now on, huh?" he said.

By "this," he meant just living on impulse, something I was terrified of doing.

"Yes," I said. I almost had to shout.

He whipped around a turn and pulled up in front of Erik's as if he had been there many times.

"Yeah, this is the view," he said, and came around to open my door, something no one else but Grandfather's driver would do.

He took my arm, and we entered the restaurant. Erik was there to greet us. He had very long licorice-black hair and was at least six foot three or four and wore a traditional Viking warrior outfit with the short pants and leggings.

"*Hei*," Kyle said to him.

He smiled broadly. "How much Norwegian do you speak?"

"That's about it, and *Hvor er badet?*"

"What does that mean?" I asked.

"'Where's the bathroom?'" Erik said, and led us to the table with the best view.

It wasn't until we were seated and had been handed menus that I realized I hadn't called Jamie. Kyle was describing his times in Norway. He could see I wasn't listening.

"Something wrong?"

"I forgot to call someone who is probably waiting for me to call."

"Oh. Well, just go call. I see a phone at the end of the bar."

I looked at it. What would I say? I went to the phone and called Jamie. He picked up before the line finished ringing.

"What happened?" he asked before I could speak.

"Sorry I took so long to call. It all went well. I'm cleared to . . . to be normal," I said. "Just routine checkups. Not much different from anyone else."

"That's so great. Are you home? We'll find a way to celebrate."

"No, I'm in Bar Harbor having lunch."

"Oh. With who?"

I paused. There were so many reasons not to do what I was about to do and so many to do it.

"Grandfather," I said. "He's done so much for me."

He was quiet. "Okay. See you on Birdlane," he quickly added, and hung up before I could say goodbye.

He knew I was lying. Jamie and I never lied to each other. I stood there holding the phone, feeling really bad. I saw Kyle staring at me and took a deep breath before hanging up.

"Everything all right?" Kyle asked when I returned.

Instinctively, I wanted to hide my relationship with Jamie.

"Yes. No," I said.

He smiled. "Did you lie to someone to protect him or yourself?"

"Maybe both."

He laughed. "Truth is the most slippery thing to hold," he said.

The waiter approached with a small bottle of champagne. And two glasses! As soon as he walked away, I leaned over.

"I'm not quite eighteen, and besides, they raised the drinking age to twenty-one," I whispered.

He leaned in toward me, our lips inches apart, and whispered, "Erik said if my glass spills into yours, it's no problem. And what's a celebration without a little champagne?"

Looking into his eyes so closely put an excited chill through me. When he put his hand over mine, I held my breath a moment. He smiled, I thought because he saw my reaction, and then sat back.

"Everything is different for you now, Lisa. The chains are off. You can be the young lady you were meant to be. My advice is *carpe diem*. It's how I've lived."

"'Seize the day.'"

"Yes, don't get weighted down or concerned about the long-term meaning of everything. A beautiful wave is a beautiful wave. It'll come again and again. Don't just discard it."

He sat back, and we ordered sandwiches.

"Tell me about your sister," I said.

"Oh, not much to tell. She fell in love about an hour after she was eighteen, was pregnant two months before she married, and—surprise—had another baby ten months after the first one, a boy and then a girl. She had intended to go to college and become an English teacher. Her husband scrounges out a living as a bartender. In her case, she took *carpe diem* too literally."

"Meaning?"

"She was promiscuous at sixteen and pregnant at eighteen."

"You never said her name."

"Oh, didn't I? Pauline. My father was hoping for a Paul, not that he was any better with boys."

"Where do they live?"

"Some small town near Baltimore. I see them occasionally."

"Do you think it's harder to be a successful woman or man?"

He smiled. "Here?"

"Anywhere."

"With the exception of Cleopatra, being a man is easier anywhere," he said. "Wow, you are like someone just born, someone who just arrived on planet Earth."

"Feels like it."

He laughed, and we ate as he told me more about his world travels. Then he paused and stared at me hard.

"What?"

"I think you already know that I believe there is such a thing as intrinsic beauty. It's why I don't paint anything anywhere just because I'm offered a big fee. You have the look of a newborn baby, fresh and pure. Most girls your age would be insulted. They want to be thought of as experienced and sophisticated. You have a great natural quality. Don't let anyone tell you different."

He put his hand over mine and closed his fingers just enough to highlight the excitement I felt being with him. Other older men had looked at me, and I could see them eyeing me for some fantasy. But as soon as they knew who I was and what was wrong with me, they quickly turned away. Most girls my age would giggle and flirt. Maybe Kyle saw the maturity in me. Maybe it was a maturity I'd had to develop. In so many ways, I did feel like I had skipped my childhood.

"No one has said otherwise," I said.

He laughed and sat back. "You mean no one has dared."

I laughed.

"For a woman your age, you have quite a strong personality. If I didn't know better, I'd say you were already in college. You have a strong sense of responsibility. It's easy to see."

Where is this going, these compliments? I wondered. And did I have any control over it anyway?

CHAPTER ELEVEN

On the way to the dock, Kyle told me he was coming tomorrow to start the painting.

"All my equipment was delivered to the Crest today. I even know where I'm going to sleep. Your grandfather's housekeeper has everything arranged. I think your grandfather has chosen a place to hang it, above the fireplace where you currently have a portrait of two ancestors."

"Yes, perfect. I never liked the expressions on their faces. They both look constipated."

He laughed. "In the early days, people didn't smile for portraits or photographs. It wasn't considered proper. Maybe they were afraid to show their teeth. What does your father think of my painting the Crest portrait?"

"He'll want to know how much it will add to the value of the Crest. He measures everything in life by P and L statements," I said, and Kyle laughed again.

"He has that look. I'd better stay clear of him. I'm not good at keeping within a budget."

We pulled up to the dock.

"I guess I'll see you tomorrow," he said when he opened my door to help me out. He paused. "Hey, don't look so serious. I won't break up your family just because mine's a mess."

Of course, I wasn't thinking of that. I was thinking of Jamie when he actually saw Kyle at the Crest and might even see how Kyle looked at me. Or maybe I'd betray a feeling. *He's been hurt enough*, I thought.

"No, not worried," I said. "A bit frightened. New life and all that."

"Understood. When we see each other again, remind me to tell you how I started a new life."

"Only once?" I asked as we walked to Grandfather's boat.

He laughed and said, "I never met a man or woman as young as you who cuts right to the chase."

"I never thought I had the time to waste on beating around the bush. Inherited that from my father, I suppose."

He and Grandfather's driver, Arthur, helped me into the boat.

"You don't realize what a discovery you are for me," Kyle said, before letting go of my hand. "Natural, honest, and beautiful."

I just looked at him. I had no idea what to say. "Thank you" seemed so juvenile. And I wasn't going to say the same thing to him even though I felt that way. Sometimes silence was the best reply.

I sat back. He stood on the dock, looking at Arthur and me as we pulled away. I felt as if he was still holding my hand. A "So long" or "Goodbye" could last a second or linger in your mind for minutes.

What a day, I thought. *What a wonderful day*. Then I turned to look toward Birdlane. It looked so small, so contained. It was, after all, where I had spent my restricted life. But it was my home. For a moment it felt like I was belittling a lifelong friend. "You're not a mainland girl," Jamie had once said, but what if I was? What if Birdlane was too small? What if it stifled me? Was it enough to be able to take trips once in a while? I looked back at Bar Harbor. I felt like I was being pulled in two different directions. Which way I would go was a mystery. How would it be solved?

Anna rushed to take my roses as soon as I arrived. She already knew all the good news. I laughed because she looked like she thought I had brought Kyle's flowers for her.

"He's such a nice man who shows appreciation," she said.

We talked about the exam, and then she told me Kyle's room was the next one after my mother's on the first floor. Anna had to show me what she had done with mine and how she had freshened up Kyle's. Everything that had to do with medicine had been removed from mine. Kyle's room looked very cozy, with a new bedspread.

"Where's my new granddaughter?" I heard Grandfather call.

I hurried down the hall. I thought my father would be there, too. But he was probably still angry about my lunch date.

"How was your lunch?" Grandfather asked.

"It was fun. Every time I go to Bar Harbor, I realize how lucky we are to live so close."

"Your grandmother would say that. So I decided to give you your birthday present early. I want you to feel completely independent."

Anna returned to the door that led to the kitchen. Her wide smile convinced me she knew what the present was. He had nothing in his hand, and he wasn't the sort who would just give me money. What would make me feel completely independent?

"What is it?"

"Let's step out," he said.

I followed him, Anna right behind us with that wide, happy smile that beamed from ear to ear.

A bright red Mercedes convertible was parked right in front of the Crest.

"Well, as your father would say, we spent all the money on your driving lessons. Better have a reason for it."

"Grandfather, my own car?"

"Well, everyone was afraid to let you drive alone, but that's over, and Birdlane's coastal highway is a beautiful ride."

"It is."

"Go on. Take it for a ride. Just drive around here for a few minutes and get used to it."

"Really?"

"You got your green light to do anything anyone else your age can do," he said. "I'm sure anyone your age given a car would be itching to get in. Anna," he called, "do you want to get in and ride around the property with Lisa?"

"Oh my, yes."

I laughed, the excitement practically lifting me and flying me to the car. There was a red ribbon on the steering wheel.

"How beautiful," Anna said, and we both got in.

I started the car and drove around the driveway and along the road around the Crest.

"Your mother is surely smiling," Anna said. She ran her hand over the dash and the radio and got out.

I hesitated for just a moment and then set off to show Jamie. I was a little afraid of what my classmates might say once they saw me in my car. I knew that many used to say I was given things to compensate for my health issue. Some said nasty things. Jamie always told me they were simply jealous. I thought it was why I didn't have many girlfriends. Who wanted to make friends with someone who could die any day, maybe right in front of you?

What would they say now?

As I drove into our old neighborhood, many memories returned. I paused to look at places where Jamie and I had played games and sat talking. *He'll be excited about the car*, I thought. *I'll tell him to drive us.* His right leg was good. I got more and more enthusiastic as I drew closer to his family home. I was hoping he might be outside when I drove up and into his driveway. The house looked so quiet. It was always so peaceful inside as well as out. I rarely ever saw a family squabble. Jamie liked to tease his sister, and his mother bawled him out for it all the time, but I knew everyone loved each other. It just felt warmer there than in my own home.

Mrs. Fuller came to the door even before I pressed the doorbell, obviously excited to see me.

"Oh, Lisa, Jamie told us the good news. Everyone is so happy for you."

"Thank you, Mrs. Fuller. Jamie here?"

"Didn't he call you?"

"No, but I've been driving about and was in Bar Harbor longer than I had expected to be."

"Driving about? Oh, is that your car?" she asked, stepping out.

"Yes, my grandfather's pre-birthday present. I wanted Jamie to see it before anyone else."

"It's beautiful. Good luck with it."

"So where is he?"

I felt her reluctance.

"Jamie left about an hour ago with Terry Duncan, his best buddy."

"Well, where did they go? I'll drive there. That will be even more fun."

"I'm afraid not, Lisa. They've gone to New York City."

"What?"

"He and Terry were planning it for years."

"I know. He talked about it all the time, but . . ."

"I couldn't deny him anything with what he's gone through. He'll probably call you when he's there or on the way," she said.

I'm not so sure, I thought.

"How long will they be away?"

"With travel and all, about ten days," she said. She leaped to change the topic. "Your grandfather's spreading the word about your good news, and you know how fast news spreads on Birdlane."

"Yes, he's very happy."

"And what did your father say?"

I looked at her. She knew my face, what an expressionless facade meant.

"He's such an unemotional man. I understand," she said.

She was an expert when it came to bailing people out of an uncomfortable moment.

"Your mother is surely jumping for joy in heaven."

"Thank you. See you soon, Mrs. Fuller."

She stood there watching me get into the car. I waved to her and drove off. All the excitement I had felt seemed to drift away. I didn't even want to look at our old neighborhood. I saw people who knew me looking at me, but I didn't turn to acknowledge them. It was a beautiful day, with the ocean so inviting, but it was as if a cap had been placed on my new enthusiasm. *I'll wait for Jamie's call*, I thought, but I doubted very much that I would get it.

I started up the hill to the Crest. When I rounded the turn, I thought I was looking up and out at a Norse god who had slid down on the wind to stand at the cliffs of the Crest. He was staring out at the sea. Of course, I knew it was Kyle. What was he doing here so soon after we had parted? He heard me approaching, turned, waved, and hurried toward me as I parked.

"Beautiful car," he said. "Anna told me about your birthday gift. It was made for you. They could make a commercial with you sitting there."

"Thank you. What are you doing here now? I thought . . ."

"The gallery had two private tour cancellations, so I thought, why waste time tomorrow by traveling, getting organized, when I could do it today and tonight? So five more days to your birthday puts me here on schedule. Right?"

"Yes," I said, and suddenly realized Jamie wouldn't be here for the birthday we had talked so much about.

"You having a big party, or . . ."

"No," I said quickly. "I had one for my seventeenth, and everyone was there to see the Crest and ooh and aah more than to be there for me. Although it seems more traditional to have it for my eighteenth, I think it will mean more if it's a family-only dinner. My friendships at school are vague and full of rivers of jealousy to cross. I'm tired of trying to act like someone I'm not. It's not my fault my grandfather created a major successful business and we have so much. I'm sure you know what I mean."

"Sure do. Good on you. Sincerity is more valuable than gold. Family dinner, huh? So if I'm here already, maybe I can get an invitation?" he said.

"Really? You want to be at it?"

"Why not?" He looked back at the Crest. "Although . . ."

"What?"

"I came outside here because your grandfather and father are having one of those famous chats you implied explode from time to time."

"Oh? What was it about?"

"I don't want to get involved with complicated family matters. I've had enough of my own and still do, but your father just discovered that your grandfather asked the business department to include you as an employee after your birthday. Your father challenged it, asking what you would do, and your grandfather said advise, consult, research. Then it got a little snappy."

"Did it?"

"Your grandfather said something about your father's trips not being only business."

"That rumor has come up to the Crest. One thing about gossip: it knows no boundaries. Even on an island this small."

"When your father complained about my fee, I think as his answer to the accusation, I disappeared. I'm an expert when it comes to getting out of the way of a hurricane."

I laughed but looked away when Jamie came to mind again.

"I'm all right with it," Kyle said, misreading my deep thought and worry.

I said nothing.

"What do I have to do to get a ride in the car?"

"Maybe . . ."

"Maybe after dinner you can show me the town of Birdlane," he said.

I laughed. "This is Birdlane, not Bar Harbor. You can see the town in thirty seconds."

"Still, time with you," he said. "I'll be busy . . . unless . . ."

"What?"

"When you're done with school, you watch me work, and I'll explain what I'm doing. Sort of a bonus that maybe will please your father."

"I doubt it. He doesn't think of art as a way to make any money."

"Well, I'll have to talk some investments with him."

"The only language he speaks," I said, just as Daddy came out of the house.

"This car is going to be registered under the business name," he told me. "Your grandfather never thinks of business first."

"Well, he thinks of me first, Daddy."

"Right. You know," he said to Kyle, "you should have room and board deducted from your fee."

"Whatever your father says."

Daddy smirked and then turned to me. "I'll see you in two days," he told me, as if it were a threat. He started for his car, then paused and turned. "And we'll talk about this research and consulting."

"I'm proud to help, Daddy," I said.

He just stared for a moment. Kyle smiled, and when Daddy got into his car, Kyle said, "Are you sure this birthday coming up is your eighteenth and not your twenty-eighth or twenty-ninth?"

"I think it's safer not to be sure about anything," I said.

He laughed. "C'mon. You can help me organize my materials for tomorrow," he said, and we walked to the house.

I looked back at the car before we entered. It really did give me a new sense of freedom and independence. For a while, it would surely feel strange to just do what I wanted and not ask permission or worry about restrictions. Anyone locked up for decades and then suddenly let out would surely stand there a little dumbfounded at first. *Make decisions*, I told myself firmly.

Maybe I will take him for a ride after dinner, I thought.

I followed Kyle to the room Anna had prepared. He opened a case containing his paint tubes.

"These come from Golden Artist Colors. Many of the most famous artists used their work. Special quality," he said proudly.

"I have so much to learn."

"And lots of time to do it," he said. "We want the colors of the Crest, but something special with them."

He studied the tubes as if he could look through them. I helped him get his tripod out of the case and the art paper he was going to use. Then, as if he was exhausted, he sat on the bed. He lifted his hand to reach for mine just as Anna called us to dinner. He rose quickly.

"You don't hafta call me twice to dinner," he said, and we went to the dining room, him talking about some of the world's famous restaurants.

Grandfather was already seated. He immediately apologized

for the "chat" with my father, but Kyle said it wasn't necessary. He understood family differences. After which Grandfather asked him even more questions about his family and background than I had. Kyle seemed to enjoy talking to Grandfather, who was pleased at the questions Kyle asked about his upbringing and ancestors. They talked about the Crest, the architecture and the location. For most of the dinner, I felt like an audience. Somewhere toward the end, they both seemed to remember I was there and talked about my birthday gift and my wonderful health report.

When dinner ended, Kyle asked if we could take that ride to see Birdlane proper and what I thought were important places. I glanced at Grandfather, who didn't say a word except "It's up to Lisa. She's her own lady now."

Kyle looked at me.

"Sure. I'll show him the highlights of Birdlane," I said. "It actually has its own atmosphere, its own sense of identity."

"Well, I'm very excited. Thank you," Kyle said.

When we walked out, I told him he could drive. He liked that. It was still a warm, almost cloudless night. I looked forward to the sea breeze in my hair when we started off.

"Your grandfather is quite a guy," he said as we headed down the hill. "I never had a grandparent for long enough to appreciate him or her. I hope you don't mind me saying he's more like what your father should be."

"I never mind the truth," I replied.

He smiled and shook his head.

"What?"

"You have all the right answers built in."

"Is that bad?"

He looked at me and smiled. "No. Scary. It's like you inherited some sort of wisdom. Maybe Birdlane is a magical place. There are places in the world where people believe there's a special energy."

"Were you ever at one?"

"Yes. But as an artist, I find special energy almost anywhere."

We rounded the curve and looked down at the lights of the houses and the village. The glow shimmered in the evening air. It all seemed suddenly brand-new, as if the town had been quietly waiting for this moment. It all felt a bit different now, probably because I was seeing it through Kyle's eyes, or maybe it was because I felt so brand-new myself.

"I'm sure it's a great feeling to be above the world you live in," he said.

"Not so much above the people. Just the view."

"Yes, of course."

I took him through the village and then on a highway that I knew would bring us to a beautiful view of the ocean. Many people went there on warm summer nights, lingering beneath the stars, alive with voices. But tonight the world felt hushed, and there was practically no one there. I showed him where to pull in, and we both sat back and just looked out at the endless horizon where the sky melted into the dark waves.

"You know, I wonder now why I don't do more night scenes. It's breathtaking."

He leaned toward me and touched my hair.

"A girl like you should have many dates that end up here," he said.

Jamie flashed through my mind, but I realized there was always some underlying tension when he and I went somewhere alone, especially at night.

"You have to make moments like this, scenes like this, special in your mind," Kyle said in a half whisper.

Then he brought his lips to mine. It was a kiss I had imagined, longer than a usual friendly kiss or even a slightly unsure kiss. This was a kiss meant to be, meant to make me feel what it did. There wasn't the slightest sense of uncertainty. His firmness and determination didn't frighten me as I'd imagined such a thing would; instead, they excited me. I didn't pull away or look in any way upset.

He smiled. "Just something I wanted to be sure happened to you," he said.

Then he surprised me. He started the car, and we drove back to the house silently.

At the house, he thanked me for the tour of Birdlane as if nothing else had happened. Was I making too much of that kiss? He took my hand, and we entered the house. Everyone was somewhere else. We paused, and neither of us spoke.

"Well," he said. "I think we should get some rest. A big, long day and lots of work ahead."

I nodded.

He kept holding my hand, and we started down the hallway. At my doorway, we stopped, but I held on to his hand, and he held on to mine. Something more was going to happen, I thought; it was more like I wanted it to happen.

"Have a great sleep, and thanks for making me part of your great day," he said, and let go of my hand, leaned over to kiss me on the cheek like a big brother, and walked on to his room.

Maybe I had misjudged him. My expectations had led to disappointment, and I wondered if that was a weakness of mine. Should I have recognized right away what his real intentions were? How much experience did a girl need before she could see the right way to go?

Of course, I hadn't been here if Jamie had called, and there were no calls for the remainder of the night. In the morning, I got excited thinking maybe things would seem different when I saw Kyle at breakfast. But when I got there, Anna told me Kyle was already outside working. He had risen practically with the sun.

Before leaving to go to school, I went around the corner and shouted to him, but he was so intensely focused on his sketch that he didn't turn. I waited another moment. I was going to approach him and then thought maybe it was wrong to break his concentration. I hesitated and then went to my car to drive to school.

At school, everyone knew about my good health report and most knew about my new car. Peggy Merton approached to tell me, "Well, maybe it was a present for getting better." And I thought, did she believe I'd had control over that and that this was my reward for having made the right decision?

"Yes, I just decided to do it," I said as sarcastically as I could.

She giggled. *She's my age*, I thought. I understood what Kyle and Grandfather saw in me.

Classes were mostly review for finals, and I found the conversation with my peers suddenly quite infantile. The giggling over what was meaningless to me made me wonder if I was feeling superior because I had an older man interested in me, but how interested? Was it showing how childish I still was to fantasize about it? I couldn't wait for the day to end so I could return to the Crest.

One way or another, I would learn if I was totally misunderstanding everything. Part of me just wanted it to be a platonic relationship, but a strong part of me wanted it to be romantic and mature. Maybe we did have two identities. We talked to ourselves, argued with ourselves. Growing up, especially romantically, meant accepting who you really were. Did I have the strength to do it?

CHAPTER TWELVE

When I arrived, Kyle was still out at his site, but this time he turned immediately, put down his brush, and started toward me.

"How was school?" he asked as he approached. He brushed back his hair and straightened his shirt. It was a little gesture, but I took it to mean he didn't want to look in any way untidy in front of me.

"Pretty boring," I said. "Review, because most of my classmates won't do it at home."

He laughed. "Well, I think we can still do it," he said, looking at his watch.

"Do what?"

"Save the day for you. I found a good place to rent a sailboat, and I thought we might go to Bar Harbor for dinner. With the weather this good, it will be enjoyable."

"Go to Bar Harbor now? Really?"

"We'll sail there, and your grandfather will have his boat ready to bring us back."

"My grandfather agreed to that? You've really charmed him."

He laughed again. "We share the same goal, pleasing you. Anyway, I was told about this small Italian restaurant with authentic Sicilian food. I've been to Sicily twice, so I can tell."

"Where *haven't* you been?"

"Topeka, Kansas."

"What?"

"Just joking. Don't worry. You'll be a traveler for sure," he said.

Would I? I wondered. Maybe someone like him with his experience could see my future better than I could. I hurried off to change my clothes while he gathered his materials. I did have a sailing outfit. It was a vintage dark turquoise dress with a large button-down collar. My cotton sailing jacket would be great for the restaurant, too.

I thought sailing or anything to do with it would never interest me again since Mommy's accident, but that had happened in very bad weather, and right now I thought I'd want to go and do anything Kyle suggested. This had a sense of spontaneity, which made it all seem much more exciting. Most of all, I wanted to do things I hadn't been permitted to do before. Flowers blossomed, doors opened, shades were raised in my new world.

I stepped out of my room and heard Kyle clapping. He was standing next to Anna and chatting near the entrance.

"The new young lady," he said, and did a full theatrical bow.

Anna laughed. "She is so much brighter that I hardly recognize her." She looked at Kyle adoringly, as though he had accomplished this.

"Sailing we shall go," Kyle sang, and took my hand as we walked out to my car.

"Have a nice time," Anna called.

"You drive," I told him. I wanted to feel more like I was on a date and being catered to. Was I going to become that spoiled brat my peers assumed I was? I looked back. Anna was still out there watching us go.

I suddenly had a new fear. Maybe Grandfather's and Anna's encouragement was part of a plan. The whole idea of doing a landscape of the Crest could be part of it. They wanted me to develop self-confidence as quickly as possible. What better way than having Kyle Wyman show me all this attention? What if even his choice of my painting was part of the plan? If I found this to be true, I didn't think anything could depress me more. Grandfather wouldn't have taken the chance, would he? I could hear my mother saying, "Why wouldn't any man be interested in a girl like you?"

It isn't easy building self-confidence when you have been kept on a shelf all your life, I thought. But I had to do it. And I had to keep from showing any doubt.

We drove to the pier and to Birdlane Sailing. The owner, Steve Rogers, knew who I was. I wasn't sure what the expression on his face was—maybe that of surprise, mostly. The gossip was sure to start. He helped us launch, and as soon as we did, I could see that Kyle was a good sailor. I sat back as the wind started us on our short journey to Bar Harbor.

"You are good," I said.

"Oh, this isn't much of a challenge today. More like a dreamboat ride."

It was for me, I thought.

He held the tiller that connected directly to the rudder and sat beside me.

"Surely you've taken lessons," he said.

"Not really."

"Oh. Let's start." He put my hand on the tiller and changed positions. "You can almost feel the wind through it, can't you?"

"Yes."

"When the boat is moving faster, you can turn the tiller less to turn the boat, so don't be afraid of the wind giving us more go."

"Who taught you?" I asked.

"Not my father. I had a cousin who was in sailboat contests. That's it. You're doing well."

He drew me closer.

"I can't feel the wind through you," he said.

I was so excited steering the boat that I didn't react, and then I thought, why wasn't this something Jamie and I ever did? Of course, I knew the main reason. He was so extra careful with me. Maybe having him hovering about me like some worried parent was not such a good thing. Romance seemed to have taken second place. That, for sure, would never happen with Kyle.

Of course, Jamie was brought up seeing the sea as his workplace, not his playground. Kyle, I thought, saw nothing as his workplace and everything as his playground.

The sea spray hit us, and we both screamed with delight. I felt so loose and free, like a kite whose string had broken and was being carried by the wind. There was laughter, there were smiles, and all sorts of feelings were suddenly set free inside me. Kyle steered us over the small waves and then turned into the calm waters of

Frenchman Bay. He kept his left arm around me the whole way. It just felt like a safe and welcoming place for me to be.

Someone from Birdlane Sailing was there at the pier to take the line and get the sailboat set so we could step out. Kyle took my hand and moved me quickly toward the taxicabs.

"When the wind is with you, go with it," he said.

I truly felt blown along. We were in the cab and on our way to the restaurant in what seemed like seconds. It was down a side street, and the restaurant looked like it didn't hold more than twenty or so people, but it was cozy and decorated with Sicilian pictures and colors. We had a side table that was clearly the most personal and private in the restaurant. There was Italian music and the scent of delicious food. *Am I in a dream?* I wondered when we sat.

When the waitress came to our table, Kyle shocked me by speaking in Italian. How did he know she spoke Italian? And how did he get so good at it?

She left quickly.

"What did you say?"

"I ordered a special red wine from Sicily. I told her only one wineglass, but," he said, winking, and reaching for my water glass, "we'll accidentally spill some in here."

"You never said you spoke Italian."

"I lived for nearly two years in Rome, studying art," he said. "Don't look so amazed. Once you break out from Birdlane, you will have wonderful worldly experiences, too."

This was the way real love happened, I thought, the romantic love you read about in books and saw in movies. First, the door opened slightly when someone physically attracted you. However, a man could look like Adonis and have a very bad personality; it only took a few moments to realize it, and you would surely turn away from that. But a man like Kyle, who was so optimistic and excited about life and loved to share that feeling, opened the door a little more.

When he then began to tell you his personal experiences, speaking in a way that seemed so honest and true to you, you were drawn further in, and when he did that while building your own self-confidence, you felt comfortable and ready to be embraced.

Then he began to offer simple little touches and smiles that excited you in deeper ways. Your own imagination began to explode with the possibilities. Even while he was talking, you envisioned yourself with him in loving embraces; you felt his kiss and his touch, and your body trembled with new excitement. All the while you were telling yourself, *Stay in control, don't be easy, be sure.*

None of these thoughts and feelings were as sharp with Jamie because I could sense his caution as much as I could sense anything in myself. I felt no caution coming from Kyle, just that confidence that came from his experiences and molded his own life.

When the waitress brought the wine, he ordered dinner for both of us after asking me about things I liked to eat. When she left, he poured the water out of my glass and poured in some of the wine. He then gave a toast in Italian to my health, explaining how important it was to make eye contact with the person being toasted. "*Cin cin,*" he said, and I sipped the wine.

Mommy used to joke and sing, "Little sins mean a lot. Throw me a kiss from across the way." I never relived her joy as much as I did when I imagined myself as being more like her.

We laughed and ate the delicious food. Every once in a while, Kyle put his hand on mine and said something warm and complimentary.

He talked about himself as though he was suddenly releasing his own hidden feelings. Was there a way not to fall in love with such a man?

After dinner, we went for a casual walk. It was as if there were no other people around us and Bar Harbor was just for us. Without realizing it, I thought, we had reached the gallery. We paused and looked at the door to his upstairs apartment. Before he could ask or say something and turn us toward the pier, I said, "I'm not going to school tomorrow."

"You sure?"

"Yes."

What we were saying, or at least what I was saying, was code for what I felt and wanted. As if the words didn't have to be spoken, he turned to the door, and we entered.

"As I said, a surprising view for something like this," he told me.

We walked up the dark wood stairs to the door of his room. He hesitated a moment and then turned the knob. The room was small, with a simple double bed, a dresser, a bathroom on the left, and a small cooking area on the right. The window to our right on entering was unusually large, stretching almost from floor to ceiling, and it offered a sweeping view of the bay. The soft glow of the evening bathed the water in a gentle haze. We walked right up to it, drawn by the quiet majesty of the view. He didn't put on any bright light; there was no need. For a moment, the world outside felt like a quiet dream, untouched and eternal.

"What do you think?" he asked.

"Exactly what you said. Amazing view."

"For something like this. I've slept in a lot worse, especially when I first started traveling."

"How old were you?"

"Sixteen. I got a job on a cruise ship drawing caricatures of the guests. I was able to do some seascapes during the day."

"Sixteen? Your parents let you?"

He smiled. "I had a fake license showing me as eighteen. I ran off for a while."

"What happened when you returned?"

"My father started charging me rent."

"What?"

"It was all right. Made me more ambitious."

He stared for a moment.

"The moonlight is dancing on your face," he said, and touched my cheek. Then he put his arm around me and gently turned me toward him, fully embracing me.

We kissed, and the feeling rippled down my body, making me feel absolutely naked, every part of me touched. His lips were on my neck and then pressed below. He lifted me gently and took me to the bed. Then he stood and took off his clothes. Naked, he knelt to take off mine.

His kisses moved as smoothly as his paintbrush. It actually gave me the feeling he was drawing me, outlining me and then filling me with his passion as his lips caressed the nipples on my breasts and his body pressed closer to mine. For a long moment, we just stayed that way, breathing hard, anticipating each other's touch. Then he kissed me again, but hesitated to do more.

"How many days again until you're eighteen?" he whispered.

"Four," I said.

"I can wait."

I felt a deep disappointment, but the way he moved and the way we satisfied each other put it on pause. For minutes afterward, we lay there, breathing heavily. The moonlight fully illuminated Bar Harbor and lit up his room.

"Better get back," he said, and reached for his clothes while handing me some of mine. In silence, we got dressed. It seemed like hours had gone by, but it had hardly been that long. Minutes later, we were walking to the pier.

We were both silent on Grandfather's boat as it returned us to Birdlane, but before we reached the pier, I turned to Kyle and asked, "Did you hesitate to please me or to protect yourself?"

He smiled. "I was waiting for that. I knew you would ask it. It's one thing for a girl who is underage to be sexually active, but when an older man is involved, the law steps in, and it can get very unpleasant, not only for him but for the girl. I mean, some things should be public and some should not. Sound right?"

"All this logic seems to take away from the romance and the mystery," I said.

"Not for long," he replied, and kissed my cheek.

I leaned against him on the ride up the hill to the Crest. When we arrived, he asked if I was still staying home from school.

"Absolutely."

"Then we'll spend the day talking art," he said.

He kissed me good night at my bedroom door. I went in, not sure how to feel. I sat on my bed and thought about Jamie and our time at the oak tree. We had been hot and heavy, as they say, and then suddenly he'd said, "I'd hate to think that I was taking advantage of you."

"You're not," I'd told him.

I had wanted him, but he'd looked around and said, "This isn't the place I envisioned for it. I want it to be ours, everything . . . ours."

Ironically, I had called him a hopeless romantic. But Jamie's hesitation was truly different from Kyle's. Kyle's was more practical. I wasn't sure which I liked better.

I didn't stay home from school the next day; I stayed home the next *two* days. Each day was exciting. Kyle took me along on his journey to create the portrait of the Crest, and every moment along the way, I learned more about art. At dinner, we talked incessantly about the experience. Grandfather roared with laughter at our enthusiasm. My father was like a child forced to attend church service. Whenever he could, he tried to turn the conversation to the company, but it was always more of a complaint. Kyle actually annoyed him one night by comparing him to his father. Grandfather was amused, but Daddy, as usual, left to do his own things, go his own way.

When Kyle returned to Bar Harbor to work at the gallery, I attended school, looking forward to his next trip to the Crest, for my birthday. Anna was preparing a wonderful feast for us. I spent time choosing what I would wear. I wanted to look older, and after I pondered and pondered, it suddenly occurred to me to look at some of Mommy's things that had been placed in a guest room closet.

I found her sequin-stitched bodycon dress, with short sleeves and about knee-length. It fit me perfectly, as if it had been waiting for this moment.

I stood before the mirror, brushing my hair so it looked closer to Mommy's. In her jewelry box, I found a perfect pair of her earrings to match, and when I fastened them in place, it was as if a part of her lingered with me. I also found a pair of her shoes that not only were stunning with the dress but fit as though they had always belonged to me. By the time I walked out to the dining room, Grandfather, Kyle, and Daddy were sitting there.

As I approached, it was Daddy who had the biggest reaction. His eyes widened, and he actually stood up, looking like he was losing his breath.

Grandfather spoke for him. "I thought for a moment your mother was approaching the table," he said.

Looking at Daddy, I realized he really had loved Mommy, and she had married him, so there must have been something between them, something they had lost, and maybe that was what made Daddy so bitter all the time. I smiled and took my seat. Daddy sat, still not talking. He looked dazed.

"I think I should present my present now," Kyle said, and reached to his side to bring up a framed picture he had painted of me. He placed it on the table. In the picture, I was standing on the cliff of the Crest and looking toward Bar Harbor.

"Very nice," Grandfather said.

Daddy looked at it. "What's it cost?" he asked.

"Cost?" Kyle looked at me and then back at him. "What do you mean? I mean, there's the materials."

"Not much, then," Daddy said.

"Well, it took me a number of hours," Kyle said. "Normally, I would get about five thousand for a picture like this."

"Five thousand? Dollars?"

"Yes, sir. Art is a very valuable investment."

"How's that?"

"Old artists and their works could bring in millions. With time, they gain value. They don't lose value. It's not like the stock market."

"Too much for me," Daddy said. "I'll stay with the stock market."

"When did you ever leave it?" I asked.

Daddy shot me a sharp, angry look, but I didn't look away.

Anna started to serve dinner, almost as if to stop any more of an exchange between Daddy and me.

Daddy had a way of making birthdays seem ordinary, even his own.

"Stores and card companies created holidays," he told me once. "Underneath everything there's a profit-and-loss layer."

"What about happiness?" I asked him.

"Profit is happiness; loss is unhappiness," he said.

I felt sorry for him, but I would never dare say it. It would say itself in time.

CHAPTER THIRTEEN

In the back of my mind, I was hearing Kyle say he would wait until I was eighteen. I went to sleep that night with expectations. And fears. Would he be more aggressive; would I be more receptive? Sometimes the hardest person to know was yourself.

What if it was not the most wonderful thing in the world? Every girl surely went through this ambivalence. I knew there were some girls in my class who knew the answers. What Kyle described as my beautiful innocence seemed more like a disadvantage to me. The first time you gave yourself to someone should be something special; it shouldn't be simply passion and the loss of control. It should be something you did willingly, but somehow planning it took away the mystery and romance. It was just another thing to do on your march to adulthood. I didn't like that thought. So much of my life was not in my control; this was one thing that should be.

When I was fifteen, I heard two of my classmates, girls, whispering about me. I was around the corner and stopped when I heard my name. I recognized Caroline Lee when she said, "I doubt Jamie would try to make love to her. She might die on the bed."

They laughed. I waited until they walked away. But the thought never left me.

I stayed awake as long as I could on my birthday night, but Kyle never came. He was out working as usual early in the morning. I walked down to him to be sure he saw me leaving.

"I'm going to school today," I told him. "They're going over the finals, what to do, et cetera."

"Sure. I'll be here today. Making progress," he said, looking at his work.

It was like he had forgotten all about me. *That's just the way real artists are when they're into their work*, I thought. *They can see nothing but their work. I'm like that. I can't blame him.*

"See you later," I said, and headed for my car. He didn't say anything more. When I looked back, he was studying his last stroke. *Men are so complicated*, I thought. Then I laughed at myself. Like I really knew anything about men.

More of my classmates spoke to me. I could see they felt less frightened of what would happen if we had a disagreement. When I thought about it deeply, I really couldn't blame them for how they were. Surely their parents had warned them not to do anything that might cause me to have a seizure or something. I tried to be as energetic and active as I could be now. The only things that slowed me down were questions about Jamie. All I could say was he was living one of his dreams.

Gossip had spread, of course. There were questions about Kyle. I referred only to my grandfather hiring him. Mr. Angelo asked me about him. He knew who he was and was excited about it.

"I'll visit the gallery in Bar Harbor," he said. "Interesting man, I bet."

"Yes," I said.

I was afraid to say anything more. I still had this guilt about Jamie. The more he heard about me and Kyle, the more hurt he would be. Maybe I was just infatuated with Kyle. But when the school day ended, I couldn't be anything but eager to see him. How would he act toward me? There was something exciting about not knowing. Jamie and I knew the ins and outs of each other. I never thought of that as anything but good.

Maybe that made our relationship too simple. Was I being ungrateful even just thinking such a thing? How I envied girls my age who had mothers or older sisters they could trust to get advice from.

I drove slowly up to the Crest. It was a warmer afternoon, with clouds like dollops of whipped cream across the blue. I had never felt so alive and free, knowing that I would soon graduate from high school and step into the adult world with a clear path to pursuing my dreams. There was no dark cloud hovering over me, not anymore. It wasn't just driving up the hill; it was like driving into the sky. Oh, how I wished Mommy was with me. I could imagine her in the passenger's seat, her hair dancing in the wind. She'd be smiling with such pride when she saw my work now, how much more sophisticated it had become, how every stroke of my brush was well-thought-out, and how I spent more time on colors.

When I pulled up to the Crest, my first thought was to go to Kyle to see his progress and, truthfully, see how he would greet me. I hurried to get out of the car and go around the house, but he wasn't there. I had been thinking so hard about him that I hadn't noticed Dr. Bush's car parked in front. My first thought, of course, was that Dr. Knox had found something new about me in one of my tests and I wasn't as healthy now as I had been told. With trepidation, I hurried to the front door.

The stillness inside frightened me more.

"Anna!" I cried.

Kyle came hurrying from the kitchen.

"What's happening?" I asked before he could speak. "Why are you in here and not working?"

"We didn't want to alarm you. About an hour ago, your father followed your grandfather here to continue an argument, and your grandfather had a seizure of some sort. Dr. Bush is in his room with him."

"Where's my father?"

"He ran out twenty minutes ago. I think he was afraid Anna might attack him with a kitchen knife."

"She should have," I said, and headed for Grandfather's room.

Dr. Bush was sitting at his bedside, taking his blood pressure. Grandfather's room was twice the size of any other bedroom. It was the size of some Birdlane homes. On one side, he still kept all of Grandmother's things: her favorite pictures and paintings, vases, and small statues of Greek characters and lovers. They had picked up so many things during their travels.

Their bed was a customized extra-king, with her side completely undisturbed as if he expected her to arrive at any moment. Grandfather told me he wouldn't get rid of her things and satisfy death.

"She'll never be dead to me," he said. I thought that was so sweet and romantic.

Suddenly, as if she had been hiding in a closet, Aunt Frances appeared in the doorway. She was in her nurse's uniform.

"Melville called and said I might be needed. I was just returning from an assignment on the coast and had the boat turn into Birdlane. Hand it to Melville, he can reach me whenever he feels like it," she said, and smirked.

"I don't need her," Grandfather told Dr. Bush.

"There's not much to do here, Frances. He just needs some rest and to take his pills."

"I'll be sure he does," I said quickly. "And Anna will help."

"Of course."

"Maybe you should get your money back on my nurse training, Daddy," Aunt Frances said. She turned to walk out, then paused and said, "I'm getting something to eat before I leave."

"Oh, I'll make you a sandwich," Anna said.

"I don't need a hired maid to make me a sandwich," she said, and left.

"Maybe you should have given her something to do, Charles," Dr. Bush said.

Grandfather sighed. "I saw how she helped Harriet. She's better with strangers."

"Okay." He stood. "Just mind what I told you . . . good bed rest."

"I'll be fine," Grandfather insisted.

Dr. Bush looked at me and started out.

"Better behave, Grandpa," I said.

He laughed and closed his eyes.

Kyle was waiting for me in the den. He was pacing and looked up when I entered.

"I thought the house was going to explode, so I ran in. I might have been a little aggressive with your father when I pulled him away from your grandfather."

"You might have saved his life. They both have fiery tempers. What did you do with your painting?"

"Put it in a safe place. Who knew what your father would do?"

I turned and looked at the ocean. I had been so high and was now so low. I could feel Kyle move closer to me. He put his hand on my arm and stroked it gently. When I looked at him, I saw how intense his eyes were. Mommy once told me that all your secrets were in your eyes. You could close them, but you couldn't wipe away what they said. Your eyes would always betray what you really felt. "But it isn't that simple," she'd gone on to say. "Sometimes we see what we want to see and ignore what eyes are really telling us, especially when it comes to love."

"This shouldn't be happening to you now. These nights should be the best, the happiest of your life," Kyle said. "You just turned eighteen, you're graduating from high school, and you had the most successful and important heart operation. There should be celebrations, not nasty arguments threatening your grandfather's health."

"I know. I'm so sorry you were brought into this."

"I never go unless I want to," he said. "Besides, I've planned for it, planned for this night."

"What do you mean?"

"I rented this inboard down at the harbor and looked into being served a lobster dinner with all the fixings—and cake, of course. We'd just take a short ride to the cove and enjoy the evening. I saw what your favorite music is and have that arranged. Tomorrow I return to Bar Harbor, so this is the only night this week I can do it. What do you think? I know it's hard with all this commotion, but . . ."

"How soon do I have to be ready?" I asked.

He laughed. "Nothing fancy. I didn't bring anything fancy. It's just the two of us." He looked at his watch. "How's twenty minutes?"

"Perfect," I said, and headed for my room, his laughter trailing behind me. I was sure he was surprised at how little it took to convince me.

I put on my favorite blouse and skirt. The colors blended in a way that felt right: not too bold or plain, just enough to make me feel like myself. I found some comfortable slip-ons and tied my favorite scarf around my neck, letting it drape gently. I kept my makeup simple, a touch of color to brighten my face, and I wore no jewelry. Somehow the absence of it felt better, lighter. Kyle was already outside when I appeared after telling Anna where I'd be. She nodded but didn't smile. Worrying about my grandfather, I thought.

"Great night," Kyle said. There were hardly any clouds now, and the breeze was soft.

"Special weather for Birdlane," I said.

"I ordered it for tonight."

I laughed. He sounded like he really could have. We got into my car, with him driving. He had such a great profile, I thought, and he had such sensible control of things. I was never as conscious of ascending and descending the hill as I was after meeting him. I didn't want to feel like some fantasy princess, but it was the way he made me feel, so special. Truthfully, I never felt like a teenager. I had to grow up faster than others; I was in a race against time, and now, being with him, someone with so much experience, I was more of a young woman than a mere eighteen-year-old. He saw someone older from the start. Otherwise, why would he want so much to be with me?

I couldn't imagine any of my girlfriends at school knowing how to go out with a man like Kyle. They'd be giggling and oohing and aahing. I was sure he'd be doing something bad. Never once did he give me that feeling.

When we stepped onto the pier, the man in charge of the boat hurried toward us.

"Your dinners are in the warmer; the champagne is on ice. Anything else?"

"No, that's good, Tony. Thanks."

I saw Kyle slip him a fifty-dollar bill. He helped us get into the boat. Kyle pulled the accelerator lever back hard, and we shot off away from the pier area so fast that I fell back in my seat. He laughed and asked if I was all right.

"I think so," I said. "I have to catch my breath soon."

He slowed down and started us in a wide circle. He slowed down even more and went to the warmer.

"It all looks good. Let's get the music going and set the table as soon as I anchor. I thought in the cove there." He pointed. It was the cove right below the Crest. Jamie and I had often gone there, mostly exploring. We'd walk down from the Crest when no one was watching and find shiny rocks and stones. It was a safe path, but still an incline, and Jamie would always be nervous about it. As always, I'd threaten to go without him, and he'd be forced to come along.

Our lobster dinner was delicious, and I drank more champagne than I ever had. Kyle lay back on his arms and stared up at the sky.

"It's when I do this," he said, "that I feel the immensity of the universe and how small we really are. Diminishes your ego."

"Yours? Why do I doubt it?"

He laughed. "I've never met a young woman so uninhibited. I knew some married women who were pretty independent."

"You had affairs with them?"

He laughed again. "Let's say they had affairs with me. I don't look for trouble. Interferes with my work." He patted the space beside him. "Look at the stars," he said.

I lay beside him. We were silent.

"You live in a special place," he said. "And you know I've been around."

"Yes. My art teacher told me he never appreciated Birdlane until he left."

"Must be something to do with us artists," he said, and turned on his side, bracing himself on one elbow to look down at me. His smile was so attractive, his eyes so mesmerizing, that I felt comfortable being so close.

"You have the eyes," he said, as if he could read my mind, or else he was used to women telling him how beautiful his were.

He reached back for our two glasses of champagne and handed me mine.

"What should we toast to?" he asked.

"I don't know. I mean . . ."

"Let's just toast to the stars."

We clinked glasses and drank. Then he leaned down and kissed me. My mind reeled with visions of passion. I felt his fingers undoing my clothing. I liked the feeling of being helpless.

"We'll be careful," he whispered, and in moments, it seemed, we were both naked. He gently moved my legs and brought himself to me, hesitating slightly, perhaps to see if I would resist.

I didn't.

The stars seemed to get bigger and brighter, filling the sky with an astonishing brilliance. I felt their warmth as if they were exploding inside me. When our lovemaking ended, I closed my eyes and took deep breaths, letting the night settle around me. Kyle lay on his back beside me, his body warm against mine. We were quiet for quite a while.

"Funny," he finally said, "but I feel the same way when I finish a work of art."

"Am I a work of art?"

"Yes, but I can't claim you," he replied, and then he smiled and started to dress.

I rose slowly. What did this mean? I wondered. Was it a confirmation of love or just a sexual incident—one of many, I was convinced, for him? He surely realized what it was for me.

"Your father definitely has a girlfriend," he said after he started the engine.

"How do you know?"

"I saw them in a sailboat going around the curve ahead. Do you want to see them?"

"No," I said quickly.

"She could become your stepmother."

"She'll never be anything to me."

He laughed and turned to the pier. "I saw you haven't hung your birthday present yet."

"I'm not sure where to hang it. I was going to put it in my room, but I thought not many would see it." What I really meant was that as soon as Jamie saw it, he would know everything.

"Maybe the den," Kyle suggested.

"Yes," I said. "Maybe."

I didn't know what I expected Kyle to say about our lovemaking. It was almost as if it hadn't happened. Was it so matter-of-fact to him? But as we approached the pier, he said, "We just made this into a perfect night."

Was that enough? How I wished I had more experience; I felt at a disadvantage, something I wouldn't feel with Jamie. Maybe Jamie put too much importance on it? Was I different now? Had I changed? Would anyone be able to look at me and know? Maybe *I* put too much importance on it.

The boat man met us at the dock and helped me out first. He and Kyle secured the boat.

"How was it?" he asked Kyle.

I looked at him.

"Wonderful," he said.

Everyone was asleep when we arrived at the Crest. Kyle kissed me in my doorway and said, "You do make it a perfect night. Sleep well."

I watched him walk off and then decided to look in on Grandfather. He was asleep, and sitting beside him, asleep as well, was Anna. I didn't think she was merely a dedicated servant; I thought for sure she was in love with him.

Kyle left early in the morning because he had an early tour at the gallery. He left a note under my door: *See you soon.*

The next day, my guilt over Jamie was too strong. I could at least talk to him, I thought. Maybe he wasn't meant to be my lover, but he was my best friend.

His mother answered.

"Hi, Mrs. Fuller. It's Lisa."

"Oh, how are you?"

"I'm good. Is Jamie home?"

"No. He's going to be a few days late, maybe three. Their car broke down, and the garage had to send out for the parts. That takes a day or so, and there's a day or so to get it fixed."

"Oh. How terrible for them. Did you tell him I stopped by?"

"Yes, and I told him about your car."

"What did he say?"

She hesitated. I could almost hear her take a deep breath. "He just said, 'That's nice.'"

"Well, if he calls, just tell him I called."

"Yes, I will."

"Thank you," I said, and hung up.

I knew in my heart that Jamie had sensed everything. We were too close to miss each other's emotional changes. But I couldn't stop thinking about Kyle. No question that he had turned me into a mainland girl almost overnight. But it was like putting on a new pair of shoes. You had to get used to it, and the question was, would I?

Before I left for school, I realized that Jamie would not be here for my graduation. We had always talked about seeing each other graduate. Today we were going through how to conduct the ceremony, so I had to go, but I was increasingly depressed about it. I stopped on my way out and down the hill and got out of the car.

There was a spot on the side where my mother and I would stand sometimes to look out at the village and the sea. Sometimes we would just remark about how beautiful it was, but sometimes my mother would bring up a serious concern, usually offering advice she wanted me to carry into my adulthood.

When I was troubled, standing here brought her back to me.

"You're moving too fast," I could hear her say. "Don't let your ego overtake your judgment. Birds should feel like gods flying and looking down at us, but they are always careful."

I stood there watching the gulls for a moment, imagining myself soaring with them. The warm spring air brought the scent of seawater up to me. Big cities like the places Kyle had been—Paris, Rome—didn't have this natural world that made you feel a part of it. The less you were surrounded by man-made structures—buildings, bridges, roads—the more free you felt. The lights, the sounds, enveloped you. I could sense that just from the city part of Bar Harbor. Could I just stop being a Birdie? Could a gull stop being a gull?

"You're thinking too hard about it all," my mother would say. "Those questions are part of growing up. Even a ninety-year-old man or woman is still searching for answers."

Mommy had a way of relaxing me, even just when I thought about her. I took a deep breath as the spring air brought the scent of the seawater up to the Crest. When I arrived at school, I learned that I had been given the English award and the math award. I knew some of the students believed it was because of my family. I called Daddy, who was too busy to pick up, but I reached Grandfather and told him. He was very excited for me and said he had expected no less, especially in math.

When I returned to the Crest, Anna congratulated me. Grandfather had already told her. But she also said there was a phone message left on my answering machine. I paused before I headed to it. Did I want it to be Jamie or Kyle? The fact that I even questioned it put all sorts of doubts in my mind. I went to my room and pushed the playback button.

CHAPTER FOURTEEN

It was Kyle congratulating me on my graduation and apologizing for not being able to be there. He said he couldn't wait to see me when he returned to finish the painting. A little while later, flowers for me arrived. Again, a part of me wished they were from Jamie, but they were from Grandfather.

He then organized a catered dinner for us, surf and turf, lobster and steak. Since it was catered, he invited Anna to sit with us. He even invited Aunt Frances. At dinner, he asked about "that nice fisherman's son." I explained what had happened to him on the way home from his trip.

"Probably not smart enough to check the car before they did such a trip," Daddy said.

Aunt Frances laughed.

"What would you say about yourself four months ago, Daddy?"

"What do you mean?"

"You rode on a low right front tire until you were down to the rim that ripped the tire. Cost you $2,456.38," I said.

There was a pause, and Grandfather slapped his knee and laughed. Aunt Frances dropped her mouth open, and Daddy flushed red.

"How do you remember a bill so exactly?" Daddy asked.

"When it comes to numbers, she's really a genius," Grandfather said. "She can balance the books better than her mother could."

Daddy grumbled and started to eat. Then he stopped and looked at me. "At least I wasn't far from home," he said.

"Just because you're eighteen doesn't mean you can talk to your father like that," Aunt Frances said.

"You've said worse things to him, Aunt Frances, and I know you're more than eighteen."

Grandfather slapped another knee.

"You're just encouraging her," Aunt Frances told him.

"I didn't do a good job encouraging you," he said.

She pulled back and stared down at her food.

"Well now," he continued, "how should we celebrate your graduation?"

"I thought that's what we were doin'," Daddy said. "You bought her a car for her birthday."

"Good point," Grandfather said. "Which was why I decided to have Arthur teach her how to sail her new boat."

"New boat!" I said.

Yes, I thought, *I can sail. I can do anything now*. All my classmates who had their own boats, who sailed, who drove motorboats, would be amazed to see me, even though they all knew by now that I had been cured. To hear it was one thing; to see it was another. Of course, I'd wave at them and see the shocked looks on their faces. Daddy wore one now.

"Is it a company boat?"

"Sure, she's an employee," Grandfather said. "Which reminds me . . ." He reached down for a folder. "Here are the accounts from one line I asked her to review for us." He handed it to me. "She found twenty-eight thousand dollars in wasted spending."

"What?" Daddy said, reaching for it and turning the pages. "This isn't wasted. I needed those things."

"Rental cars when you had a car."

"It was inconvenient at the time."

"In my time, a windstorm was inconvenient, not an effort to get your own car."

Daddy slapped the folder down. "I don't like her looking over my shoulder," he said, glaring at me.

"She's not looking over your shoulder, Melville. She's looking over mine, for me."

Daddy closed his mouth and stabbed his steak.

Anna began talking about the weather and comparing it to that in England, and she and Grandfather began talking about the English countryside and Ireland. For some reason, the mention of Ireland brought Daddy's attention back to the conversation, but he said nothing.

"Tomorrow morning about nine o'clock, you can meet Arthur at the dock with your new sailboat. Good weather predicted. He'll start your lessons."

I was going to tell him that Kyle had already done so but didn't mention it. Then I thought about how this was something Jamie and

I had put on our wish list, and he wouldn't be here to see it. Maybe he wouldn't care now.

After dinner, I went for a walk with Anna, who had become my true confidante. We went to my mother's and my favorite spot. Of course, Anna knew that.

"This older gentleman, the artist, he's fond of you, I think."

"I think so, but I don't know how you know for sure."

She laughed. "Another million-dollar question. My mother told me this: older men have fewer dreams. You have to figure out how that would apply to you."

I looked out at the sea and the way the wind was sending the ripples to the mainland. Was that a sign of where I should go? Why trust nature? Look what it had done to my mother and to Jamie.

"Why do you think my father is the way he is, Anna?"

"He knows he's not his father, and that depresses him and makes him angry," she said.

I wondered how much she really knew, but I knew I wouldn't break my promise to Grandfather.

"Night's falling fast now," Anna said. "Here come the stars."

I laughed, thinking of what the stars had meant just recently. She put her arm around me just the way Mommy had and turned me toward the house. We stopped because Aunt Frances came charging out of the house, jumped in her car, and sped off, kicking up dirt behind her.

"Anna, what kept you with this family so long?" I asked.

"Easy question to answer . . . your grandfather, your mother, and you," she said.

I smiled, and we continued on. Daddy came walking fast toward the door when we entered.

"Congratulations," he said to me, as if someone was choking the word out of his throat. We watched him go out.

"The thing about men," Anna said, "is they never let go of being boys."

We both laughed. *Laughter*, I thought, *takes the sting out of family pain.*

No one called me that night. Right after breakfast, I drove down to the pier to meet Arthur and see my new sailboat. All these wonderful gifts made me feel so special—not spoiled, special. My life just seemed to burst into itself, not like I was unchained but more like I was reborn to be who I really was.

Arthur was very impressed with how I handled the rudder. I didn't say anything about being with Kyle. It felt dishonest, but Arthur was so proud of how he was teaching me. Why diminish that?

"It's in your blood," he said.

Was it? I wondered. Daddy wasn't a Baxter, but he was brought up to be one. Could you inherit that? The wind did feel different; the sky looked more beautiful. The bounce on the water was more exciting than usual because I was doing it. Maybe just living on Birdlane instilled it all in you.

"You look like you belong," he said. "It's like you were born for this, not just because you're a Baxter, but because you are who you are."

"Where did you get such wisdom, Arthur?"

"Where everybody does these days, from my grandfather."

I laughed, but, boy, was he right, I thought.

I was actually disappointed when we turned for the home port.

"Enough for one day," Arthur said, "but it won't be long before I'll tell your grandfather that you're ready to go out on your own."

He had no idea what the words "go out on your own" meant to

me now. But I loved hearing it. I spent the next few days practicing with Arthur. I was still thinking I would attend the art school at the College of the Atlantic in Bar Harbor, but that wouldn't start for months. In the meantime, I waited anxiously for Kyle to return to complete the landscape painting of the Crest.

The day before Kyle was supposed to come, Jamie called. He had come home, and as I expected, he knew all about Kyle and me.

"It's all right," he said after telling me what he knew. "We don't own each other."

"I know that, Jamie. I just didn't want to hurt you in any way."

"A man has to contend with disappointment as well as success. Daddy says that practically every day he goes out with the boats."

"You're luckier than I am."

"Meaning?"

"You have a father you enjoy quoting."

He laughed. It made me feel so good.

"Let me know when you have time, and we'll catch up on my New York trip."

"Oh, yes. I want to hear about that."

"And your new car and now a new sailboat?"

"Yes."

"I bet it all came from your grandfather."

"You'd be right."

He laughed again.

I felt so comfortable talking to Jamie. But did that mean we were lifelong lovers or just lifelong friends? I wondered if there had ever been a time when Mommy and Daddy were comfortable talking to each other. How could you fall in love without being able to do that? My parents were a puzzle. But Grandfather didn't seem to know the answers. Or if he did, he was still holding that back.

"I've got to get back to therapy for my leg. They're angry about all the time I took off."

"Sure."

"I'll call, and we'll . . ."

"Make a date," I said.

"Good. See you soon, then."

I felt better than I thought I would. That was Jamie's doing. After we spoke, I had an urge to go out to the oak tree and just sit there awhile. There was something magical about the spot. It gave me not only a good view of the whole house but also sort of a portal through which I could see so many important parts of my life. While I sat there, the weather changed to cloudy, and the sea became rougher. It actually grew cold for this time of the year. I was just getting up to get a sweater when Anna called for me.

"What, Anna?"

"Your grandfather just called. Your father was in a traffic accident. He was speeding. Imagine, here on Birdlane, where you can't drive faster than people walk. Someone was hurt badly."

"How horrible!"

"Your grandfather wants you to go to the office and man the main desk. He has to deal with the legal matters, and your father's at the police station."

"Okay. Any other instructions?"

"He said you'll know what to do."

I put on a sweater, raised the top of the car, and headed for the office building. Mrs. Hegal, Daddy's secretary, was at the door when I arrived. She was a tall, stout woman with graying brown hair she kept cut short. She wore a gray and black skirt suit with a wide-collared blouse. I didn't think she knew what makeup was.

"Terrible," she said. "They're blaming it on him."

"Grandfather says he was speeding."

"Only for a few seconds, maybe, trying to get by a bad driver. Now they want to charge him with manslaughter."

"You mean the person died?"

"They just want to make money," she said.

"By dying?" I walked past her to the office.

Daddy's desk was a mess, papers pushed over each other. I realized how many calls he hadn't made. I organized it and began. Mrs. Hegal stood in the doorway.

"When I finish one call, put through the next," I told her.

"How would you know what to do?" she asked.

"I passed kindergarten," I said, and began my first call.

Grandfather called an hour or so later. "I've gotten the manslaughter charge dropped," he said. "But it cost quite a bit. When he finds out, he'll carry on, but he doesn't know how lucky he is. He killed the son of one of the oldest families here, the Shanes."

"Oh."

"There's surely somebody in that family you know from school. How is it going there?"

"Daddy left ten accounts on hold. Just finished."

"Knew you would. I told him to take a vacation until things die down a bit. You don't have to cover. I'll be there."

"Okay, Grandfather."

By the time I got to the Crest, Daddy had come and gone, slamming doors and cursing aloud. Anna said she had just stayed out of his way. Jamie called to see how I was. We talked just like old times, trying to cheer each other up. I felt better when we hung up.

The news spread fast to Bar Harbor. Kyle called an hour later. But it was a different conversation. It was all about how he would cheer me up and get me to forget.

"Can't have anything messing up our beauty," he said.

He said the gallery was busy and he would have to move his arrival at the Crest another two days forward. He said he had already informed my grandfather and promised not to disappoint him.

I smiled. Grandfather? "What about disappointing me?"

He laughed and promised he wouldn't. I then thought about something that would be a lot of fun.

"Can I pick you up in a Baxter company boat at the pier where you took me sailing? About nine thirty?"

"Sure."

"See you then," I said, and began to plan how I would sail myself to Bar Harbor that day.

When my grandfather came home, he looked exhausted.

"Lawyers," he said. "When they see a good fish, they go after him. No worries, Lisa. All will be well. Everyone was impressed with you at the office."

"I'm glad, Grandfather. It makes me feel . . ."

"Like your mother is still here."

"Yes!"

"It's the way I feel, too," Grandfather said. "People like her never die. They live on in us."

"Yes," I said.

He walked away, looking older, sadder even. Could you cry on the inside and not shed tears on the outside?

All night, I thought and dreamed about my surprise sailing. I practiced continually with Arthur during the days I waited for Kyle. Arthur finally approved my solo sailings and told Grandfather. I took the boat farther out than I had imagined I would. With this kind of perfect weather, I felt safe. I had thought I would always fear the sea because of what had happened to Mommy and Jamie, but in a strange way I took joy in overcoming that fear—strange because it became so important, even though my real love was art. This was more like putting a life's importance on recreation, but also the sea inspired. While I was sailing, I was imagining paintings I could do.

Just before every solo sailing, I thought about inviting Jamie, but then I thought that it might be tormenting to him, and I didn't want to have him hurt any more.

The morning I set out for Bar Harbor was extremely beautiful, with a calm sea. I brought along a bottle of good champagne and glasses, knowing Kyle would like to celebrate the surprise. I didn't know he would have his own way to do that. I should have expected it.

The wind couldn't get me there fast enough, but I arrived a good five minutes or so faster than the time it usually took. As I drew close to the pier, I saw him looking out and not yet realizing it was me. How fun that was. He looked like he was pacing, and then finally he realized it was me. He burst into a smile of surprise and delight. It filled me with a new sense of power. Look what I could do—me, who had had to be careful not to exert myself too much going up a hill or get too excited at things others my age could enjoy without any worry or restriction! This really was the start of a new life.

"You amaze me every time I see you," he said as I reached the port, and he took my line so as to be able to board. "Never thought you'd get here this fast."

"Lot of time to make up," I said after he hugged and kissed me.

He got into the boat, and the man on the pier threw the rope to us. In moments, we were on the way to Birdlane. I showed him the champagne.

"Wonderful idea, even this early, and I have one, too. Head for that inlet we found."

I knew exactly what he intended, and it sent a chill of excitement through my body. When we got there, we opened the champagne and reclined in the boat beside each other. He talked about some of the visitors to the gallery, sharing his stories and feelings about it as if we were already a married couple. I felt so comfortable that when he kissed me, I seemed to settle into my own body like I would into a warm bath. In moments, he was caressing me and running his lips over and down my neck. I leaned farther back, and our clothes seemed to fly off us.

At one point, the boat rocked so hard we both laughed. Afterward, we lingered for a while, both of us breathing hard but happily. Realizing the time, I rose and said, "We should get back. I don't want Grandfather to worry."

"Grandfather? What about Daddy?"

"He's in hiding, and besides, I don't think he would worry much."

He laughed but said he understood.

Arthur was waiting for us at the dock and helped tie up the boat and helped us out. We got into my car, me driving this time, and headed to the Crest. I noticed that Anna saw us and disappeared, surely to call Grandfather. Kyle went to get his work, and I changed into a more conservative outfit to go to Daddy's office. Kyle was outside when I headed off.

"See you later," I said.

"Oh. I forgot to mention I made dinner reservations for us at the Sea Breeze at the dock."

"You did? When?"

"Last night. Don't worry, Anna knows."

We kissed, and I left for work, smiling to myself and playing my radio too loud. I felt like I was lifting off from the earth and flying ahead. Grandfather and I did some of the work together. I couldn't wait to get back to the Crest to dress for dinner. I wanted to do something special.

I told Grandfather, who just nodded. Why did he have such faith in me? I wondered, and before I left, I asked him.

"Because you've never behaved like a silly teenager. I think of you as a woman already well into her twenties, at least."

Was that good or bad? I wondered. Shouldn't I regret growing up too fast? No time to think of it now.

I did dress specially, choosing another of my mother's favorite dresses, a green taffeta and black velvet with puffed sleeves. After I fixed my hair and put on some light makeup, I looked into the full-length mirror and for a moment saw my mother looking back at me. If I could only hear her voice, hear her advice. Kyle knocked on my door.

He was wearing a black blazer with a gray turtleneck. He had never looked more like a movie star.

"How beautiful you are," he said.

"My mother's dress."

"I can see why people say you inherited the best of her."

He took my hand, and we started out. Anna waited for us at the door. She pressed her hands together and smiled.

"I love when you dress up," she said. "You know why."

"Thank you, Anna. Where's Grandfather?"

"He's resting. Takes a while to get over dramatic things when you're his age."

"Sometimes any age," Kyle said.

She nodded. "You're a very handsome man," she told him.

"Thank you. I work on it. We're all pieces of art."

She laughed, and we headed out. He drove down the hill to the Birdlane pier. It was a perfect night to have dinner near the ocean, and he had reserved the best table, looking out on the breakers and the lights on the horizon from the ships passing.

At dinner, Kyle talked more about his youth and the trials and tribulations he'd had with his father. It was like he was peeling back the layers of his life for me to know him more and more deeply. It felt like the kind of dinner conversation that tied two people closer to each other, as if they knew the future was waiting for them.

The restaurant was filled mostly with tourists, but I recognized a few local people who were looking at us and whispering. The only real reason I hated that they gossiped about me was that it would reach Jamie.

"So," I said, "that is all why you ran away from home at sixteen?"

"Sure is."

"You weren't afraid to be on your own?"

"Are you?"

"I was, but . . . not now, not that I want to leave Grandfather."

He laughed. "I have little doubt you can be on your own now. I never saw you as a teenager."

"I never had a chance to be, but I don't seem to regret it anymore."

We had a wonderful dinner, and when we drove home, I leaned against him and clung to his arm. When we arrived, he surprised me again. He had made a reservation at the Bird's Haven Café almost all the way across the island. If every time he was here I could look forward to these romantic nights, I couldn't see not really falling in love with him, especially if I believed he was really falling in love with me.

Both of us went to work in the morning. The difference this time was he kissed me goodbye and said he was afraid he would lose his concentration on his painting thinking about me too much.

"I bet you don't lose yours at work," he said. "You are too determined."

"Maybe, maybe not," I teased, and was off.

I didn't think that I would be as efficient as usual, but once I was at work, I thought of nothing else.

The day went fast anyway, and almost before I knew it, I was dressing for dinner again. Anna watched us leave, and we were off on the long but most beautiful ride along the Birdlane coast, with so many turns taking us to what looked like fifty feet from the ocean waves coming into shore. We passed the beach I had shown him, the place lovers went, the place where he had kissed me so romantically. I saw him smile to himself as we went by.

The restaurant was different from the one on the beach. It was a lot more elegant. When I asked him if he had ever gotten really close to marriage, he was silent for a moment. I thought he wouldn't answer.

"Yes, there was someone once. She was from India, and when her parents found out about us, they sent her back. I was shocked, of course, but I realized it wouldn't work to go there searching for her and try to bring her back."

"India."

"Let's not talk about sad things in the past. Let's talk only about the future. I wonder what your first international holiday will be, where you will go."

"I don't know. I never thought . . ."

"I'll give you a few ideas," he said, and began to describe beautiful places. It all sounded wonderful, but not by myself, I thought. That would be more sightseeing than imprinting a loving memory on my mind.

After dinner, we headed home, but he surprised me by turning into the "lovers' beach" and pulling into a well-hidden spot. He got out of the car and went around to the trunk. After opening it, he took out a blanket and came around to lay it on the beach just to our right.

"How did that get there?" I asked.

"I snuck it in just before I got dressed," he said. He held out his hand. I just stared for a moment. "Worried about your dress?"

"Yes," I said.

I got out and took it off. I saw the glimmering smile on his face.

"Come over here and pinch me so I'll know I'm not dreaming."

I walked over, and he kissed me while brushing back my hair.

"The best dessert after a wonderful dinner is making love," he said.

"I guess I'll know," I said, and we lowered ourselves to the blanket.

Afterward, we both lay back and looked up at the stars, which for me were shining more brightly than ever.

"Well, I bet someone out there is looking at us with a telescope. He'll see we aren't a star, but we have bright spots." He turned to me. "One of them is you."

"I bet you've said that to other women."

He laughed. "Yes, but none understood it."

I laughed, too. And then we scurried back to the car, dressed, and headed for the Crest.

"Ditto for next week," he said when we entered. "Down to the smallest detail."

"Okay. I'll pick you up at the pier."

"And we'll stop at the inlet. I did say 'ditto.'"

I laughed. We kissed and went to sleep.

The week couldn't go by fast enough for me. I knew the best thing to do was to throw myself into work. Kyle didn't call until two days before I was to get him, and all he talked about was his work, so maybe he was feeling the same impatience. At the end, almost like an afterthought, he said, "See you soon."

Somehow I was able to keep my mind on my work. The morning of the day I would pick him up was a little windier than usual. For a fleeting moment, I thought of my mother and how the wind had turned against her that day, how it had taken her away from me. But I wasn't afraid. Arthur was there to give me some helpful hints for a little rough weather, and in minutes I had set sail. It was as hard as I had feared, and I reached the port just about nine thirty as planned.

But as I sailed in, I saw Kyle wasn't there waiting. I tied up and sat. Twenty minutes passed. I got out of the boat and walked up to look at the street in the hope of seeing him coming. I didn't see him. A small panic began in my chest. Had something happened to him? After a good fifteen minutes, I headed for the gallery.

When I arrived, Eddie Doyle was surrounded by people complaining. He saw me and excused himself.

"Lisa," he said. "I already spoke to your grandfather."

"About what? Where's Kyle?"

"Exactly. These bohemians . . . they might be talented and even make money, but they never stop being who they are."

"What do you mean?"

"He had to go to Boston. He was about to be subpoenaed."

"Why?"

"He had relations with a seventeen-year-old girl. She became pregnant, and her parents found out and went to the police. He had promised her he'd marry her and care for their child. He went home to do that. He said he had no choice. Now I'm stuck for a . . ."

He paused as though just realizing he was talking to me.

"Oh, Lisa, I'm sorry. I didn't realize . . . are you okay?"

Okay? I thought. *When will I be okay again?*

I turned and walked out and almost in a hypnotic state walked to the cemetery. I fell to my knees at my mother's grave and put my hand on her stone. Only then did I release my tears. Anyone watching me would think I was mourning her terribly. I was, but for more reasons than they could know.

After a while, I rose, wiped away my tears, and started for the pier. I was surprised Arthur was waiting there for me.

"Why are you here, Arthur?"

"Your grandfather wanted me to be. That's all I was told. He wanted me sailing back with you."

Mr. Doyle had called Grandfather, so he would be worried.

"Okay, Arthur. Thank you."

I sat back and let him do all the work. When we passed the inlet, I took deep breaths and closed my eyes. Grandfather was waiting at the Birdlane pier. He helped me out.

"I'm sorry, Grandfather. I let you down."

"No. Someone let you down, and me, but now we will see how you handle it. My father loved the expression 'What doesn't destroy you makes you stronger.'"

I nodded.

"You going up to the Crest?"

"No, I'm going to work," I said.

He smiled.

"What about the money for the landscape?"

"Well, let's not tell your father. He'll gloat."

I laughed and went on to the office. I tried not to think of it all. Difficult, if not impossible, but I would go on.

Just turn the page, Mommy would say.

And so I did.

CHAPTER FIFTEEN

When I arrived at the Crest after work, I went to where Kyle kept his supplies and the unfinished landscape of the Crest. Looking at it now, and not because of what he had done and the person he had proven to be, I did not like it. It was too cold. It didn't have the feeling of being a home, just that of being some sort of monument, despite his claim of showing it from some unique perspective.

When I went to my room, Anna was waiting.

"How are you?" she asked.

"I'm good, Anna. Life, especially now for me, goes on."

She smiled. "Your mother could have given that answer."

She hugged me and went off to prepare our dinner.

I looked at the drawing Kyle had made of me. How ironic that Aunt Frances had been right. I took a sharp bread knife and tore it up like she had. At dinner, I told Grandfather about the landscape painting.

"I think I'd like to do it, Grandfather."

"Good idea. I should have let you from the start. See, we both learned lessons," he said, smiling.

"What do you hear from Daddy?"

"Threats of returning every day. We'll see."

Despite my strength, I couldn't help wondering if Kyle would call one day and come up with some excuse. He never did, but I read in a newspaper that he had gotten married and was making art in New Jersey. He was getting more involved with New York exhibits.

Jamie eventually heard about it, but he didn't call to ask how I was. I knew what he was going through. He wanted me to call first. I hesitated. The one thing I didn't want was for him to feel like he was second prize. I wasn't sure about any of it anyway.

I finally called him and, without saying anything more, asked him if he would like to go out on my sailboat.

"Sure," he said, and we set the date and time.

I was in the boat waiting for him and saw him coming down the pier. I hadn't seen him for a while and thought he looked stronger and was walking better. He was in a bright turquoise light sweater and jeans and wore his sailor cap. When he saw me, he brightened and walked faster.

"You look like you're doing so much better," I said.

"Went at it vigorously. Beautiful boat."

"Well, you're going to take her out," I said, sitting back.

He brightened even more and got in. It was a good sailing day, with clouds peppering the sky. The wind was strong but not strong enough to make the water rough. I saw the pure pleasure in Jamie's face as he navigated us northwest of Birdlane.

"This is like sailing a Cadillac," he said.

"I brought us lunch and drinks."

"Great. We can go to Captain Blood's Inlet."

"Oh, I forgot about that. Yes, beautiful."

He stared at me for a moment, and when he realized I could see him staring, he turned away. I lay back and closed my eyes. It was, at least for the moment, as if nothing had changed between us.

I knew what he was wondering, but he wouldn't ask specifically. Finally, he asked something that would give him the answer.

"I guess you're going to Bar Harbor a lot these days, right?"

"Not as much," I said. "But I am looking more seriously into classes at the school of art."

"Oh."

"I sorta take things day by day."

"Understood," he said.

"So, tell me about your New York trip," I said, hoping to leave the topic.

He became more animated, describing the lights and the excitement.

"But after a few days, we grew tired of the crowds and noise and set out for home early. You heard how we broke down. We took an off-the-beaten-track route and ended up in a small town with the car. Pretty boring few days. I guess I am truly a Birdie," he said.

I knew what he wanted to hear from me.

"I do enjoy the excitement of Bar Harbor—more restaurants, stores, things to do—but I have to admit that when I am heading home to Birdlane, I feel a breath of fresh air, comfort, and warmth. So I'm a little mainland but mostly Birdlane."

Jamie liked that answer. I could see it in his smile.

"I like occasional trips to Bar Harbor, too."

"Great," I said, and we headed toward Captain Blood's Inlet. We had lunch and talked about things we often did. It was like old times and comforting, but I was careful. I didn't want to start a deeper relationship until we both felt certain about it. *No more hurting Jamie*, I thought.

For some of the time, we just sat quietly and enjoyed the beautiful day. The ocean gleamed, and the birds seemed excited about life. We watched ships off in the distance, and, like always, we talked about the exotic places they were sailing to.

On the way back, Jamie asked me more about Daddy. I told him everything I knew. He paused and then said, "Some people are calling him a stain on the island."

I nodded, but I didn't say anything more. We made a date to sail again, hugged, and parted at the pier. It all felt a little strange to me because we were both hiding our emotions.

After work each day, I started on my landscape of the Crest. I used the materials Kyle had left since we had paid for them. Getting deeply involved with the work helped me to ease back more to a new version of my life. The only tension both Grandfather and I felt was anticipating Daddy's return.

He didn't arrive until a day after we had both expected him. Grandfather was very suspicious about it, but he was suspicious of Daddy continually. And continually upset with things he had done at work. The day before Daddy's return, Grandfather called me into his office to tell me he had a special assignment for me.

"The Johnson fishing group is considering another distributor because of the way your father talks and deals with them. I've asked Matthew Johnson to stop by today to talk to us before he leaves us. I'm giving you this assignment," he said. "He'll be here in fifteen minutes."

"Fifteen?"

Grandfather smiled. "You'll be fine. Go familiarize yourself with the account."

I returned to Daddy's office and did just that. About fifteen minutes later, Matthew Johnson arrived. He was surprised, of course, to see me in Daddy's chair. Grandfather had given me my own office, but for this meeting I thought I had to be here. Matthew Johnson was a tall, gruff-looking man with a full reddish-brown beard. He looked poised to leap over the desk at me.

"This isn't very respectful," he said. "Having me meet with Melville's daughter."

"Oh. Sorry. No offense intended. I've been put in charge of accounts for now. Please, have a seat," I said.

He sat, but he didn't look any more relaxed.

"All I know is we can't survive with the deal you are offering and that your father said is firm. The supply isn't as plentiful, and we have to work harder to acquire what we need."

"I imagine so," I said. "I know about the supply. You do have a bigger overhead now."

He sat back, surprised.

"If you don't produce, we have nothing to sell," I said. "That's why we have this new offer for you." I handed him the paperwork. "There is a ten percent increase."

"Ten?"

For a moment, I thought that wasn't enough, and then he smiled.

"Well, okay, this is fair."

"I'm glad you feel the same," I said.

He looked at me harder. "How'd you get so grown-up?" he asked.

"I had no choice," I said.

He liked the answer and signed the paper.

"My grandfather would like you to stop by his office on the way out."

"Will do," he said, and left.

I let out a deep breath.

Ten minutes later, Grandfather came to the office doorway and stood there smiling at me.

"I like it when I'm right," he said, and returned to his office.

Daddy returned home that night, and during dinner Grandfather told him I had saved the Johnson account. But when he found out how, he ranted, saying it was nonsense. "Fishermen know their risks and costs. We shouldn't coddle them."

Grandfather's face turned red. "I was a fisherman first," he said. "You don't really know anything about it. You took rides as a child but never showed any interest."

"Whatever," Daddy said, and soon retreated.

I saw how he had gotten to Grandfather this time and tried to console him.

"The man doesn't realize this is more like a partnership, us and the fishermen. I don't think he's capable of understanding."

He left to go to sleep, grumbling to himself.

I fell into my routine of work and painting. About a week later, Jamie proposed that we go to Bar Harbor for lunch. "We can pretend to be tourists," he said.

I liked his upbeat mood and agreed, even though I feared how I would react to the fresh memories of being with Kyle. I had mixed feelings during the sail over to the pier, almost expecting Kyle to be standing there waiting to give me some sort of an apology. What would I do if that really happened? Fortunately, Jamie's laughter and continued excitement took my mind off all that.

We tied up at the pier, and Jamie took over the visit. He wanted us first to walk the streets and gawk through store windows, wondering if we would wear this or that. I sensed he was trying to keep me from dark thoughts, just the way he had when Mommy died. He pulled me into a Bar Harbor souvenir shop and got us Bar Harbor caps.

"One of the fishermen on my father's boats, Skip Carnesi, told me a great new restaurant here is Mamma DiMatteo's. How about lunch there?"

"If we can get in."

"I made a reservation," he said, and I laughed.

"You did plan this."

He shrugged.

We headed for the restaurant. I was quite proud of Jamie for doing the research. One thing that cheered me was that Kyle had never mentioned the place. It gave me the feeling he planned every move strategically to overwhelm me. I had to admit to myself that he did.

Mamma DiMatteo's had pizza on the menu, which was delicious.

While we ate, Jamie talked a blue streak about every subject under the sun. It was as if he was terrified of a long moment of silence between us. I understood and contributed to the conversation. Toward the end, he sat back and smiled.

"What?"

"You won't remember this, probably, but when you were about ten, we walked the beaches looking for precious stones, and I found two that I thought matched your eyes."

"I think I remember that."

"I still have them," he said.

I was speechless for a moment. He looked through the window and then proudly paid our bill.

We continued our walk until we were close to the gallery. When I paused, Jamie said, "We can start back."

I thought for a moment. *If I don't confront this emotional event, I'll always retreat.*

"Don't you want to look at my painting? It's still on the wall."

"Sure," Jamie said, surprised.

We headed to the gallery. Eddie Doyle stepped out of his office just as we entered. He looked from me to Jamie.

"Lisa. I was afraid you wouldn't come back."

"It has nothing do with my love of art," I said, and he smiled.

We went to my painting.

"I don't know much about it," Jamie said, "but it sure looks professional to me. I always believed you'd be famous someday."

I laughed. "I have a ways to go yet, Jamie."

"You'll get there."

We left, but I could see that he was troubled and debating whether to ask me anything. I helped him out.

"I made a mistake in judgment, Jamie. My grandfather tells

me what my great-grandfather told him: what doesn't destroy you makes you stronger. I'm not going to feel sorry for myself."

"Good," he said, lighting up.

"Let's have a good sail home."

We walked faster to the pier.

That night, Grandfather said, "Why don't you invite the fisherman's son to dinner one night?"

I went ahead and did so. Jamie was now able to drive his father's truck. He came the next night. When Daddy heard he was coming, he suddenly had an important dinner meeting. Neither Grandfather nor I said a word.

What surprised me was how much Grandfather enjoyed talking about fishing with Jamie. It brought him back to his earlier days. At times it was like I wasn't there, which made me laugh.

A few days later, Jamie and I had a picnic at the Crest. We were both careful about talking about ourselves and the future. He was more optimistic when it came to the work he could do with his father, but he didn't bring up the cottage. It was just very comfortable for me being with him. I wasn't quite ready to talk about emotions and deeper feelings for each other. I had already burned myself rushing to do that.

We made dates to continue doing things together, but I kept my mind on my work and the landscape painting. One night, I saw Daddy brooding about something in the living room. He just stood by the window looking out. We had had few personal conversations these past few months. He was seemingly always in a rage. Was I partly to blame? Was I being unfair?

I decided to try.

"How are you, Daddy?"

He turned and stared at me for a long moment. "The last time your mother asked me that, you weren't yet a year old."

"Why was that? Why were you two so estranged? You were in love with her, and she must have been with you."

"We each had different ideas about love," he said. That was the most he had ever said about it.

"Well, what was different?"

"I don't like retreading the disappointments of the past. Just know that it wasn't all my fault. Your mother was far from perfect."

"I don't think that you should say that. She's not here to defend herself."

He smiled. "Sure she is. There's you," he said, and walked out.

I searched my mind for instances when he had acted like a loving father. They were few and far between. Most of the time, it seemed like my mother had protected me from him, from his sarcasm and his superior attitude, especially when it came to ordinary citizens of Birdlane. I think I understood it all better when I realized he was treating me more like a possession than a daughter.

Days of summer moved on. The work at the business did seem to grow. Grandfather complimented me often, and I could see that Daddy was annoyed. If I corrected something he had done, he would almost explode.

"She shows no respect," he once told Grandfather, who was sitting at his desk.

I came up behind him to defend myself.

Grandfather raised his eyebrows and glared back at him. Then he said, "If that's true, where do you think she got the idea?"

Daddy turned and walked out, nearly knocking me over.

Grandfather looked at me and shook his head. "Tantrums. Both he and his sister grew up having them, but your grandmother always smoothed it over. There's such a thing as being too good," he said. "I loved her to death, but she was stubborn about satisfying them."

"I'm sorry, Grandfather."

"Me too. Back to work," he said.

I tried to concentrate on that and not think of what was my family. The summer days were beautiful, and when I was off and not working on the landscape, Jamie and I sailed, took walks on the beach, and seemingly relived our youth together.

One day, I paused while looking back at a business account. The payments to the company were consistent, but I couldn't find them on the received side. Why had we been paying them, and for a number of years? They were called Shell Fish Ltd. The oddest thing was that the payments had stopped just after I had come to work.

I didn't want to bring this to my grandfather's attention without doing more research. I decided to talk to our attorney, Mr. Orseck. I explained why I wanted to hold back on mentioning anything to Grandfather until he and I researched it. He was a perfect attorney, never showing his thoughts. Gray-haired, with a neatly kept beard, he was a tall, lean man in his late fifties. I liked his down-to-earth but factually supported statements.

"No address?"

"No. Just the name, really. And the fact that the payments stopped recently."

"Let me look into it. I'll keep it between us until I know something concrete."

"Okay, thanks."

"You might have done good work here," he said as I rose to leave.

"I hope it is good," I said.

He called me two days later.

"What we have here is a shell company located in the Cayman Islands. There's only a door with the name on it."

"What is that?"

"A way to avoid taxes and hide what you've socked away," he said. "We'll have to tell your grandfather. It looks like your father has been basically stealing from the company."

"Oh, it will kill him. He's fragile now," I said.

"He'd be angry if we kept it from him."

I nodded. He was right, of course. Had I done a good thing or a bad thing? What was going to happen now?

"I'll tell you what," Mr. Orseck said. "I'll call your father in, confront him with what we know, and give him the opportunity to put the money back. Then no harm will have been done."

"Thank you," I said, breathing easier.

"I'll let you know," he said. "Don't blame yourself."

"Okay," I said, and left.

Every day at the company, I was filled with anxiety and tension. Whenever I saw Daddy, I expected him to burst into a rage at me. I first saw that the money had been returned to the company account, and then, hours later, I saw Daddy. His eyes were filled with such anger that I could easily imagine fire coming from them. He said nothing, but he nodded to indicate that he was never going to forget what I had done.

Nearly a week later, Grandfather called me into his office to thank me for the mature way I had handled the shell company issue.

"Right now," he said, "he thinks I don't know. We'll keep it that way, but you let me know if he does anything to harm you in any way."

"Okay, Grandfather," I said.

He gave me a hug.

I went home that night feeling protected but expecting that my father would find a way to get revenge. He was that kind of man.

It wouldn't be long before I found out.

CHAPTER SIXTEEN

It was three days later when Jamie called me early in the morning sounding quite upset, even a bit hysterical. He had gone down to the pier to go on one of his father's boats when he had seen it.

"What are you saying, Jamie?"

"Your beautiful sailboat. Completely sunk."

"How could that be?"

"They were pulling it up. We'll see. Your grandfather is down here with the police chief."

"He is?"

He must have received a call from the police and left without telling me.

"I'll call you as soon as I know anything more."

I sat back, stunned. My mind was racing with possibilities.

Naturally, my first thought went to Daddy. Would he do such a thing? How could he do it? He was already out of the house, too. I got dressed quickly, grabbed a muffin and a coffee for breakfast, and rushed out to go down to the pier. By the time I got there, the boat had been removed. I saw Jamie off to the side, talking with other fishermen. He spotted me and hurried over.

"I was just about to call you."

"I wanted to see what was happening myself. What do you know?"

"Someone cut an oval hole in the bottom of the boat. It had to have been done during the night and had to have been done by someone who went underwater and could work on it. No one knows who might have done it. The police have opened a full investigation. Sorry, Lisa. Could be a very jealous person."

I nodded. "Birdlane might not be paradise after all," I said bitterly.

Jamie looked pained but reluctantly agreed.

"I'll talk to you later," I said, and headed for the office.

On arriving, I saw that everyone was in Grandfather's office, so I hurried to it. Daddy was sitting off to the right, scowling. It had become his normal expression. Grandfather was behind his desk, and the police chief, Ralph Barber, was in front of the desk reporting.

"Lisa, here, sit," Grandfather said. "The chief has some things to tell us."

I slipped into the seat. Daddy sat back with a deep sigh.

"Billy Thomas, who mans the pier, might have dozed off while this was occurring, not that he would necessarily have seen or heard it. What we are sure of is that someone skilled in underwater maintenance or construction attacked the sailboat at about three or four in the morning. He carved out an oval opening, and the boat filled quickly. Because it was tied up, it sank vertically. We're reviewing any possible suspects on the island. I have everyone at the department on this."

"Think we should bring in someone from Bar Harbor?" Grandfather asked.

"I have put in some inquiries with the state police," Chief Barber said, "but we might get this solved on our own."

"Of course." Grandfather turned to me. "So sorry about this, Lisa."

"Just one of those jealous Birdies," Daddy said. "These people have been envious of us for as long as I know."

"So jealous that they'd hire a professional?" Grandfather said.

"Wouldn't surprise me," Daddy said.

"Well, we'll leave it up to the chief," Grandfather said.

"I'll get back to you this afternoon and keep you constantly updated," the chief said.

"Thank you," Grandfather told him.

He left the office.

"Maybe we've wasted enough time on this nonsense," Daddy said, following him out.

Grandfather sat looking after him for a moment and then turned to me.

"If he had anything to do with this, I'll personally wring his neck," he said. "He always needed more discipline, but he knew how to play your grandmother. I know it's hard, but put this aside for now. We'll fix things."

"Okay, Grandfather."

I rose and went to my office. He was right. There was no point in dwelling on it. I buried myself in paperwork. Later Jamie called, obviously very concerned about me.

"My mother feels very bad for you," he said. "She'd like you to come to dinner at our house."

"Oh. Thank her, Jamie, but I won't be good company. I want to go home and meditate on everything, not just this. Ask her for a rain check."

"Sure. You think that's best, to be alone at this time?"

"I have some things to work out, and I can only do it myself. Sometimes your life seems like it's free flying, but I have to be more like the seabirds and work my way through and around the winds."

"You are something," he said, "but you always have been."

"Have I?"

"Don't blame yourself for any of this, Lisa."

"Okay," I said, not very convincingly. "Thank you, Jamie."

After work, I did exactly what I had told him I would. I went home and sat by myself at a place near the cliff where my mother and I had had picnics once in a while. I sat staring at the ocean, mesmerized for a while by the rhythmic movement of the water.

How had things changed so quickly for me? I had been in an ecstatic, wonderful place after my operation freed me of a restricted and maybe shortened life. The world had opened up for me. I had never enjoyed colors and sounds, birds and nature, as much. I had truly been reborn.

Perhaps this joy had blinded me to the dangers of life. I couldn't imagine for the moment anything worse than what I had endured. Why wouldn't I want to open myself up completely? Yes, it had made me vulnerable, but that sense of freedom and being in charge of my own life had been too strong for me to pause out of caution. I had been doing that my whole life.

I was starting to move forward despite the setback. I had seen another beginning and rushed to claim it. But I had disregarded my knowledge of how complicated and in some ways twisted my family life was now because of my father. If anything, we were more alienated than ever. How could I change that trajectory?

What I had feared came the following morning. Daddy had left for work and then come speeding home before Grandfather and I had finished our breakfast. He charged into the house and slapped a newspaper against the wall, jolting the both of us.

"What is it?" Grandfather asked.

"The *Bar Harbor Times*!"

"What about it?"

He walked toward me.

"This story about this so-called famous artist. A journalist got wind of it and pursued it, found out he impregnated a girl who was seventeen. He left rather than fulfill his obligation to her and the child and, according to the article, was about to be arrested for sex with an underage girl when he returned and married her. Some deal made, probably."

"So?"

"So the story tells about his work here and," he said, turning to me, "his relationship with Lisa. Which apparently started before she was eighteen. Expect to be visited by the police," he added.

Neither Grandfather nor I spoke.

"Why?" I finally asked.

"Why? He's a sexual predator. They'll want your testimony. Look what you've done to the Baxter name," he added, slapping the paper down on the table in front of me. "You're mentioned. You're eighteen now. They can do that."

I unfolded the paper and looked at the headline: "Are the Baxters of Birdlane Island the Latest Victims?"

I skimmed the article. It was very specific when it came to Kyle's relationship to us and especially me. There were witnesses who had seen us out together, and, matching that with the date, it had been before my eighteenth birthday.

There were quotes from Eddie Doyle complaining about Kyle and how much money he had lost because of him.

"This is a big story for them," Daddy said. "They won't stop with one. I can just imagine the chatter downtown."

"Just go to work, Melville. What will be will be."

"Great philosophy," Daddy said, glaring at me, and then he turned and marched out.

Grandfather sat back. "Maybe you should stay home today. Let this blow over," he said.

"Daddy thinks it's just beginning."

Grandfather hesitated. I knew what question he was going to ask, and I knew how painful it was for him to ask it. I jumped ahead.

"I had no relations with him before I was eighteen."

Grandfather nodded.

"Oddly, he was the one who was insistent about that," I said.

Grandfather thought for a moment. "He was smart, knew he could get into even bigger trouble."

"I guess I . . ."

"No, don't start blaming yourself," he said sternly. "He was quite a charming man. I had no such suspicions about his past, and I've been around a lot longer than you have."

"It's not the same, Grandfather," I said, smiling. "Female experience."

"You sound like your grandmother. Okay. Let's wait and deal with whatever we have to," he said.

Before he left, however, it began. I was informed that two detectives from Bar Harbor had requested an interview with me. I was shaking but replied that it was fine. They could come to the Crest. Grandfather wanted his attorney, Mr. Orseck, present. That made it seem more serious to me. But I couldn't disagree. It was all arranged for two o'clock. I sat on pins and needles until then.

The two detectives arrived shortly after Mr. Orseck. He and I sat in the den and waited for Anna to bring them to us. There was a man and a woman who quickly introduced themselves as Detective Burton and Detective Williams. Detective Burton was a well-built man at least six two or three. Detective Williams was rather attractive, I thought, with her perfect nose and soft lips. She had really sparkling greenish-blue eyes. She wore a skirt suit, and I thought she wasn't more than thirty.

"We just have a few questions," Detective Burton said, "and then Detective Williams would like to ask Lisa some very personal things. She could do that somewhere else if you like. We'd like to respect her privacy, but please understand our mission here."

"So far, I have no objections," Mr. Orseck said.

They sat down, and Detective Burton began. It was a review of the facts that were commonly known about Kyle and me. I confirmed it all. I knew this was a lead-in to a more intense set of questions.

"These questions now are quite personal," Detective Williams said. "Would you rather we went somewhere else?"

"No," I said. "I'm ready here and now."

"Oh. Fine," she said, surprised at my firmness. "We know you began a relationship. Did it become intimate, and did that begin before your eighteenth birthday?"

"Yes, and no, not before my eighteenth birthday."

"There were no sexual relations before you were eighteen?"

"Asked and answered," Mr. Orseck said. "Dwelling on it won't change the answer."

"I can add something," I said. Mr. Orseck looked concerned. "It was Kyle Wyman's idea to wait for any intimacy until after I was eighteen."

She looked very disappointed. "Many young women who have been abused protect their abuser, maybe hoping to continue the romance."

"That," I said, "is not me."

"It's best to talk it out," she said.

"Do you want another language?" Mr. Orseck asked her.

"Pardon?"

"She gave you her answer in English, but you don't seem to get it."

She bristled and stood. "This is an intensive investigation. We may be back to speak with you again," she said.

We watched them leave.

"Okay," Mr. Orseck said. "Let's go report to your grandfather."

Grandfather was in his home office, having stayed here only because of this police interview; otherwise, he would have been at the company. Daddy always whined about not having a real home office, too. Grandfather wouldn't let him redesign one of the bedrooms for that purpose.

"You don't need to work from home," Grandfather had told him. "You're not my age."

Daddy had grunted and mumbled under his breath as usual. He had glanced at me at the time. I think he was bothered by the fact that I had witnessed Grandfather denying him things and chastising him from time to time.

"Charles," Mr. Orseck said now.

Grandfather turned his chair around to face us. He had been staring out of his window.

"All went well. She did excellently."

"Knew she would," Grandfather said.

"I doubt they'll bother her again."

"Okay, Gerald. Thank you."

Mr. Orseck left. I stepped toward the desk.

"What is it, Grandfather? There's something else. I can tell."

"You could. Always. So could your mother. The publisher of the newspaper is a friend of mine. He told me the source of the story."

I held my breath. It wasn't simply Eddie Doyle.

"Which was?"

"Your aunt Frances," he said. "I just got off the phone with her. I told her never to set foot on this property again and that I was ending all her financial aid. She has deliberately diminished the reputation of our family."

"Why?"

He sighed deeply. I could see he was having a very bad physical reaction. He was taking short breaths, overheating, and probably having skyrocketing blood pressure.

"She's always been a spiteful child. I never knew what she was going to do from one moment to the next. Your grandmother always believed in sympathizing with her and feeling sorry for her. You know the reason," he said.

"What did she tell you in response? How did she defend what she has done?"

"What difference does it make? She is not a reliable advocate for this family. She's gotten worse than ever, thinking only about herself. Don't think about it anymore. This will blow over."

I saw he didn't want to spend another word on it, so I said it would all be fine and left him. But I couldn't just forget about it. I arranged for Arthur to take me over to Bar Harbor. An hour later, I was at the pier.

I knew where Aunt Frances's apartment was located. I had been there only once before, to get something for Daddy. It was a very simple two-bedroom apartment with furniture that looked as if it had been bought secondhand. She did little to dress up her home. There were almost no pictures on the wall, certainly no pictures of our family anywhere. For all intents and purposes, it could have been a motel on some back road. The dreariness of it in a place like Bar Harbor had disturbed me. I had never really wanted to return and hadn't attempted to visit her ever.

She answered the door. She wore a drab yellow nightgown and looked like I had woken her by ringing the doorbell.

"What do you want?" she asked in her snappy, sharp tone.

"Answers," I said, and walked past her and into her apartment.

She closed the door and turned to me, her arms folded.

"Why did you do it?"

"Do what?"

"Don't try to deny it now. Grandfather is close friends with the newspaper publisher, and I know of his conversation with you."

"I told you clearly not to have anything to do with that man. I saw what sort of man he was, but no one in this family ever listens to me. I might as well talk to the wind," she said and walked into the kitchen, taking a defiant position near the counter.

"I have a right to live and learn from my own experiences," I said.

"No. You don't listen to me because you don't have an iota of respect for me. You're just as arrogant as Melville, only you pretend you're not. You've been spoiled by my father. You think you're some sort of princess on the hill with the Crest as your castle. I was never treated anywhere near as royally as you've been. My father resented me from the start. I could see it in the way he looked at me from when I was a child until now. Nothing's changed."

"That's not what I was told. Your mother coddled you and made excuses for all the bad things you did."

"Oh, is that what he tells you? He was never much of a father to me, and actually not to Melville, either. We just didn't fit his picture," she said. "Anything he did for me was half-hearted. Why do you think I worked at supporting myself and living away from the Baxters?"

"You're not supporting yourself. He's been helping you."

"What, did he tell you every dollar he gave me? Has he been keeping the books? I'm sure he's not doing that with you."

"If you had shown more affection for him, maybe things would be different."

"Affection? He took Melville places. Melville went on his boat. I was always left behind because women couldn't do anything but be nurses, secretaries, or just wives."

"That's not the way he thinks," I said.

"Maybe about you. I've been with him longer. The bottom line is, I might as well have been adopted and forgotten," she said.

The reality that I knew took my breath away for a moment. She would surely explode when or if the truth ever came out, and especially if she found out I knew but she didn't.

"But what you did hurts us all, even you. Why do such a thing?"

"Maybe now I'll be listened to."

"Now? Now you're even more of an outsider than you thought you were. Grandfather wants nothing to do with you. I'm sure my father is beyond rage. He treasures the Baxter name more than anything else. If I were you, I'd work on some sort of an apology."

"You're not me. Go back to your castle and live like a princess," she said, and turned her back on me.

I stood there for a long moment and then left. There was so much about her youth I did not know. I knew she had never had any real friends and had never had a boyfriend, but I couldn't find the compassion to feel sorry for her.

I started back to the pier. Along the way, I saw the newspaper on the stands with the article about me on the front page. I wondered if anyone looking at me connected me to the story. What would I do? Would I become what Aunt Frances had said, a princess holing up in her castle? I was afraid of the immediate future now on Birdlane and headed home with a heavy heart.

To my wonderful surprise, as we approached Birdlane Island

pier, I saw Jamie waiting for me. He helped me off the boat and hugged me, holding on to me longer than usual.

"I'm okay, Jamie," I said. "How long have you been waiting?"

"Not long. I know you will be fine; I just want you to know that I'll always be here for you."

"Thank you."

"See your aunt?"

"How did you know?"

"I know you. You won't ever back away from a confrontation when it comes to your family, especially your grandfather."

I smiled. "Are you free?" I asked. "Let's just go to the Crest and enjoy the rest of the day."

"Oh, yeah, I'm free for that," he said, and I hooked my arm to his and walked to his truck.

For a while, at least, I felt safe and even hopeful. Was this enough to convince me it was love, a better love than I had imagined with Kyle? Everything got so complicated, I thought, when you reached a certain age, especially what your deep feelings were and should be. The future was always tottering, shifting.

When we arrived at the Crest, Anna told me Daddy had created another crisis, getting into a bad argument with one of our clients based in Bar Harbor.

It was beginning, I thought, the potential crumbling of all Grandfather had built, and there was no one really to blame but me. I walked off, Jamie beside me, to sit at the oak tree and try desperately not to cry.

Jamie simply sat beside me. Neither of us spoke. Then he slipped his hand into mine. I felt an overwhelming sense of comfort. Again

I wondered if this wasn't true love, something I should have realized and not risked losing. I had faith that time would tell.

We both turned sharply as the police chief's car pulled up to the Crest.

"What now?"

We both stood and headed for the house.

CHAPTER SEVENTEEN

The police chief and a deputy had gone to Grandfather's home office. We approached. The door was partly opened. Grandfather saw me there and told me to come in. He didn't say Jamie couldn't. I took the seat on the left, and Jamie stood beside me.

"The police chief is making a report update concerning your boat," Grandfather said.

The chief looked at me and nodded. "We were able to confirm that someone had come from Bar Harbor and attacked your boat around two in the morning. This was obviously someone with underwater experience when it comes to these sorts of things. We know everyone on this island who has those skills. So we pursued the theory that this was an outsider. We tracked him to a boat rental at Bar Harbor. He paid with cash and had what we've determined was a fake ID. We believe he left the area immediately, maybe even the state. Whoever wanted this done was willing to spend considerable money on a professional," the chief said.

There was a long moment of silence as both Grandfather and I digested the information and then looked at each other, speaking through our eyes. Our unspoken words were chilling.

"It's not simply someone envious of you," the police chief told me. "That's big money spent on jealousy, so we're kind of dubious of that as the motive. Did you have any arguments with anyone on Birdlane, anyone who would want to hurt you in this indirect but meaningful way?"

"No one I know of," I said.

Grandfather looked even more disturbed, his eyes narrowing and his lips pressed so firmly against each other that it highlighted some of the wrinkles in his cheeks and deepened the lines in his forehead.

The chief appeared to pick up on our expressions and silence.

"Do you want me to follow up on this, Mr. Baxter?"

"Yes," Grandfather said. "But let's keep the information tightly between us."

"Will do. I think I'll have something more for you soon. A friend of mine at the FBI is looking into it, too. The only thing to be thankful for is that the boat wasn't sabotaged to cause trouble when you were out on the sea. This was more of a dramatic statement. Otherwise, we'd be talking about an attempted murder," he said.

"Murder?" Jamie said aloud.

No one spoke as it all settled in on the three of us.

"Rest assured, we're on it, Mr. Baxter," the police chief said.

He rose, and the deputy stood.

"Naturally," the chief said, "there's a lot of nervousness at the pier concerning other boat owners. I'll let it leak out that this is looking like a one-time deliberate act and not something others have to be concerned about."

"That's fine, understandable," Grandfather said.

The chief nodded, and then he and his deputy left.

Grandfather sat back. "This family," he began, "has taken some serious body blows recently. We need to take deep breaths and give it time. Take a few days off from the company and enjoy the summer on Birdlane. Go to the beach. Our motorboat is always there for you if you want to just ride the coast or go to Bar Harbor. Meanwhile, why not have Jamie to dinner tonight? Anna is making her famous cottage pie. As to your sailboat, I'd be more comfortable with just replacing it."

"Oh, Grandfather, that's . . ."

"Perfect," he said before I could say it was too much.

Jamie laughed.

"Okay, Grandpa," I said. He always felt the affection I had for him when I said "Grandpa" instead of "Grandfather."

His eyes brightened with his smile, but it was short-lived. He looked down, and I knew what was troubling him, troubling me. We were both refusing to believe in the possibility.

"I'd better get home," Jamie said, "and change for dinner at the Crest."

His excitement brought us both, Grandfather and me, some relief.

I walked him out. I could see he was in deep thought and debating if he should say something.

"What is it, Jamie?"

"Am I reading too much between the lines," Jamie said, "to think your grandfather and maybe you believe your father had something to do with what happened to your boat?"

"I thought you were a country bumpkin," I said.

"What?"

"Yes, that's very astute of you to pick up on the possibility. Let's hope it's not true."

Jamie nodded, got into his truck, and said, "See you soon."

"Bring an appetite," I said. "Anna goes overboard."

He laughed and drove off. I went to the cliffs and sat on the grass. So much had happened since my successful, life-renewing operation. I couldn't help wondering if all the negative stuff was really my fault because I had rushed headlong into a normal life. I had been like someone dying of thirst swallowing buckets of water when I had the opportunity. Too much too soon? The tempo of it all was far faster than the normal tempo of people living on Birdlane. Maybe I was becoming someone else too soon.

On the other hand, it had opened me up to good possibilities, and I was working well with Grandfather and the business. I was still as enthusiastic about my art. I wouldn't let Kyle destroy that ambition.

As the sun waned, the color of the ocean turned a darker purple. The breakers, in contrast, looked whiter. The ocean was truly unpredictable, but that made it more mesmerizing. How could I ever even think of living somewhere else? Other places were just places to visit, temporary memories. Where you lived, where you grew up, was too deeply a part of you. *Jamie has nothing to fear*, I thought, then smiled to myself and headed back to the house.

I was getting myself ready for dinner when I heard the shouting. Anna came to my doorway, looking very concerned.

"They're at it again," she said. "Only I'm worried about your grandfather. His lips are trembling and he is gasping with anger."

I hurried out and to his home office. Daddy was just inside, raging.

"Can you imagine how embarrassin' it was for me to have the police come to our offices and question me about that damn boat? You sent them there. I know you did."

"They're following up on all possibilities," Grandfather said.

"Why am I a possibility? How deranged are you? You know nothin' about me."

"I know you can be very deceptive, Melville. You were like that as a child. You had no trouble deceiving your mother, but you had and will always have trouble deceiving me."

"Stop!" I commanded, coming into the room. "You're making him sick."

"I'm makin' him sick? You see this face?" he said, pointing to himself. "Every wrinkle and every gray hair has his initials on it."

He stormed out.

Grandfather closed his eyes and sat back. I could see him aging right before me, his lips sagging.

"Grandfather?"

"I'm all right," he said. "I'll just take a short rest before dinner."

He rose slowly. I hurried to help him. He smiled and put his hand on my shoulder.

"I'm fine," he said.

A man with his pride wouldn't accept old age, I thought. I could only love him more for it.

"Did you send the police to question Daddy?"

"I might have dropped a suggestion or two. He can be vindictive, my Melville. He'll calm down."

"But do you think he did it?"

"Let's let it go, Lisa. There is enough to overcome as it is."

"Okay, Grandpa," I said.

He went to his room, and I returned to mine to get dressed. Anna had told Daddy Jamie was coming, and he told her he had a dinner meeting. It was the way it would always be, I thought.

At dinner, Grandfather was more subdued than usual. Jamie tried to get him to talk again about his early fisherman days, but he simply smiled and ate. We looked at each other. Jamie knew how worried I was. Grandfather looked like he was struggling to finish his meal. I nodded at Anna, and she suggested that Grandfather get an early night's rest. He didn't resist.

We watched him walk off with Anna at his side.

"Let's go for some frozen custard at the pier," I said.

"Sure."

"We'll take my car. You drive," I told him.

As we headed down the hill, I could see the look of simple pleasure on his face and thought about the difference between him and Kyle, who had acted as if he belonged in this car and expected nothing less.

"Beautiful," Jamie said. "I never really rode in something as smooth and sweet."

"I'm glad you enjoy it."

"Smooth and sweet. Just like you."

"Jamie Fuller. Are you flirting with me?"

Even in the shadows, I could see him blush.

I laughed and then thought about Jamie and Kyle. Jamie was all innocence and sincerity. What woman wouldn't want that? But there was a part of people that enjoyed the excitement of surprise. Someone mysterious might seem more attractive. Every day was different.

But different didn't automatically mean good or even fun. Deception was almost a requirement for a relationship like that. A man or a woman could exaggerate, distort, and even lie about what he or she had done in their lives. You had to be so much more doubtful, controlling your urge to believe it all because it was exciting and made you feel more like being in your own movie. When I had been with Kyle, I had even imagined music in the background. Who was more to blame, him for his dishonesty or me for being so gullible, so eager to believe him and turn him into a romantic hero? My mother used to say things like "Buyer beware," clearly saying you had to consider yourself at least partially to blame.

I had been trapped, held prisoner by my body. Freed of it and all restrictions, I longed for a world without cynicism. I was eager to fly, but, like Icarus in the Greek myth, I had steered myself too close to the sun. My wings had melted, and a dark, disappointing, even shocking reality had burst around me and in a real sense sent me back to hovering in my imprisoned world.

I did what I could to live with it and start anew. When I was bound and tied to my health, I wasn't as aware of my family tensions. I had always felt the estrangement between Daddy and Mommy, but it was tolerable because Mommy had compensated and always made it seem as if my concerns were minor. She had always been there to protect me from everyone and everything, even my own family.

But she was gone, and even with Anna and Grandfather always being there for me, I was really on my own, joyful at being able to fly but nowhere near as prepared as I should have been for the world beyond Birdlane. I could see it from the cliffs of the Crest—the horizon, the promises, and the discoveries to make—but like a seabird who had gone out too fast and too far, I struggled to find a safe place to land.

Was it with Jamie, or was that just too simple and convenient?

The pier was busy with tourists and locals. Actually, I had never seen it bustling as much as this. All the restaurants and shops were crowded. We met some of Jamie's friends and a few of the fishermen who worked for his father. I saw how they all looked at me, making me feel as if I was some sort of celebrity who had to grant permission before anyone could speak to her, especially if they had questions.

Jamie was amazing, behaving as if nothing had happened between high school and now to either of us. It had a way of relaxing me. The frozen custard had never tasted better.

We walked the pier and then decided to take a ride to one of our favorite spots on the west side of the island. From it we could clearly see all the lights of Bar Harbor. There was a large rock formation that separated and had a level pocket between the two sides. We could sit there and simply look out at the ocean, the stars, the mainland. We had never really told anyone about it; it was sort of our secret place.

For a few moments on the way, I felt juvenile going to it. We were being kids again, me being the protected one. We climbed into our spot and sat. Neither of us spoke for a good two minutes; we just sat there and absorbed the scenery.

"I'm glad you're not going to Bar Harbor as much," Jamie said.

"Going to Bar Harbor" had become code for me seeing Kyle. For a while, it had been a tinderbox to talk about it or even make a slight reference to my affair. It seemed better to pretend it had never happened, but maybe that was wishful thinking and just not possible.

"Not as much, no," I said.

"For a while there, I was thinking of taking a dinghy out and heading for the horizon, but then I would think of you and how you dealt with your heart issue until you had the operation. My problems were nowhere near as difficult as yours."

"I worried about you. All the time," I said.

"Did you? That's nice."

"It's not just nice, Jamie. You have always been close to my heart."

He was silent. Then he said, "I don't want just to be your friend, Lisa."

"I know. Let's give it a little more time."

He nodded, I was sure with disappointment.

"What was that quote Mr. Feldman, our English teacher, liked to use all the time?"

"'Fools rush in where angels fear to tread.'"

"Very good, Jamie. You were a better student than you give yourself credit for."

"I would never be a fool rushing to you, Lisa."

I reached for his hand. He brought mine to his lips.

"This is our island, Lisa. It will always be our island."

The purity of Jamie's heart felt like a wave washing over me. I couldn't resist leaning in to kiss him. He held me tightly.

"I thought I'd lost you," he whispered.

I was silent. *I can't hurt Jamie. Wait*, I told myself. *Be sure.*

A little while later, we left to return to the Crest. Jamie talked about all the things he was going to plan for us to do.

"Got to keep your mind off all this trouble," he said.

Good luck, I thought, especially with my father raging at everything.

When we arrived at the Crest, Jamie wanted to come in to see how Grandfather was. Anna told us he had fallen asleep quickly and she was keeping an eye on him.

"Good," Jamie said. I walked him back out. We paused at his truck.

"I had a good time tonight."

"Me too."

He leaned in to give me a friendly kiss on the lips, then paused and leaned in again to give me a meaningful, passionate kiss. My mind was spinning with images of Kyle's dramatic kisses. Jamie was nowhere near as histrionic, but this was the most passionate kiss he had ever given me. It took my breath away. We paused and just looked at each other.

"See you tomorrow," he said, and got into his truck. He waved, and I watched him drive off.

In the morning, Anna told me Grandfather had listened to her and decided to take a full day of rest. He was not going to the office. I ate breakfast alone, as Daddy, Anna said, seemed energized today and had hurried to go to work. When I got there, he was locked in his office. I asked one of the assistants, Heidi Peterson, to bring me copies of the documents I was reviewing for Grandfather. She told me my father had said everything had to go through him.

I went directly to his office and entered without knocking.

"Why are you holding the documents I am supposed to review for Grandfather?" I demanded.

"I'm reviewing them first."

"But—"

"You'll have them shortly," he said.

Frustrated, I returned to my office to wait. When almost an hour had passed, I rose to go back and make my demand stronger, but just then the phone rang. It was Anna.

"Your grandfather would like you to come to the Crest right now," she said.

"Is he okay?"

"Yes." She was silent a moment and then said, "The police chief is here."

I hurried out and drove home.

It was only the police chief there this time. Grandfather sat behind his desk in his bathrobe. He looked pale and very disturbed. I just sat.

"We have a major decision to make," Grandfather said, nodding at the police chief.

"My FBI friend was much more successful than I had anticipated," he began. "I should have realized the culprit had to be close to the sea and shipping. He was picked up yesterday, and the boat rental employee identified him. The district attorney immediately offered him a deal if he revealed who had hired him."

"And?" I asked.

"He did. I'm sorry to say it was your father."

I knew the blood drained from my face even though I had anticipated hearing it.

"The chief has brought up a major issue," Grandfather said, "but I'm going to let you decide, since this was done mainly to you."

"What?"

"Families have issues," the police chief said, "and sometimes things like this happen. The Baxters are the biggest employer on the island. If this is aired and your family in any way crumbles, it will affect many people. I think this is a matter better settled among yourselves than in the courts and newspapers. But if you insist, we'll issue an arrest warrant for your father today."

"No!" I said. "You've actually done Birdlane Island a great service by coming here first. You're right. This is an internal family issue and not one for the courts. Grandfather and I will handle it."

Grandfather smiled.

The police chief nodded and rose. "Matter closed as far as our department goes," he said. He shook Grandfather's hand, nodded at me, and left us.

For a moment, we just stared at each other.

"As I told you many times," Grandfather said, "Melville was always a spiteful and deceitful young boy. He carried that into his manhood. I was very pleased that your mother decided to marry him. He could be a bit charming back then, always arrogant, but in a gentler way, if you could understand."

"I saw some of that when I was younger, but not very much."

"I've always lived believing you can't pinpoint exactly who people are. Everyone is complicated, and it's best to react to what they do and who they are at any given time. Preconceived visions make it harder to see the truth. That's a piece of wisdom I'll share with you."

"What will we do?"

"I'll have one of my frequent heart-to-heart talks with Melville. He'll have to apologize to you."

"He'll never do that."

"We'll see. I still have some cards to play when it comes to him,"

Grandfather said. He held up some papers. "This is the chief's report with all the evidence, so there'll be no denial or games played."

"Okay, Grandpa."

I didn't return to the office. I returned to the landscape painting. Art was truly therapy for me right now. Later, just before dinner, Daddy stopped in my doorway and said, "Sorry about your boat."

Before I could respond, he walked off, and nothing more was said about it. I didn't know what to expect at dinner. He did sulk until Grandfather started to talk business. He even mentioned giving some of the work to me.

Afterward, I decided to tell Jamie. He was, after all, the most trustworthy person besides Anna and Grandfather.

"I'm sorry, Lisa. That's hard to take."

"We both believed it even before this confirmation."

"Yes, we did. That is mean."

"He is who he is. I'll just go on doing what I want to do."

"Sure. As long as I'm part of it," he added, and laughed nervously.

"When I start doing portraits, you can pose," I said, to get over the moment.

"Will do."

We made a date to have lunch at the pier the next day.

For the next few days, Daddy didn't seem different. He wasn't remorseful as much as he was careful about what he would say to me. He did give me work at the office and looked satisfied with how the business was doing. I wondered what promises Grandfather had made.

Meanwhile, I was getting more and more excited about my landscape painting of the Crest. I felt my version captured it more as a home than as some monument, even though Kyle had a style. Mr. Angelo stopped by to look at my work and raved that it was the best thing I had done. I knew he was full of questions about Kyle and what he had taught me, but I avoided the topic. I thanked him for making the trip.

Maybe life was taking a turn and it would be easier for us, I thought. Grandfather had seemed to regain his strength and was at work regularly again. Jamie and I did more and more together, always reaching that point when something very serious could be said about us, but I always pulled back.

Would I ever be able to love again? I would have other things to think about, love being at the bottom of my list.

CHAPTER EIGHTEEN

Just as I emerged from my bedroom and headed to breakfast, Anna came running, wearing the most terrified expression I had ever seen her have.

"Your grandfather," she said, gasping. "He got out of bed and collapsed on the floor."

"What? Call Dr. Bush," I said. I started for Grandfather's bedroom. "Where's Daddy?"

"He never came home last night," she said.

I hurried on. Grandfather was on the floor struggling, one side of his body trembling. I grabbed a pillow and put it under his head and then lay down beside him. He turned to me and tried to speak, but his lips were twisted and he made only guttural sounds.

"Dr. Bush is on his way, Grandpa."

I put my arm around his shoulders and cradled him to my breast. I could hear his heavy breathing. We were like that when Dr. Bush arrived with assistants carrying a stretcher. I got up quickly, and he examined him.

"Get him to the ambulance," he told his assistants.

"What's wrong with him?" I asked. Anna was embracing me.

"He's had a stroke," Dr. Bush said. "I need to get him to the clinic. There's no time to travel to Bar Harbor."

Anna and I followed him out and then got into my car to follow the ambulance to the clinic. For a small clinic serving Birdlane, Dr. Bush's facility was as good as it could be. In his emergency room, he began to do as much as he could, easing Grandfather's breathing, dissolving blood clots, and maintaining observance of his blood pressure.

Of course, we called Daddy, who rushed over and almost immediately began to complain. "Why wasn't he taken to Bar Harbor?"

Dr. Bush was never intimidated by Daddy, or anyone for that matter. He stood calmly in front of him and said, "There was no time. He probably wouldn't have survived the trip. I have him resting comfortably, but you should all know that he won't return to the way he was."

There was a saying about Dr. Bush: he never beat around the bush.

"What do we do?" I asked.

"Once we are done here, you'll take him home. If you don't have one, get a wheelchair ASAP. I'll start to arrange for nurses around the clock. They will administer medications, and I'll arrange for a therapist to start therapy and see what we can restore in terms of movement and speech," he explained.

"I'll get the wheelchair," Daddy said, welcoming a reason to leave. "It will be at the Crest in an hour." He hadn't even asked to see Grandfather. I watched him leave, knowing he was really elated, believing now that there was no check on what he could and would do at the business.

Anna and I sat and waited. One of Dr. Bush's assistants brought us some coffee. I didn't know how news spread so fast on Birdlane. Sometimes I thought a seagull told another bird who told another, and all those birds sitting on telephone wires were transmitting the news around the island. Twenty minutes later, Jamie appeared.

"How is he?" he asked immediately.

"A stroke. Looks like his right side is damaged, and his speech."

Jamie sat beside me and took my hand. I wondered if Kyle, even at his best moments, would have spent any time beside me in a clinic. It just didn't seem to fit his image.

Dr. Bush emerged again to address us.

"Anna, you should return to the Crest and prepare his room. I'm going to have some equipment brought there to monitor him. He won't be able to stand on his own or walk at all right now. We'll see what therapy can do. Actually, you should all go to breakfast. It will be a while yet."

"Okay," Anna said.

"I'll take you back," Jamie offered. "In a truck, I'm afraid."

I had my first laugh of the day.

"Anna and I will ride in the back."

"What?"

"Just joking, Jamie. Thank you."

The gray, overcast sky seemed perfect for the mood we were all in. The silence was like a door slammed on any joyful thoughts.

I could almost see the shadows deepening over the Crest as we approached. This was, after all, Grandfather's home. To me, the house was a living thing, its walls absorbing happiness and sadness, and the halls and stairs, even the pictures on the walls, seeming to darken with the trouble and brighten with the joy we experienced while there. I was hoping I had captured that in my landscape. It was something Kyle didn't feel in his work.

Daddy was true to his word, out of either real concern or eagerness to relegate Grandfather to this new isolation. The wheelchair, a very comfortable and expensive one, was waiting in the entryway. Anna took it to Grandfather's room, and I went to the kitchen with Jamie to work on some breakfast. He got right into it, preparing a new pot of coffee and toast while I made scrambled eggs with cheese.

We ate in the kitchenette, whose paned panel doors and windows looked out on the rear of the house, Grandfather's view from his office. Anna was too nervous to eat anything and wanted to get Grandfather's room spick-and-span. She put all her nervousness and sadness into her vigorous cleaning. I wasn't hungry but knew I had to eat. This was not the time to be weak and tired.

Late in the afternoon, Dr. Bush called to say Grandfather would be brought back in the ambulance, and the first of three nurses, Mrs. Cohen, would accompany Grandfather and get him set up with the monitors. Jamie and I sat outside, watching the hill for signs of the ambulance.

"It's easier for someone who hasn't done half of what your grandfather has done in his life to shift into sitting in a wheelchair and staring at the grass," Jamie said. "In a sense, that's where they already were."

"Funny way to put it, but makes sense to me," I said. I looked at him. "Where did you suddenly get such wisdom, Jamie Fuller?"

"From the sea," he said. "If you look at it enough and watch all the sea life and the way the water changes, you think about things in your own life more."

"My goodness, what am I going to do with you? An old man already."

He laughed.

What would I do without him? I thought.

We saw the ambulance. I had been wishing this was all a nightmare and I would soon awake, but the sight of it coming up the hill was like a drumbeat culminating in a loud clash of cymbals when it came to a stop in front of the house. We rose as the attendants came out and opened the rear. I wanted Grandfather to see me immediately and know I was there for him.

But he wasn't looking at anything. His eyes were closed.

"He's asleep, which is good right now," Mrs. Cohen said, coming around to me.

She was a woman in her fifties, with graying black hair she apparently didn't care to hide. She kept it short like Aunt Frances. Maybe it was a nurse thing.

They brought Grandfather to his room, and Mrs. Cohen began to set up the equipment.

"I'll let your father know he's home," Anna told me. "I suppose he will want to know."

I nodded, not imagining him sitting on pins and needles, waiting for the news. I told Jamie he didn't need to stay, especially if he had things he was supposed to do.

"This is what I'm supposed to do," he said, which made me laugh.

I hugged him. "I'll be fine. Probably should take a rest. There will be lots more to do now."

"Sure. Okay."

"Come back for dinner," I said.

"Really?"

"Grandfather thinks you're part of the family." It was a half joke, but he liked the sound of it. We hugged again, and he left. I did go to my room to lie down, but not because I was physically tired. I was emotionally exhausted. Nevertheless, I did fall asleep for a while, and I woke up abruptly when I heard Anna talking loudly to someone. I rose after I heard her say, "He won't like you doing that!"

"He won't realize anything anymore," I heard Aunt Frances say when I stepped out into the hallway. She was at the bottom of the stairs, holding two cloth bags in her hands.

"What is going on?" I demanded, and approached them.

"She's taking your grandmother's jewelry," Anna said. "She knew where your grandfather had stored everything."

"She was my mother. I should have these things; they shouldn't be going to you. He's stopped all financial support for me. I need this," she said, holding up the bags.

"But Anna's right. He should know first."

"He can't understand anything anymore. I know he'll leave me out of his will."

"He's not dead yet," I said, feeling my eyes widen and bulge with anger.

She laughed. "I know what a stroke like that is. He's as good as dead," she said, and started for the front door.

"I'm going to tell my father," I threatened.

She paused and smiled. "Go ahead. Who knows what he's taken

already," she replied, and left without even taking the time to see Grandfather.

I ran to the door as she was getting into the car she had rented at the pier.

"You'd better not have taken anything of my mother's!" I screamed.

She looked at me and shrugged. I watched her drive off. *I hope Grandfather didn't leave her anything in his will*, I thought.

Daddy didn't come home until just about dinnertime. He looked at me as if he was about to say or ask something and then went to speak to Grandfather's nurse. I followed him. She explained everything that was being done. While she spoke, Grandfather opened his eyes and looked at Daddy.

"You should have retired years ago," Daddy muttered.

"Can't you say anything loving to him, especially now?" I asked him.

He looked at me. "I just did," he said, and walked out.

Grandfather put his whole smile into his eyes.

I went to him and held his hand. "We're here for you, Grandpa. Don't worry."

He tried to speak but stopped and leaned toward me so I could kiss him.

"You're a very sweet granddaughter," Mrs. Cohen said.

I hugged Grandfather and went out because I could hear that Jamie had arrived. Anna had prepared a roast chicken dinner.

When Daddy came out to eat, he paused when he saw Jamie. Then he smiled coolly. "You know," he said, "maybe it's a good idea you've become attached to Lisa again. She could be a good fisherman's wife and learn to enjoy it."

"My mother does," Jamie responded.

Daddy grunted and sat at the table. We sat, and Anna began serving.

"Did you hear about Aunt Frances and what she did?" I asked Daddy.

He shrugged. "None of that stuff is as valuable as she thinks." He smiled. "Wait until she tries to sell it."

"Did you ever think of yourselves as brother and sister?" I asked.

"To tell you the truth," Daddy said, thinking, "no. She never understood what it means to be a Baxter."

"What does it mean?" I asked him, thinking about the documents Grandfather had given me.

"It means havin' self-respect and never lettin' anyone make a fool of you or get the better of you. We are privileged people. We have a responsibility to be successful for ourselves and those who are dependent on us. It's sort of America's version of royalty," he added, liking what he'd said. "Yes, that's it. The king is dead. Long live the king."

He laughed and ate with more enthusiasm. I had never really liked my father, but I wouldn't admit it to myself because I thought it was too unnatural, my fault, but at this moment, I felt myself slipping into hating him.

"I'll be at work tomorrow," I said.

"Sure. But I'll warn you now so you won't be shocked. I've moved into my father's office."

I put down my fork.

"He's not coming back, Lisa, and I need the room. We've got to face reality and deal with it like Baxters do."

I fumed inside but just continued to eat. The silence was deafening. I could see how uncomfortable Jamie was. After dinner, he and I went for our usual walk around the Crest. He could sense how deeply annoyed and sad I was. We didn't speak much until we paused at the oak tree where he had once proposed that we spend our lives together.

"What are you going to do, Lisa? I know you. You're thinking about a major decision."

"You do know me. Yes. I'll remain working at the company for Grandfather's sake, but I can see where I would not want to be working full-time with my father. I'm still interested in art school."

"Yeah, I thought you were going in that direction," Jamie said.

"It won't change anything between us."

"Hopefully not, but the mainland has a way of swallowing up people."

"You think Birdlane will never be enough for me now?"

"Let's just say I fear it. And don't make any promises," he added quickly. "It makes it all worse. Just let's see how things go."

I hugged him. "We've known each other all our lives," I said, "and until now, I really never knew you or appreciated who you really are."

I kissed him. He paused, smiled, and kissed me. It was almost as if we were back to the very day we had talked about a future together.

"Just hold me," I said. "For a little while."

"No," he said. "Forever."

We kissed again, and he left.

My days seemed to run into each other. I went to work in the morning and then returned to sit with Grandfather, who was having trouble with therapy, mainly because he was too angry to cooperate. I had the day nurse wheel him around to watch me working on the landscape. It was easy to see when he was pleased and when he would drift off, probably reliving the moment he had collapsed.

Daddy strutted about with his new sense of authority, talking more sharply to Anna and even to me. At dinner, he would brag about something else he had done brilliantly at the company. There were nights when he didn't come home. I never asked him about it; frankly, I didn't care.

I did look into more classes at the college's art school and registered to start them in the fall.

In late July, Grandfather had another seizure, which resulted in his being totally bedridden. Whenever I looked at him, I could see his wish to go to sleep permanently. I tried talking to him constantly, but even that became depressing for us both.

Jamie constantly worked at cheering me up, buying me funny things and taking me places.

"Funny," I told him. "When I lost my mother, I thought the world wouldn't go on. How could it? She was so important to me, so she had to be that important to everyone else. But the days went on, and I realized I had to go on as well. Grandfather has been such a powerful force on Birdlane."

"Yes, people talk about him every day. He's one of those men who are destined to become legends. That's what my mother says."

"Probably true," I said.

One day about a week later, Eddie Doyle called me, very excited.

"I have an offer on your painting," he said. "Substantial. Twenty-five hundred dollars."

"Wow. I didn't know you had put it up for sale."

"I didn't. The offer came on its own. It's from an attorney in Ireland. I don't know who's buying it. Everything goes through him."

"Ireland?"

"People come and go through here from all over. Whoever it is just didn't say anything to me at the time."

"I'm so surprised."

"It's good. I'll get you the money less my commission when it comes."

"Thank you, Eddie."

I waited to see if he would say anything about Kyle, since he had chosen my painting, but he didn't. Actually, I was glad he didn't.

I hurried to tell Anna, of course, and even told Grandfather, whose eyes brightened. When I told Jamie, he was very happy, but there was always that holdback, that fear that my art would take me away from Birdlane.

When I mentioned it to Daddy at work, he looked stunned for a moment. *Yes*, I thought, *art can make money*, but that didn't seem to be his thought.

"Ireland?"

"Yes." I explained what Eddie Doyle had said and told him about the attorney.

"Let me know if you learn anything else," he said cryptically.

What else was there to learn? I shrugged and walked away

About a week later, the money came with a note from Eddie saying he had shipped the painting. He included the name of the lawyer in Galway, Ireland. I thought about writing to him to ask who the buyer was but decided to leave it anonymous, as that was what the buyer wanted. It just thrilled me to know that my work would be hanging on someone's wall as far away as Ireland.

I kept thinking about Mommy and how proud she would have been. One day, I made a private trip to Bar Harbor and returned to the cemetery to sit next to her grave and talk to her as if she were still alive and could hear everything I was saying, telling her what had happened to me and how I had dealt with it. She had given me the strength. I wanted so to believe that.

Afterward, I went right back to Birdlane. I didn't want to walk through Bar Harbor and revive any of my memories of Kyle. Despite what had happened to Grandfather and how both my father and Aunt Frances were behaving, I wanted to be at the Crest more than ever. I had never felt the sense of home more strongly than I did now.

The lazy days of summer were slowly slipping behind me. I was close to finishing the landscape. Whenever Grandfather was wheeled out to watch, I could see the pleasure in his face despite all the physical changes due to the stroke. Strong emotions could not be denied.

"It's very difficult to make any sense of what he tries to say," his daytime nurse told me, "but I would swear he is telling me his wife would be very pleased with your picture."

"I hope so," I said.

It was impossible under the circumstances to be very happy any day since Grandfather's stroke, but I did try to look at what was positive. I thought I was settling into some sense of peace when, early in August, I had gone to sleep and was in a deep dream, so deep that I thought the knocking on my bedroom door was part of the dream.

It wasn't.

I put on my table lamp and called, "Come in."

Mrs. Cohen stood in the doorway.

"I'm afraid your grandfather has expired," she said.

For a moment, I had no idea what she meant. Expired?

"Dr. Bush is still here confirming arrangements. I called him about an hour ago. Anna is beside herself, and apparently your father is on a business trip?"

I sat up, her words finally having meaning to me.

"I'm not sure. He comes and goes without explaining anymore."

"I'm sorry. I'll be with Dr. Bush."

"Okay," I said, choking back my tears.

I rose slowly and began to dress.

Dr. Bush was on the phone in Grandfather's room. Anna was in the chair at the foot of the bed, bent over, her hands over her eyes. Grandfather's eyes were closed and the blanket was pulled up to his neck.

Dr. Bush hung up and turned to me. "I'm sorry, Lisa. The stroke did too much damage. Your grandfather made all his arrangements a while back. The funeral director is sending his hearse up here and should be here in twenty minutes. He'll discuss it all with you later in the day."

"Okay," I said. "Thank you."

"Anna and I will leave you to have your private moments with your grandfather," he said.

Anna looked up quickly and then stood.

"Thank you. Thank you both."

They left, and I sat in the chair beside Grandfather.

I slipped my hand under the blanket to find his. It was cold, but it was his hand.

"Grandpa, you became my whole family. You were more of a father to me than my own father was, and I will always cherish your love and wisdom. Nothing will be the same without you, but because of you, we have so much, and I will be able to go on to make you and Mommy proud. I know, as you always said, Grandmother is waiting for you. She has a smile on her face, and now you can smile forever, too."

I leaned over and kissed his forehead, and then, not really knowing how my legs were holding up, I walked out, hugged Anna, and returned to my room. I didn't want to see him being taken out.

I didn't go back to sleep. I did doze on and off and was awoken when my phone rang at about seven thirty in the morning.

It was Grandfather's attorney, Mr. Orseck.

I wasn't surprised that the news of Grandfather's passing had spread with electric speed throughout Birdlane Island.

"Lisa, I'm sorry. This is a terrible time for you, but I need you in my office as soon as possible. There's going to be a lot of trouble," he said.

"I'll come right away," I told him.

I headed out and didn't even stop to tell Anna.

I knew in my heart of hearts that "trouble" was really an understatement.

CHAPTER NINETEEN

On my way down the hill, I saw that Jamie was rushing up it. I stopped, and he stopped.

"Where are you going?" he asked, obviously surprised to see me leaving the Crest.

"I have to go to Grandfather's attorney's office. There are problems."

"I'll be right behind you," he said.

I continued on.

We both arrived at Mr. Orseck's office at the same time. When we entered, he looked up, saw Jamie, and said, "This is a confidential meeting. Only Lisa."

"Okay," Jamie said. "I'll wait for you outside."

I sat quickly, my heart pounding. What would turn my life upside down now?

"What I'm about to tell you I've known for the last four years. Now that you're over eighteen, you don't need anyone acting as your surrogate in these matters. There will be a formal reading of your grandfather's will tomorrow at ten a.m. I did reach your father, who is on his way back to Birdlane Island. It was the first question he had. He doesn't know anything I'm going to tell you, but I want you prepared."

"Okay," I said, still holding my breath.

He opened a file and took out what I assumed was my grandfather's will.

"Your grandfather was a special man. He was truly what you would call prescient. He knew exactly how you would turn out, and he was not unrealistic about his children the way some parents can be. We discussed all this at great length, and the conclusion he reached was truly his own. I watched you grow with responsibility. Your grandfather and I often met to discuss this again and again and confirm his wishes. To get right to the point, your grandfather made his will to provide the following:

"One. You inherit fifty-one percent of Baxter Fish Enterprises. Nothing can be done or agreed to without your consent. Of course, we know how your father is going to react to this. His attorney is Ron Cutler, who has a reputation for being aggressive, often bordering on what's legal and ethical. He could be Satan's lawyer. So expect that. Just know that I'll be there for you, a promise I made to your grandfather. At this moment, I do not know what tactic they'll employ to challenge the will. Your grandfather was fully in charge of his business when he made his will. No one can claim he was incompetent or incapable of knowing what he was doing. I would be witness to that, of course. He's left everyone some money, but you the largest portion, something close to two million."

"I'm overwhelmed."

"Well, there's more," he said.

"More?"

"Number two. Your grandfather left you the title to the Crest. You own the home," he said.

Now I truly lost my breath.

"I know your father. He's going to see himself as your employee and your tenant."

"Yes."

"This is why I wanted you to know all about this ahead of time, Lisa."

"Yes, thank you."

"Try not to worry, but call me anytime," he said.

"I will."

I rose and he escorted me out. Jamie stood quickly. I said nothing, and we started out.

"What happened?" he asked.

"I'm still trying to digest it. Come up to the house," I said.

All this the same day Grandfather died, I thought. I didn't know which of my emotions to subdue first. They were all in a panic.

The Crest already had a dark, vacant, lonely look to me. Anna had been lying down but heard us come in and hurried out.

"Come into the living room," I told her. "Daddy will be here soon, and he doesn't know what I'm going to tell you."

Neither Jamie nor Anna spoke when I finished. They looked as overwhelmed as I felt.

"The house, too," Anna had to reconfirm.

"Yes."

"How will he live with this?" Anna wondered aloud.

"He won't. Mr. Orseck thinks he will fight it in court, so we'll have to be ready for all that. Meanwhile, we don't reveal anything. It will all be known after the reading of the will tomorrow. Anna, you'll be there, because Grandfather left you something."

"Oh my," she said. "Oh. The funeral director is coming here in a few hours to go over things with you and your father. He called from the office, and I told him."

"All right, thank you," I said, standing. "I think I need a few quiet moments." I looked at Jamie.

"Okay," he said. "I'll be back later."

"No, you can come to my room. I'd just like to lie down and would like you there."

His smile widened.

We went to my room. Jamie sat as I lay down, my right hand over my forehead. *How am I going to process all this*, I wondered, *especially when Daddy finds out? Will he take one look at me and know?*

"He'll rant and rave," Jamie said, as if he could read my thoughts. Sometimes I was sure he could. "You'll just have to say, 'It's what Grandfather wanted.'"

"I know."

"Don't let him bully you."

"I haven't for a very long time," I said.

Jamie smiled and reached for my hand.

"This isn't going to change who I am," I said, "or what I want."

"Good."

We were silent.

Then I said, "Poor Grandfather. He had to suffer for a while."

"Sometimes when I looked at him, he seemed at peace with it."

"You think so? I hope," I said.

We sat quietly. I closed my eyes again. I guess I drifted off, because when I opened them, Jamie was standing by the window looking out.

"Oh, did I fall asleep?"

"For a while. Your father's back. He came in ranting a bit, not about what you know. He blames your grandfather for not waiting for him before he died. He declared there would be changes made here. I heard him tell Anna he wants to modernize the Crest. He made reference to someone, a woman."

"He did?" I rose.

"We'd better get out there. The funeral director will be here soon anyway."

Daddy saw us coming and stepped forward.

"Do you bring him to everything that's private in this family?" he asked, nodding at Jamie.

"Yes," I said firmly.

He shook his head. "All right. Once everything's over, things are changing here. I've already given Anna some idea of it." He turned to her. "You might think of retiring, Anna," he said.

She looked at me. I shook my head.

"All right. I'll get changed, and we'll meet with the funeral director," he said, and left.

"It's not going to be very pleasant," Anna said, and then surprised me with a smile.

Jamie laughed. "I guess not," he said. "Maybe it's best I leave for a while. Reduce the tension."

"You'll return for dinner?"

"Your father . . ."

"Has nothing more to say about it," I said.

He smiled. "Sure. I'll return."

The funeral director arrived and laid out Grandfather's plans. He wanted a memorial ceremony on Birdlane Island and a religious ceremony at the gravesite in Bar Harbor. We organized the times and announcements. The moment he left, Daddy turned to me and said, "From now on, you don't invite anyone here without my permission. I don't care how old you are. Understood?"

"No," I said.

"And you don't have to return to work at the company. You're just doing redundant reviews anyway. Return to your art, and if you want, marry the fisherman's son and become a Birdlane housewife."

He rose and left.

I started to fume and then laughed. *Wait until tomorrow*, I thought.

Jamie came for dinner. Daddy apparently had a date with the woman he had been seeing. It was a well-kept secret. No one seemed to know any details, or else most were afraid to gossip about him.

That night, Jamie and I sat outside after dinner. It was one of those glorious Birdlane Island summer nights, with the sky ablaze with stars, the ocean waves softly stroking the shore. There were the lights of ships in the distance and the sounds from Birdlane that rose up the hill, including some music.

"Thinking about tomorrow and what you'll be doing?" Jamie asked.

"Not fully. I know I'll have to be on the defensive, but I think we'll be fine. Nothing seems the same without Grandfather now, so it will all feel different."

"I'm sure. I think I'll start working regularly with my father again," he said. "I'm strong enough now, and I think I'm taking advantage by acting so tentative about myself."

"You have to be honest, even about yourself," I said. "Jamie, did you love me right from the start?"

"I did; I do. Something lit up in me when we started to be together. It's like a flame burning inside, warm and bright. I know that doesn't sound as romantic as things you've heard, but it's the truth."

"More important than stylish love words."

"I'll never lie to you, Lisa. Deceiving you will always be the worst sin to me."

"I know."

It was a hard time to think about my feelings for him. Was it love or just a sense of comfort? In the end, what was more important, chasing some movie dream or finding a wholesome life? Few, if any, of the fishermen on Birdlane Island divorced or even cheated on their wives. The sense of family was just something you breathed here. That didn't sound very exciting, but I felt so much older because of all that had happened since the operation had freed me.

I could feel as free as any of the seabirds, but I realized the wind could stop or change direction and, in a moment, could change your life. Was it better on the ground or in the air? Where did birds spend most of their time? Where did they feel safer? Where would I?

I didn't go to Mr. Orseck's office with Daddy, not that he asked me to. I took Anna in my car, and we headed out just after he did. Aunt Frances was there. I knew Grandfather had left her a significant amount of money, contrary to what she believed. Daddy was already seated and looking impatient when we arrived. He looked at Anna with a sullen expression.

"Actually, what is she doin' here?" he asked.

"I asked that she come," Mr. Orseck said. "Your father left her some money."

Daddy scowled. "I'm not surprised," he said. "She's a clever lady."

"What? What does that mean?" Anna asked.

"Let's just get to it," Mr. Orseck said, and began reading the will.

Watching Daddy, I imagined an iceberg melting. His complexion got so red that I thought he would burst into flame.

Then he shot up and screamed at Mr. Orseck. "This is a load of fish guts, crap! It won't stand in court!"

"Your father was of sound mind and body when he wrote this will. He was managing the company. I will be a witness to that," Mr. Orseck said.

"You send a copy of that hogwash to my attorney, Ron Cutler, this morning, and expect to be in court."

"Well, don't throw out what he gave me," Aunt Frances said.

"You idiot," he told her, and charged out.

"All right," Mr. Orseck said. "We'll proceed as your father and your grandfather wanted until told by a court otherwise. For now, Lisa, you can announce the results to your employees at the company. Take whatever action you want."

I rose. I couldn't say I wasn't trembling with the authority and new wealth. Could I live up to this?

Anna took my arm and smiled. "It will all be good," she said.

I looked at Aunt Frances.

"Well, he did surprise me, the old coot," she said, and left.

I drove Anna back to the Crest and then decided to step up to my new responsibilities and went to the company. I informed the employees we'd be closed for Grandfather's funeral and told them what he had left me. Daddy was still with his lawyer, plotting, I imagined.

By late afternoon, Mr. Orseck called me to tell me Ron Cutler had filed in civil court and the case would be adjudicated in two days. He said he had no idea what their strategy was. "But we'll be there to counter it. Don't worry," he said.

Daddy did not come back to the Crest, which was a relief to both Anna and me. Jamie came to dinner both nights and promised to be at court. The community was already buzzing about it.

Anna decided to attend court with me as well as Jamie. I could see from the way Daddy was behaving with his attorney that he felt confident. What did he know that we didn't? The preliminary information was presented to the judge, Victor Collins, who had Grandfather's will before him. Mr. Orseck stood and commented about Grandfather's state of mind at the time he had helped him create his will. He thought he might quickly shut down their line of reasoning if that was what they had intended.

Ron Cutler stood and said they had no intention of proving Grandfather incompetent but simply intended to show that the decision he had made was based on false information.

What information? I wondered.

"At this point," Mr. Cutler said, "we would like to enter into the record the following information that Charles Baxter did not have at his disposal. It is our argument that he would not have made the decision he did if he had known it."

"What is the nature of this information?" Judge Collins asked.

Ron Cutler held up some documents. "We will show that Charles Baxter was unaware that his supposed granddaughter was not his granddaughter, that she shared no blood relationship with any Baxter. This document is a legal agreement between Theresa Baxter and Melville Baxter, in which Theresa Baxter agreed never to reveal the true father of her child but instead to support Melville Baxter's paternity in exchange for which Melville Baxter would support both Theresa and Lisa Baxter and pay for all the expensive medical procedures Lisa Baxter required. This additional document is Rudy Clancy's agreement never to claim fatherhood of Lisa Baxter if Melville Baxter did pay for all Lisa Baxter's needs. He wasn't in any condition to support himself, much less a needy child. Melville Baxter and Theresa Baxter never revealed this to Charles Baxter. He was under the misconception that Lisa was his true granddaughter. It is our contention that he would not have designed this will if he had had a full understanding of his bloodline."

The papers were presented to the judge. I was speechless. Daddy was not my daddy. Mommy had never told me. She had kept to the bargain, probably afraid Melville Baxter would stop supporting my medical needs if she didn't. I couldn't deny that Grandfather hadn't known. In light of the secrets he had shared with me, what would we do?

Mr. Orseck rose. "Your Honor, we'd like to request a postponement of these proceedings so that I can look at the documentation and prepare a response. We had no knowledge of this prior to today's hearing."

Judge Collins thought a moment and then nodded. "This hearing will resume at ten a.m. two days from today."

"I'll see you in my office tomorrow, same time," Mr. Orseck said. He sounded very depressed.

I looked at Daddy joking with his attorney and Aunt Frances smiling beside them. I couldn't stop myself. I marched across the room to his side. He turned, that cold smile on his face.

"Why?" I asked. "Why would you make such a deal and cover up your wife's betrayal? Don't you have any pride as a man?"

He stopped smiling. "You miss the point. It's exactly my pride that made me decide. I wasn't going to let your mother and some transient bum embarrass me. I don't lose; I don't get betrayed."

"Except by yourself," I said, and walked back to Jamie and Anna. "Let's go home," I told them.

An air of gloom filled with dark silence followed us all the way. When we arrived at the Crest, I decided to just walk about the property. Jamie stayed with me, still silent.

"In a way, I'm glad you're not his real daughter," he finally said.

I laughed. "You won't believe it, but, deep in my heart, I never thought I was."

"Well, you really can't blame anyone. Your mother thought she was making the right decision for you, and Grandfather Charlie, believing you were a true Baxter, arranged his will that way."

"What did you say?" I asked.

"What?"

"A true Baxter."

"Yes, isn't that the point?"

I smiled. "It sure is," I said, and started for the house.

"Where are you going?"

"To win our case, silly. Come on," I urged.

He rushed to catch up. "I don't get it," he said.

"You will."

We hurried through the house to Grandfather's office. Jamie watched me pull out the desk drawer to find the key to the safe-deposit box. I held it up. Of course, he didn't understand. I picked up the phone and called Mr. Orseck.

"Can you meet me at the Birdlane National Bank as soon as it opens tomorrow morning?"

"Sure. Why?"

"I have what you need," I said.

At dinner, I explained it to Jamie and Anna.

"Well, you know who is in for a big surprise," she said. "It's like an Agatha Christie novel," she added, and began to describe the Agatha Christie house, the old railroad used in movies, and the countryside. She missed it.

"Maybe we'll all go there someday with you," I said.

In the morning, I gave Mr. Orseck the papers at the bank.

He read them and looked at me. "It's amazing," he said. "It's as if your grandfather knew this day would come."

"Maybe he did. Maybe he knew more than Melville Baxter thought."

He laughed. "Let me go work on this for tomorrow," he said.

The next day couldn't come fast enough. I could hardly sleep that night. My stomach was so in knots in the morning that I could barely swallow some coffee, much less eat. Jamie met us at the courthouse. There was already a bigger crowd than on the first day.

Judge Collins called the hearing to order.

Mr. Orseck stood up. "Your Honor, we do not wish to challenge any of Mr. Melville Baxter's documentation."

Daddy smiled widely.

"However, we would like to present our own documentation, provided to Lisa Baxter by her grandfather. It was kept in his safe-deposit box at the Birdlane National Bank. May I approach?"

Judge Collins nodded, and Mr. Orseck handed him the envelope. The judge read the papers.

Daddy's face grew somber, as if he wondered what this could be.

The judge put the papers down. "And your point, Mr. Orseck?"

"As you can see from all the documents presented, Mr. Baxter's and ours, none of the parties in this hearing had a blood relationship with Charles Baxter and his wife. Charles Baxter was quite aware, obviously, of his son's and his daughter's true origins. He provided Lisa with this information anticipating a situation like this, which only reinforces his decisions in his will."

Ron Cutler rose to read the documents.

"Mr. Cutler?" the judge asked.

The attorney looked speechless. "Well, if no one is blood-related, why grant the benefits of the will to one of them?"

"Because that's what my client wished," Mr. Orseck said.

The judge nodded. "Since I see no viable reason to deny the authenticity or intentions of this will, I uphold its desired result."

He banged his gavel and closed the case. Daddy's body seemed to sink in his chair. Jamie hugged me, and the visitors cheered.

"Birdlane loves you," Jamie said.

I could feel it.

For the first time, I could feel it.

EPILOGUE

About three days after the court decision, Daddy took one of the Baxter motorboats and went out to sea. He did not return. The coast guard was informed and told us they had found the boat just west of Captain Blood's Inlet. A search for his body was undertaken, but nothing was found. Suspicious, I began to dig deeper into the books and found where he had worked the money that had been in that shell company back into it.

"Whoever he had been seeing probably met him at the inlet," I told Jamie. He agreed.

Once I took full reins of the company, I saw Jamie's elation move slowly into despair. One night in late August, we sat at the oak tree on a blanket and just looked at the stars.

"I know something is bothering you, Jamie. You can read me and I can read you. We can't hide anything from each other."

"Somebody, one of the jealous guys, said I was being kept."

"Kept?"

"I wasn't earning enough to take care of you ever. I never would be, so I would always be the kept husband, wearing the aprons."

I laughed.

"It's not funny."

"No, it isn't. I know Birdlane."

I thought deeply about it. What was the solution? What did I feel would make me complete?

"Well, there seems to be only one solution," I said.

"What's that?"

"Marry me. That way, you own half of what I have, but you can't get away with just that. I've thought about our need for an office of customer relations and realized, who better than you to run it? You know more about our suppliers and customers than I do. I'm not making up a job for you; the company needs it. We have to look forward. Daddy, or whoever we want to call him, was stuck in his own ways. We're not that far from the twenty-first century," I said.

He was silent. Then he asked, "Did you say 'Marry me'?"

"You idiot. Yes."

He hugged me quickly and kissed me and said, "You took the words right out of my mouth."

"They were stuck there so long that I was going to send you to a dentist."

He laughed. We kissed again. I looked out at the sea and the stars and thought, *I'm here; I'm really here.*

Two and a half years later, I gave birth to Ishmael. We both loved *Moby-Dick*. For us, Anna now became a wonderful nanny.

Just before our third anniversary, I told Jamie I wanted to take a trip.

"To where?"

"Ireland," I said.

"Really? Any particular reason?"

"Let's just leave it as a surprise. For us both."

He shrugged. "I'm okay with it."

I arranged the trip. We flew into Shannon Airport, where I had a driver who knew the address just outside of Galway. The grass was truly kelly green, and the streams and hills were breathtaking. Jamie kept asking me where we were going.

"I don't know," I said. "Not until we get there."

We pulled up to a sheep farm with a sign that said it was Clancy Lane.

Jamie's eyes widened. "Are we where I think we are?"

"I don't know."

We got out and entered the property. We could hear children's laughter coming from just behind the house. Jamie carried Ishmael, and I walked ahead.

I saw him playing soccer with two young boys who looked about ten or eleven. One of them saw me first and stopped playing. Then they all stopped, and he turned. He looked awestruck for a moment and then smiled and started toward me.

"Lisa," he said. "I thought your mother was walking toward me."

"She is," I said, and we hugged for the first time.

"This is my husband, Jamie, and our son, Ishmael."

"So good to meet you," Rudy said, shaking Jamie's hand. "Boys," he said, turning to his sons. "Say hello to Lisa and Jamie. This is Boyd and Connor."

"Hello," they said. "Pleased to make your acquaintance," Connor added. They both had reddish-blond hair and sparkling greenish-blue eyes.

"This is your half sister," Rudy told them, and their eyes widened with surprise. "My wife, Shannon, is making cottage pie for us for dinner. How about staying for it? Start a catch-up. I'm sure there is lots to tell."

"Oh, yes," I said. Jamie smiled. "Lots to tell."

We had a wonderful visit. I kept thinking about all the time I had lost with my real father. Could you catch up on all that, or was it gone forever? His joy in seeing me gave me the feeling it wasn't lost. I knew every time he looked at me, he saw my mother and his memories were revived. There it was . . . another gift she had given, both to me and to him. Of course, I promised we would see each other again. I invited them to the Crest. I really looked forward to hearing more from Rudy about his affair with my mother. I knew that was something we had to discuss privately someday.

A day after we returned home, I went to the cemetery in Bar Harbor and told my mother and my grandfather all that I had done. I went alone.

Afterward, I headed back to the pier and found that I was walking quickly. I realized when I reached the boat that I was so eager to go home, to get back to Birdlane Island and my family and my life. It was enough after all.

The next day, almost as if it was a ritual for us, Jamie and I climbed to the Birdlane Crow's Nest and sat watching the geese heading south. I would swear that some of them turned slightly to look at us. I thought they were as happy to see us as we were to see them.

All of life was a set of journeys for a variety of reasons.

But in the end, you always went home, not because it was the place you knew but because it was the place you needed, the place that reminded you who you really were.

We held hands and watched the geese disappearing, knowing in our hearts that they would be back, and we would be here to greet them.